THE SECRET HEART

Unmarriageable
Book 6

Mary Lancaster

ARE YOU SIGNED UP FOR DRAGONBLADE'S BLOG?

You'll get the latest news and information on exclusive giveaways, exclusive excerpts, coming releases, sales, free books, cover reveals and more.

Check out our complete list of authors, too!

No spam, no junk. That's a promise!

Sign Up Here

www.dragonbladepublishing.com

Dearest Reader;

Thank you for your support of a small press. At Dragonblade Publishing, we strive to bring you the highest quality Historical Romance from the some of the best authors in the business. Without your support, there is no 'us', so we sincerely hope you adore these stories and find some new favorite authors along the way.

Happy Reading!

CEO, Dragonblade Publishing

Additional Dragonblade books by Author Mary Lancaster

Imperial Season Series
Vienna Waltz
Vienna Woods
Vienna Dawn

Blackhaven Brides Series
The Wicked Baron
The Wicked Lady
The Wicked Rebel
The Wicked Husband
The Wicked Marquis
The Wicked Governess
The Wicked Spy
The Wicked Gypsy
The Wicked Wife
Wicked Christmas (A Novella)
The Wicked Waif
The Wicked Heir
The Wicked Captain
The Wicked Sister

Unmarriageable Series
The Deserted Heart
The Sinister Heart
The Vulgar Heart
The Broken Heart
The Weary Heart
The Secret Heart

The Lyon's Den Connected World
Fed to the Lyon

Also from Mary Lancaster
Madeleine

CHAPTER ONE

Gazing out of the landing window, Lily's heart gave a little flutter of gladness. It was *him.*

He rode alone into the inn yard, as he sometimes did, without any servants or companions, and dismounted with an air of weariness she had never seen in him before. But he still had a smile—and a coin—for Jem, who led his horse away to the stables.

He began to walk to the front door, then paused, almost as if he sensed Lily's observation. She had no time to draw back before his gaze found and trapped her.

Something is wrong, she thought in dismay.

And then his lips quirked, and he touched his hat, just as if she were a great lady instead of the innkeeper's daughter, and walked out of her line of vision and into the house.

Pulling herself together, Lily hurried along the passage with her tray for the grumpy merchant in the small bedchamber. Escaping swiftly—for he was not the sort of man to chat—she hastened downstairs, trying not to run, in time to see her mother show his lordship into the private parlor.

"What's his pleasure?" she asked cheerfully as her mother closed the door.

"A bottle of claret. He claims he isn't hungry, but I suppose it's early still for an evening meal. We'll talk him into it later. Make sure the best glasses are clean, and don't give him that chipped one."

"I won't," Lily assured her and went to fetch a bottle of the best claret which she set on a tray beside one of the good glasses. As she crossed the hall to the parlor, her heartbeat quickened.

He sat in the armchair by the fire, leaning forward to warm his hands. But when she entered, he stood and came to take the tray from her before she could lay it on the table. Their fingers touched, and she treasured the thrill that sparked through her hand to her heart.

"You look well, Lily," he remarked.

He was taller than she remembered. It made her somehow afraid to look up.

"Thank you, my lord, I am." She picked up the bottle and poured the red liquid into the waiting glass before finally raising her gaze to his face. "Are you, sir?"

She had no idea why he should affect her this way. He must have been at least thirty-five years old, and he was not the most handsome man she had ever met. He was not even the most handsome lord she had ever served. A straight and well-built figure, in a lean kind of a way, he possessed unremarkable brown hair, cut in a fashionably short style, a thin, aristocratic nose, and a wide mouth with a ready smile. Not everyone would have described him as distinguished, but something about his pleasant face always stayed with Lily. And left her wondering.

If Lily had a gift, she knew it was reading people's characters. It was this that led her to nudge certain people gently toward certain other people, thus increasing the inn's reputation as the "lucky house" her father always called it. But this man, Lord Torbridge, had always eluded her. He was kind, polite, amiable. He had been to the Hart several times, and yet she could not read him. His light eyes were secretive, as though they only cast back one's own expressions, and yet below that was a world of intelligent thought she had never come near. Perhaps it was that which fascinated her so. Or perhaps it was the contrast between the mild-mannered, proper gentleman he had always appeared and some of the things she knew he had done.

Like killing the traitor Pierre de Renarde. Like questioning her and everyone else at the inn after the French raid.

With something close to shock, she found weariness in his eyes, strain in the lines around them. Sadness.

He blinked. "Am I what?"

"Well."

"Of course." He picked up the glass from the table and walked back to the chair by the fire.

"You seem tired, my lord," she said with a hint of desperation.

He rested his head against the back of the chair and smiled. "I was. I feel better for being here."

"The Hart has that effect on people."

"I wonder why that should be?"

"It's a lucky house," Lily said lightly. "Can I get you anything else, sir?"

"No, I believe I have all I need, thank you."

He had a particularly sweet smile that drove straight to Lily's heart, depriving her of words and breath as she all but stumbled from the room. Pulling herself together, she went to help her mother prepare the evening meal.

"Ned said he would call this evening," her mother remarked as she energetically rolled out pastry for the pigeon pie.

"Oh?"

"You needn't sound so surprised. You know he comes to see you."

"I can't imagine why," Lily said ruefully. "I've never given him any encouragement."

"Maybe you should." Her mother glanced up with a scowl. "You could do worse, Lily. He's a good man, young and strong, and it's a tidy bit of land will come to you both."

"I can't marry for such reasons, Mother."

"I think, if you spent time with him, those other reasons would come. Your father likes him."

"My father wants me within walking distance of the inn!"

Her mother slapped the pastry into a dish and began pressing it into the edges. "Don't you want that?"

"Yes," she admitted. "But not if it means marrying Ned."

"Don't be so set against him! Just consider him while he's here. You might find things change."

"I might," she allowed peaceably.

In fact, she knew she would not change her mind about Ned. Or her heart. Not that night. And definitely not while *he* was here.

DAYLIGHT WAS FADING as she lightly knocked and entered the private parlor. His lordship appeared to have fallen asleep in his chair, the empty wine glass still in his hand. The bottle now stood on the hearth beside his chair, less than half-full.

Lily hesitated. She had come to persuade him to eat dinner, but perhaps she should leave him to sleep. Certainly, he seemed much more peaceful than when he'd first arrived. She walked quietly across the room.

It was odd, but in repose, his classic good looks were more obvious. Almost as if he deliberately changed his appearance when he was awake. Ignoring such fantasy, she closed her fingers around the wine glass, trying to ease it out of his grip.

His eyes opened at once. He smiled. "Lily."

She jumped back. "I'm so sorry, my lord. I thought you were asleep."

"You needn't be sorry. I was just thinking."

"You're a gentleman who thinks very deeply," she said because it was in her head. She blushed, but he didn't appear angry, just curious.

"Why do you say that?"

"I don't know. You just give me that impression."

"There aren't many people who would agree with you."

"More fool them."

A smile curved his lips, lit his eyes. Perhaps it was the firelight, but he seemed warmer, less aloof than usual. And his gaze was fixed steadily on her face.

"Shall I light the lamps, sir?" she blurted.

He inclined his head. "If you please."

She lit a spill from the fire and walked around the room, lighting the lamps and the candles on the table. His gaze seemed to follow her, but he didn't speak. In the silence, she heard only the beating of her own heart.

She turned to face him, and he lifted the glass to his lips. "Would you like dinner, sir? There's an excellent ham soup and a fresh pigeon pie."

His gaze dropped to the glass, almost as though he expected it to answer for him. Then he glanced back up to her. "Yes, if you please. But there is no rush."

She curtseyed and left him. But someone was waiting for her in the hall.

"Ned," she said and closed the door. She didn't know why she was surprised, for her mother had told her he would come. Lord Torbridge seemed to have the effect of knocking everyone else from her mind. Which was not only rude of her, it was stupid. "Did you smell my mother's pie?"

Ned grinned. "That I did. Will you eat with me?"

"I can't right now. We have guests to look after. But I'll be popping in and out of the kitchen, and of course, there will be my mother and Bessie for chatter. Or Matt Barnes is in the taproom tonight if you prefer male company."

He didn't even glance toward the taproom, from where a convivial hum of conversation was already flowing. "Yours is the only company

I want," he said in a rush and took a step nearer her.

She laughed as if he were joking. She wished he was. "Why, you will hurt Jack's feelings! To say nothing of my mother and Bessie's. Come to the kitchen, and you can tell us about your day and—"

"Lily," he broke in, with just the sort of desperation she had been trying to avoid. "Lily, I wish you wouldn't dodge being alone with me. You must know how I feel!"

"How we both feel," she said lightly. "We have always been very good friends and always will be. We've no need to be alone."

She made to step around him, but he anticipated her and blocked her path.

"Yes, Lily, we have," he argued, capturing her hand. "How else can I ask you to marry me? How else can I convince you it's the right thing to do?" He glanced warily toward the open taproom door.

"You can't," she said bluntly, trying to draw her hand free. "Ned, I like you, but I don't love you in that way, and I won't marry you. Ever."

"Don't say that, Lily." He held her hand tighter, desperately tugging her toward him.

"Let me go, Ned," she warned before an undignified tussle broke out.

"Never," he said fervently.

She pushed him in the chest to show that she meant it, but it seemed only to inflame him. His arms went around her, and she had had enough. She raised her hand and dealt him a ringing slap across the cheek, just as the parlor door opened and Lord Torbridge stood there.

Ned dropped her like a hot cake.

Lord Torbridge said nothing but continued to stand in the doorway. Large, still, wordlessly commanding.

Ned swallowed, then gave a jerky bow, and dashed out of the inn by the front door.

"Thank you," Lily whispered in an agony of embarrassment and gratitude. She fled into the kitchen.

RANDOLPH MERRICK, VISCOUNT Torbridge, closed the door of the parlor once more and dragged his hand through his hair with irritation. He had no business interfering with the private lives of the inn staff.

But this was Lily. The first time he had seen her after he had brought the wounded Verne here last year, he hadn't been able to look away. And God help him, the fascination had only grown worse. She was the secret of the Hart's success, both commercial and otherwise. And yet, she carried no airs, no ambitions. She was the heart of the Hart.

His smile twisted, and he swiped up the bottle from the hearth and poured himself another glass. Of course, he would have intervened to prevent any man importuning any woman of whatever class, but he should not have felt the despair he did when he overheard her conversation with her admirer. Nor such rage at the young man's temerity in touching her. In all, there had been far too much relief at her rejection of her swain, far too much emotion altogether.

He should not have come here. And yet, he could not stay away. He drank half the glass in one swallow and walked to the window. Well, he would accept the peace and comfort she gave without knowing and remain the perfect gentleman. And tomorrow, he would return to London and the task in hand.

He half expected one of the elder Villins to serve him, but it was again Lily who entered to set the table. And although he would have been happy never to mention the matter again, she brought it up almost immediately.

"I'm sorry you were disturbed by that...incident."

He glanced at her. "I trust that will be the end of the matter?"

"I imagine so. At last."

He frowned. "Then this has been going on for some time?" What the devil was her father about to permit it?

"Oh, no. Well, that is, I suppose I knew it was coming, but I've been avoiding it, avoiding him. Now, at least, it is in the open, and I have made my position plain."

"That you do not favor the young man? Is there someone else more to your liking?"

It was none of his business, of course, and she flushed as she shook her head. "I am in no rush to be married. I'm happy where I am. Would you like another bottle of wine, sir?"

With relief he had no right to, he accepted the change of subject along with the bottle. The wine was, no doubt, a waste because he probably wouldn't drink it without company, and the company he wanted was hers.

But he hadn't come here for her company, just her presence, and that was enough. So, he sat down at the table and let her serve him dinner. She drifted in and out of the room, helpful, friendly, and infinitely soothing. When prompted, she told him the latest news about the inn and the surrounding countryside, including the new tutor at Audley Park since Miss Milsom had left and was now Lady Dain.

"And to think, sir, she first met Sir Marcus in this very room," Lily said, "when I asked him to give up his bedchamber to her."

He glanced up at her. "Why does that not surprise me?" He laid down his fork, regarding her. "What exactly is it you do, Lily?"

She laughed, a soft, infectious sound that made him smile. "I? Nothing! The Hart is simply a lucky house. Why, the Duke and Duchess of Alvan met here when *none* of us were present."

"Hmm." He reached for his wine glass and discovered it was empty. Before he could remedy the matter himself, she hurried forward and refilled his glass. He inhaled her fresh, subtly feminine scent. How could anyone smell of happiness?

She straightened and left him with a smile to finish his dinner.

Eventually, he sat back in his chair, replete. He half-expected Lily or Mrs. Villin to come and clear away the remains of the meal. But after a few moments, when no one did, he rose and took his wine to the hearth. For comfort, he removed his coat, loosened his waistcoat and cravat, and sank into the armchair.

After about ten minutes, a knock at the door interrupted his somber and difficult thoughts. It was Lily.

"Let me clear these things away for you, my lord."

"Thank you. And my compliments to your mother. The meal was excellent, as always."

"Thank you, sir, I'll tell her." She piled the plates and serving dishes on a tray with quiet efficiency. He found himself watching her small, deft hands, hands used to work, not pampered every day in gloves and idleness.

They stilled, and he glanced up, meeting her gaze.

"What is the matter?" she asked, almost like a plea.

His eyebrows drew up involuntarily. "Nothing. I am very comfortable."

She waved that away. He was rumbled. They both knew she referred to a deeper comfort, but he held her gaze without difficulty.

"A trouble shared is a trouble halved, my lord," she murmured. "I am a good listener, and if there is anything I can do to help, I will and gladly."

He smiled, resigned to the gentle ache, which one day would become so severe that it would outweigh the comfort. He would have to stay away, then. "You are very kind and sweet, but what troubles could I possibly have? I assure you, I am perfectly at ease."

A moment longer, she stared at him. He thought, ruefully, that he had disappointed her. In fact, as she picked up the tray and turned, he realized he had hurt her. From nowhere, emotion bombarded him. He didn't want her to go.

For once in his life, he spoke without thinking first. "My father is dying."

CHAPTER TWO

A S SOON AS the words were out, he stared at his hands, appalled. Because, of course, she laid the tray back down and walked back to him.

She sat on the footstool, close to his knees, and gazed up at him. God, she was beautiful, with her raven-black hair and brilliant, green eyes, and she had no idea. She would not let anyone suffer if she could help.

"I'm sorry," she said quietly. "That must be very hard."

Again, he was surprised, for he didn't mind the sympathy at all. "We aren't close," he hastened to assure her. "Never were."

"Still, he is your father."

"Still," he agreed, "he is my father." He looked into the fire, allowing himself just a moment to remember everything. "In my mind, he is still a big, strong, roaring man. It's hard to see him brought so low, so weak." He broke off before he said too much. God knew the girl always *saw* too much anyway.

He felt rather than saw her nod. "Will his death change your life?"

He glanced up, startled, searching her face. "Yes," he admitted. "I will be the Marquess of Hay with responsibility for huge estates and hundreds of dependents."

"And what you do now, you will no longer be able to do?"

"You mean fritter my life away in the clubs and ballrooms of London, interspersed with hunting parties and visits to my tailor? I'm sure

I'll fit in a little."

Even though he smiled deprecatingly, she didn't smile back, which gave him his first moment of unease.

"No," she said flatly. "I don't mean that."

"Then I'm not quite sure to what you do refer," he said hastily. "But yes, it seems certain that being the marquess will interfere with my life."

"I suppose you will have to marry and settle down."

"I suppose I will," he sighed.

Her gaze searched his. "I'm sorry. Did you mind very much when Lady Cecily married Lord Verne?"

He blinked, for it seemed a long time ago. And of course, the world had known he was at Lady Cecily's feet. He hadn't been acting either. Or at least, not entirely. "I believe I did at first, but in truth, we would not have suited."

"No, you wouldn't," Lily agreed.

"She is happy with Verne."

Lily nodded and gazed into the fire. "Is there no lady with whom you *could* be happy?"

An ache began deep in his chest. Ignoring it, he said lightly, "I think the question is rather if there is no lady who could be happy with me."

"It is *part* of the question," she allowed, surprising him again. "And the truth is, if you guard your heart, shroud it in secrecy, it is never truly given, and so unlikely to be accepted."

Feeling his jaw drop, he recovered it hastily and rose to his feet, walking to the table where she had earlier left the port. "If you are going to talk like that," he said, picking up the unused port glass and returning to his chair, "you will have to drink with me."

"Oh, no, sir, I couldn't," she said, shocked.

He paused, one brow raised. "We are friends, are we not?"

She flushed in the firelight, causing the ache in his heart to intensify. "I like to think so," she said so quietly, he could barely hear.

His heartbeat quickened. Could that be an admission that to some extent, she shared his wayward attraction? Or was she simply humoring the noble customer? He should send her away, back to her father, who would surely not be pleased to see her sitting down and drinking wine with the patrons. But he had begun it and would condemn her to one glass, even if she never drank it.

He poured a little wine and gave her the glass. She took it nervously.

"To secret hearts," he said sardonically, clinking his glass against hers.

As he sat, she raised the glass to her lips and sipped dubiously. She looked surprised and took another. "Why this is much more pleasant than the wine I tasted when I was fourteen. I've always avoided it since."

"Your father keeps a very decent claret. Several decent wines, in fact, to say nothing of the brandy."

She grimaced. "I'd better not get a taste for it."

"Why not? When the war ends, you can travel all over Europe in search of superior wines, instead of depending on smugglers."

"I don't know what you mean," she said with dignity, presumably on the subject of smugglers. "But I rather like your idea of buying the wine!"

"You have a taste for travel, then?"

She wrinkled her nose. "I would like to go further than Finsborough." She took another sip from the glass. "Sometimes," she confided, "I feel trapped. By the inn, by everyone's expectations of me. As if it's all written in advance and what I must do. Marry a local man and bring up his children and one day inherit the Hart, which I shall give to my second son. The first, you see, would follow in his father's footsteps."

"That doesn't leave much room for traveling," he agreed, frowning in sympathy. "It sounds as if we are both a little trapped."

"Well, I have made myself a breathing space by rejecting Ned."

"Perhaps you could try something else? Seek a different sort of position with one of the local gentry families? You might get to travel with them."

"I think I'm too managing to be a chambermaid, too young to be a cook. And I don't have the training to be a lady's maid."

"You could be a different kind of assistant. Like a secretary. I know you keep the accounts for your father."

She appeared to consider that with some interest, then sighed. "I can just imagine the gossip if I did that. *Quite a decent girl, I admit, but my dear—the innkeeper's daughter!*"

A burst of surprised laughter escaped him, for not only her accent, but her voice and mannerisms were a perfect replica of a confiding Lady Overton.

Lily flushed. "I'm sorry. I shouldn't have done that. I think I shouldn't have drunk the wine!"

"I won't tell Lady Overton," he assured her. "But you are far too good at that. Who else can you be?"

In rapid succession, she said a few words as Lady Barnaby, Lady Cecily, and Mrs. Lacey.

As his laughter faded, an idea nudged at him.

"A challenge," he said. "Hold a conversation with me as Lady Lily Villin, a sweet young debutante being charming to her old uncle."

Leaning forward, she slapped his hand playfully. "My dear uncle, you are not old," she scolded. "You have been so kind to me. I was just wondering if you could see your way to buy me this bonnet? I shall wear it when we visit you on Sunday."

"You are a wicked girl," he said, amused.

"Oh, no, Uncle, merely a trifle extravagant." She batted her eyelashes. "It is the fault of my upbringing, but I really cannot do with less than twenty bonnets each Season, a dozen pairs of boots, shoes, and dancing slippers. And gowns! A different ensemble for every morning and every evening. You are such a *good* uncle."

He leaned forward, controlling his rising excitement, for her accent held true throughout her grasping little speech. She could be the perfect solution to at least one of his problems.

"Would you really like these things?" he asked.

"Of course not," she scoffed, Lily once more. "Where on earth would I put them? Besides, I've always found something slightly sickening about *wheedling*."

"But you *would* like to see more of the world?" he pursued. "At least travel to London, and perhaps a different county to Sussex."

The smile died in her eyes. She looked wary, which hurt.

He sat back, deliberately clearing all expression from his eyes, his face. "Compose yourself. I am not offering you a carte blanche, but a position. A temporary position."

Her breath caught. "In your household?"

"Sort of, but not quite. I would pay you. You'd live with my sister, go into society, cultivate certain friendships and, hopefully, discover some things I need to know."

She closed her mouth, staring at him. "With my Lady Lily voice?"

"It would be better for our purposes than Lady Overton's."

A choke of laughter escaped her, but she said with regret, "I don't think I could keep it up."

He shrugged. "A matter of mere practice."

She searched his eyes, his face, where she should have been able to read nothing but what he allowed her to see. But with Lily, he had no confidence in his powers of concealment. Besides, common sense was returning, reminding him of what he was really asking of her. The thought of putting her in danger made him feel queasy.

And yet, this was the girl who had chased across the county after thieves, stood up to noble hostage-takers and French raiders. She possessed no shortage of character, courage, or ability to think and act for the best.

But it seemed he did. "I'm sorry. I should not have asked it of you. It would not be right. Forgive me."

She did not drop her gaze. She drew in a deep breath. "But I want to do it. Give me a chance."

THIS WAS HER chance. To be close to Lord Torbridge. To help him in whatever it was he wanted. It was also a way to see a different kind of life, but mostly, she would have done anything for him.

His gaze was locked to hers, turbulent, almost fierce.

"It would be rude," she pointed out, "to withdraw your offer."

"But it would be sane." He nudged the wine bottle with his foot. "I should not have opened the second bottle. And perhaps I shouldn't have given you any."

She held up her glass, which was more than half full. "I hardly think I'm foxed. And if you are, you hide it very well," But then, he hid most things very well. "I accept your offer. When do you want me?"

Heat flared in his eyes, and she hastily dropped her gaze, realizing what her words could have been construed. Did he want her in that way? Her stomach dived with excitement, with nerves, with hope.

And yet, she had always known where such an attraction would lead. She brushed that aside, concentrating only on the immediate benefits. Going with him to London. Helping him.

He dragged one long, elegant hand through his hair. "If your parents permit and you can be ready in time, we'll leave tomorrow. Early enough to reach London by nightfall."

She smiled from pure happiness. "Tell me about the work I would do for you."

"Tomorrow will be time enough. I will need to speak to your father."

She nodded, trying to contain her elation, though she was sure it shone from her eyes, from her whole being. She raised the glass to her lips, then frowned and laid it on the hearth beside his. "I have been away too long. They will need me. But we will talk tomorrow?"

"Tomorrow," he agreed with odd reluctance as she all but danced toward the door. She had reached it before she remembered her tray and had to go back and pick it up with an apologetic smile.

His lips quirked in response, which made her happy, even though she could not read his expression.

She rushed to catch up with her work, clearing the remains of meals from the taproom and the coffee room, serving ale in the taproom to help her father, then returning to the kitchen to help Bessie with the washing up.

Only when Bessie had gone home, and things had quietened down, did she make a cup of tea for her mother and herself, and sit down at the kitchen table.

"Lord Torbridge has offered me a position," she said.

Her mother paused in the act of lifting her cup. "What sort of a position? You already have one!"

"Yes, I know. This would just be temporary, helping him with some problem in London."

Her mother stared. "In what capacity?"

"I'm not quite sure yet, but I would be staying at his sister's house."

Her mother's shoulders relaxed slightly. "For how long?"

"I don't know yet. He said he would speak to you and Dad in the morning."

"Then we'd better warn your father now, give him time to come around," She frowned at Lily. "You want to do this?"

"More than anything."

Her mother reached across the table and squeezed her hand. "Lily, men like him do not look at women like us. At least, if they do, it is only for one thing."

"I know that," Lily said steadily.

"Do you? Guard your heart, love, or you'll lose everything."

"Don't, Mother." She snatched her hand back. "He does not see me in that way."

"Tell that to your father," she said grimly.

As it turned out, there was little opportunity to tell her father anything, for he flatly refused to allow it.

"Flying off to London with you, from right under my nose?" he raged. "Who does he think he is? Of course, you will not go, not tomorrow, and not any other time either! By Christ, I would have thought better of him than this!"

"No, no, Dad, you don't understand," she pleaded.

"No, Lily," he thundered. "In this case, it is *you* who don't understand! I've known gentlemen like him all my life, and you will go nowhere with him! Never! And that is the end of the matter. I'll hear no more about it."

He stormed off, leaving Lily staring after him in dismay. She couldn't remember him ever opposing her with such certainty before. He truly meant it.

Lily was gentle in nature and slow to anger. Moreover, she loved and valued her parents and had no desire to displease them. But anger that they would deprive her of this opportunity surged. How dare her father doubt Lord Torbridge? Or his daughter, come to that. In her not infrequent dealings with entitled young noblemen, she had more than once had to turn aside indecent proposals and had managed in such a way that preserved their good humor and their custom. Why should Torbridge be any different?

Well, he *was* different. Her father probably knew that, as her mother obviously did, although she had never said a word on the subject until now. Still, he should trust her, trust his lordship, and keep his vulgar suspicions to himself! He just didn't want her to leave. He wanted her to stay here forever and ever and marry Ned Bunton to give him an heir for the Hart.

She rushed out of the kitchen and upstairs, meaning to go all the way to her chamber at the top of the house. But halfway up the second flight, she paused and ran back down to the guest chambers on the first floor.

Lord Torbridge had been given the best one as a matter of course, and she knocked on his door without hesitation.

It opened almost immediately. Torbridge stood there, his eyes widening at the sight of her, so stunned that he didn't even move when she brushed past him into the room. He closed the door and swung around to face her.

He wore only his loosened shirt and pantaloons. His waistcoat and cravat had been thrown over a chair, and his boots resided on the floor beside the bed, as though he'd just taken them off.

She gave him no time to ask what she wanted at this hour. He had sent for nothing, merely gone up to his chamber without touching the rest of the wine. She knew that because she'd cleared away the bottles and glasses when the parlor was empty.

"My father won't let me come," she blurted. "So, we'll have to leave secretly."

He blinked. "We'll do no such thing."

She almost laughed, rubbing her fingers across her forehead. "You don't have to pretend with me. I know you are not exactly the prim and proper gentleman you pretend to be."

"I'm not sure I care for prim, but I hope I am proper. In any case, I will not take you without your parents' approval. I'll speak to them in the morning. If I try tonight, I imagine I'll get nowhere with your father, except kicked out."

"Could he?" she asked, distracted from the main point.

"Could he what?" Lord Torbridge demanded, frowning.

"Kick you out."

"He's a big man," his lordship said vaguely. He glanced at her, and his eyes softened slightly. "Don't be upset, Lily, I will sort something out. But you should go before your father finds more cause to distrust me."

She bit her lip, mortified to be shown how coming here could be interpreted by anyone else, by him.

"I'm sorry I disturbed you," she muttered, moving almost blindly to the door.

She found him ahead of her, his fingers wresting on the latch as he frowned down at her. "I am not disturbed." His hand lifted, and she held her breath as his fingertips brushed her cheek in a brief caress. "Don't worry."

A girl could drown in those eyes, she thought. So deep, so fathomless, so... fascinating. His gaze dropped away from hers, looking somewhere in the region of her lips. Flame licked through her body. She had never let any man kiss her, but with *him*... How would it feel to have his lips pressed to hers? In that instant, she wanted nothing more. Her lips parted in sheer desire.

Butterflies soared in her stomach as his head inclined toward her.

Then he paused and straightened, his breath rushing out in something that was not quite laughter. "Lily, Lily, you will be the death of me." He opened the door, peered into the passage, and stood aside.

There was nothing she could do except whisk herself out of his chamber and rush up to her own.

CHAPTER THREE

IN THE MORNING, Lily and her parents worked more or less in silence, none of them referring to last night's argument or the proposal that had set it off. And it was her father who carried breakfast into the parlor to their noble guest. Fortunately, he forgot the plate of toast, so, getting there just before her mother, Lily swiped it up and trotted after her father into the parlor.

Lord Torbridge, once more properly dressed in coat and cravat, was seated at the table, reading a newspaper that had come down from London yesterday.

"Ah, good morning, Villin," he greeted her scowling father in his usual, amiable manner. "Glad to see you so early because I wanted to ask you about borrowing your daughter."

"I can't spare my daughter, sir," her father said woodenly, placing before his guest the plate piled high with ham, kidneys, and eggs, and another with honey cakes.

Lily set down the toast, and he gave her a quick, civil smile of thanks.

"Well, no, of course you can't," Lord Torbridge said, taking Lily *and* her father by surprise. "Which is one reason we need to talk. I realize it would be mightily inconvenient to you, so I would propose to pay the wages of whoever you need to replace her while she is away. And obviously, I would pay Lily for her service to me."

Lily's father, who could appear almost too respectful on occasions, was actually afraid of no one. He met Torbridge's gaze with open hostility. "What service?"

"To my sister," his lordship said in surprise, "Did Lily not explain? Shut the door, Lily, for this is between us and the walls. My sister, Lady Masterton, is in need of an agreeable person to sort out her accounts, take care of her correspondence, that kind of thing. She has a massive backlog and has got herself in a bit of a fankle, financially speaking. Lily, with all her talents, and being used to all kinds of company through the Hart, would be the perfect person."

"Sounds to me like her husband would be the perfect person," her father said bluntly.

"She would rather manage it herself," Torbridge said delicately. "Or, at least, have Lily manage it for her, for she does not, sadly, have an organized mind. However, as I'm sure you know, she is of the first respectability and would take excellent care of your daughter."

Lily could see from her father's slightly less rigid stance that he was softening toward the idea. However, he said suspiciously, "Then how come you are paying for all this and not her ladyship?"

"Well, that is between my sister and me," Torbridge said pleasantly. "But if you are imagining I haven't yet told you the whole truth, you are correct."

"I am?" her father said ominously.

Torbridge stroked his smooth chin. "I have been here a few times in the last year," he pointed out. "Often at moments of…excitement, shall we say? You have probably guessed I am involved in matters that also involve some of your other occasional guests."

"Like Lord Verne and Captain Cromarty?" her father hazarded.

Torbridge smiled benignly. "It is possible that while she is with my sister, Lily might assist me with such matters—matters that concern the Crown and the security of our country. I want you to understand, I shall not fritter her time or waste it."

Lily's father closed his mouth. "And her safety?" he demanded after a moment.

"If I thought there was any risk, I would not have asked her. If that changes, I shall send her straight back to you. With her full remuneration, of course."

Lily's father glanced at her, then back at Torbridge. He tugged indecisively at his lower lip, scowling once more. "You want to do this?" he flung at her. "Truly?"

"Truly," Lily said earnestly.

Her father threw up his hands. "I don't like it," he exclaimed. "For any number of reasons, all of them concerned with Lily. Have you even considered, my lord, how placing her among such high and mighty folk will affect her? Make her discontented with the reality of her life? Which is, she's a common innkeeper's daughter!"

"Villin," Torbridge scolded. "There is nothing common about you or Lily. Or this inn, come to that. Why do you think I keep coming back?"

Again, her father fixed Torbridge with his stare. "Oh, I know why you keep coming back. My lord."

To her surprise, Torbridge allowed a rueful twinkle into his eyes. "I expect you also know that I have never given anyone an excuse not to call me a gentleman. I don't intend to change that. Even for her."

Lily's father groaned. "Let me speak to her mother," he growled and strode out of the room.

Lily lingered, gazing after him in wonder. "I think you did it, sir."

"Then, I hope it doesn't take you long to pack."

She turned to him, frowning. "What did the pair of you mean, just at the end? Why do you come here?"

"Peace," he said ruefully. "God help me."

IF LILY HAD wondered how she was to leave the Hart without causing a lot of hurtful local gossip for her parents to contend with, the problem was solved by the time she came downstairs. She descended with her few belongings—a wooden hairbrush, a toothbrush and powder, a change of linen, and her Sunday gown—in a rather smart valise unexpectedly provided by her mother.

"I didn't know we had this," Lily had said in surprise.

"There are many things you don't know," her mother had said briskly. "Hold on to your common sense, and don't forget to come home."

"I'll write," Lily said huskily, her throat suddenly closing up.

The front door was open when she descended to the hall, and she saw a luxurious traveling carriage waiting in the yard. It had, apparently, just caught up with its owner, Lord Torbridge, who had expected it to pick him up this morning. It came with his valet, who sniffed as he climbed onto the box with the coachman.

Lily hugged her parents fiercely—for this was the first time she had been apart from them for longer than a night—and found herself handed into the coach by Lord Torbridge himself. Jem, the ostler, closed the door, his eyes round as saucers, and the horses leaped into motion. Lily waved out of the back window until she could no longer see her parents. And the enormity of what she had done hit her like a blow.

She turned back on her luxurious, velvet cushioned seat, feeling very small and very out of her depth. Lord Torbridge gazed at her, his eyes more veiled than usual.

"You can still change your mind," he said. "In fact, you can change it at any time, and I'll send you safely home."

"Of course, I don't want to change my mind," she said valiantly and realized something else. Lord Torbridge sat with his back to the horses, rather than facing the direction of travel. "Oh, I am in your place!" She half-stood as she spoke, but he waved her back down with some amusement.

"Stay where you are, there is plenty of room. Besides, you are a lady. Remember?"

"But I'm not, am I?" She spread her hands, encompassing her bright but well-mended red wool cloak and the work-a-day gown beneath. "And no one will believe it."

"Which is why you had better practice being Lady Lily."

"That isn't really my name, though, is it?" she said, self-consciously, like one of the Maybury sisters.

"Perhaps, Lady is too much, but there's no reason why you shouldn't be Miss Lily…Darrow. You belong to the Irish branch of my family, which in fact, should take care of any minor slips in your accent. Following the death of your father, you have come to your distant cousins in England for a few weeks."

"Being in straightened circumstances," Lily contributed.

"Exactly," he said, pleased. "But my father is too ill for you to stay at Hayleigh House, and so I have brought you to my sister. Where you may make yourself useful as a companion to Millicent."

"Yes, but were any of those things you told my father true? Will your sister not object to me being foisted upon her."

"Lord, no. Millie rarely objects to anything, which is how she got into this mess in the first place. She will be delighted if you can help her out of it."

"Could you not?"

He shrugged. "She won't let me pay her debts. And frankly, I don't have the time to sort it all out. You really will earn your salary even if you do nothing else."

"Tell me about that *nothing else*," she said, all her eagerness returning as their distance from the Hart grew.

He shifted in his seat and glanced out of the window. "It's complicated," he said with apparent reluctance.

"You're not used to telling anyone what you do, are you?"

"No," he admitted.

"I'm impressed you even told my father as much as you did,"

"So am I," he said ruefully. "But he is not a man who would have put up with vague nonsense and lies. A little truth was the best I could do. I will tell you this much. Information—important information, such as certain correspondence with Wellington and with foreign leaders—has been finding its way to France."

Her eyes widened. "How do you know?"

"I know," he said firmly. "In some cases, because the documents themselves are missing from the Foreign Office. In others, because my...because *our* people in France have told me so."

"But who could, who *would* steal such things? Is some spy or traitor working at the Foreign Office?"

"My money, sadly, is on the latter. In particular, upon one Mr. John Hill. He is the only link to all the missing documents, and yet I can find nothing else to implicate him. He is from a respected family, the brother of Lord Pennington, and is a pleasant, apparently open-natured young man. He has no unexplained absences, no sudden jaunts to the coast, or even to the London docks. And he has never once slipped or given any information to...informants. I have placed servants in his house, clerks in his office, even pretty women to—er—entertain him, and none of them can implicate him."

"Then what is it you expect *me* to do?" she asked helplessly.

"You will be something else entirely. A respectable young lady he'll wish to court, or at least have around him. My aim is for you to be invited to Pennington's house party next month."

"Won't you be there?" she asked, bewildered. "Your sister?"

"Probably. But Millie is too scatterbrained, and I am not a woman. Men let down their guard with women, often because they underestimate them."

"You said you'd tried that," she pointed out.

"Not a woman of his own class," he said hastily. "Which you will be, to all intents and purposes. You can be in the right place when he receives messages or gives orders, that sort of thing. Anything that would give us a clue as to the route this information is taking from the Foreign Office to France."

She thought about that for a while, as the carriage bowled through Finsborough. It was market day, and stalls were being set up in the square. "Why would he do this, though? Why would he betray his country, his family, his friends?"

Lord Torbridge shrugged. "I don't know that either. He is a second son, so short on wealth, status, prospects, forced to work for his living. And I don't think his salary covers his extravagant lifestyle. Maybe Pennington's tired of bailing him out. Or perhaps he's tired of asking."

"You mean he'll be paid for this information? Who pays him, and how?"

"I can't find any trace of that either," Torbridge confessed. His lips quirked. "You see, I am floundering in the dark and ready to try even this mad start. If nothing comes of it, then we have lost nothing. But if anyone can pry Hill's secrets from him, it is you."

LILY WASN'T QUITE sure what she expected of the journey to London. Her prime motivation, after all, was simply to stay close to Lord Torbridge. And she achieved that, although there was nothing remotely lover-like in his behavior toward her. Mostly, he was her teacher, correcting her words and accent, explaining the customs and expectations of society, and family history that she might be expected to know. In between times, he was an amiable friend.

They did not alight from the coach when the horses were changed—which they were frequently—except once to stretch their legs and be comfortable. Nor did they pause at any of the coaching inns to eat. Instead, Lord Torbridge's valet brought them some choice morsels, which they ate inside from napkins as they traveled.

"Are you ashamed to be seen with me?" she asked once.

His eyebrows flew up. "Of course not. But I don't want anyone making connections between the innkeeper's daughter who left the Hart and my cousin Lily from Ireland. Also, I would like to catch Millie—your Cousin Millicent—before she goes out for the evening."

"How do you know she plans to?"

"I'm not sure planning comes into it, but she will almost certainly go."

Dusk had fallen by the time they reached London, but there was more than enough light for Lily to stare out of the window at the massive buildings so close together, the crowds of people, and traffic swarming in the streets. The noise was incredible.

Eventually, the carriage bowled along broader, quieter streets and squares, lined with large, tall houses, and it was outside one of those it eventually stopped.

"Here we are."

The steps were let down, and the door opened. Lord Torbridge handed her out and called up to the coachman. "Don't wait for me. Give me the valise, Higgins, and go home with the carriage."

And then, with her hand on his arm like a great lady, she was ascending the steps of a grand house. The front door was flanked by pillars and opened by a liveried servant, who immediately bowed them into the house, welcoming Torbridge as "my lord." He seemed to avoid looking at Lily after the first flickering glance.

"Is her ladyship at home?" Torbridge asked cheerfully, handing him his hat and traveling cloak.

Taking her cue from him, Lily unfastened her own cloak, and the footman whisked it over his arm.

"Yes, my lord," he replied.

A superior, well-dressed gentleman appeared, crossing the entrance hall toward them with a stately gait. Lily's mouth went dry. This must be Sir George Masterton, the husband of Cousin Millicent.

"In her boudoir, my lord," he said grandly.

Torbridge said to her, "This is Gatting, who has been my sister's butler forever. Gatting, ask her ladyship to join us as soon as she may. Is Sir George at home?"

"At his club, my lord."

"Then we'll wait in the library. This way, Cousin."

She was afraid to look to see how the servants took the news that this shabby girl on his lordship's arm was their employer's cousin. Instead, trying not to stare, she walked up a carpeted staircase. Everything, stairs, ceilings, passages seemed to be built on a larger scale than anything she was used to.

He led her into a room lined with full bookshelves from floor to ceiling.

Her mouth fell open. "Goodness, it would take a person their whole life to read all of these."

"In most cases, it would probably be a complete waste, too," Lord Torbridge said. "Masterton's father bought them by the yard."

A giggle escaped her, hastily swallowed back, though she saw the gleam of response in Torbridge's eyes.

Lily wandered about the room, gazing around her, touching the luxurious softness of upholstery, the shining wood of the tables and shelves.

"Don't look so frightened," Torbridge advised. "You haven't come from a mud hut, you know, but from an Irish gentleman's country house."

"Oh, I'm not frightened," she assured him. "It's just all so *beautiful*."

"Lady Lily's voice," he reminded her.

"Oh. Sorry, of course," she said, returning to more refined accents at once.

"Why don't you sit down and be comfortable?"

"I have been sitting all day." She frowned. "I don't think there's a polite way to say how I feel."

Torbridge laughed, just as the door opened, and an extraordinary lady flew in amidst a waft of delicious perfume. She wore layers of diaphanous silk and gauze and a stunning, jeweled turban from which the most enormous feather waved, curling about her head. Her age was impossible to guess.

"Torbridge, what is this nonsense about a—Oh!" She broke off, blinking as her gaze fell on Lily.

"Millie, this is Lily," Torbridge said. "I would like you to be kind to her."

Millie, however, looked more wrathful. "No, Dolph, that is too much!" she exclaimed. "I will not have you bring your—"

"Millie," he interrupted with a sharpness Lily had never heard before. "Be sensible. Why the devil would I bring such a creature to your house? This young lady is perfectly respectable and is here to help both of us."

Lily blinked to stop herself from staring in bewildered fascination and dropped a curtsey.

"Lily, this is my sister, Lady Masterton. Your—er... Cousin Millicent," Torbridge said.

"Cousin?" Lady Masterton exclaimed, peering at Lily in astonishment. "Oh, dear me, no. Wouldn't it have been just like Grandpapa to do nothing for the family? But I don't think she needs to stay here, Dolph."

"On the contrary," Torbridge interrupted. "She *does* need to stay here. For although our late and lamented grandparent was at fault in many ways, he is not actually responsible for Lily. Sit down, Millie, and I'll tell you how it is."

Millie sat down obediently, her wide eyes fixed on her brother with more curiosity than astonishment. After an instant, she blinked and looked up at Lily, who stood rigidly where she had curtseyed to her hostess.

To Lily's surprise, the lady's eyes softened. "Come and sit with me, child. We can support each other through whatever mad start Torbridge is involving us in."

Hesitantly, but with some relief, Lily walked forward and sat on the sofa beside the grand lady. In her eyes was the same basic kindness she had always seen in Lord Torbridge.

"To my knowledge, Lily is not remotely related to us," he said apologetically, "but society needs to believe that she is. Therefore, she is Miss Lily Darrow."

"Cousin Paul's daughter? Didn't he die last year?"

"Fortuitously, God rest his soul. He left behind a large family if you recall, and poor Lily was not well-provided for. She came to England, but obviously, our parents are not really receiving visitors at this time, and so, I have brought her to you."

"Not sure you should use Papa's illness as quite such a convenience," Lady Masterton objected.

"We must make use of reality," he said vaguely.

"Must we? But why is it so important Lily is here with me? Are you hiding, my dear?"

"Oh, no," Lily replied. "I am to help his lordship. And your ladyship if you will let me."

"Cousin Lily," Torbridge said smoothly, "is very good with numbers and accounts, and is, generally, a very organized person. The world knows that you are not, so no one will think it odd that you take Cousin Lily as your companion."

"They will in that dress," Lady Masterton said bluntly.

Lily flushed.

"A dress allowance is available," Torbridge said carelessly.

His sister beamed. "Oh, well, that's different! We shall go to the dressmaker's first thing tomorrow." She looked Lily over critically. "You are very pretty, and your figure is excellent, so it will be a pleasure to dress you. How old are you, Cousin?"

"One-and-twenty."

"Really? You look younger. But in the circumstances, it is probably a good thing that you are not."

Torbridge stood up. "It would probably be best if you spend the first couple of days quietly to show Lily how things are done in society. You must keep her right about matters of accent and language, as well as dinner etiquette and so on. She has naturally good manners, and she learns quickly, so I don't foresee much difficulty. Just remember the story, Millie, or we are undone."

"I'm not an idiot, you know," Lady Masterton said, glaring at her brother, who was already walking toward the door.

Lily jumped to her feet in alarm and all but ran after him. "Are you leaving?"

He turned back with a faint smile. "Yes, but you needn't worry. Millie will look after you, and I will look in tomorrow." He took her hand and squeezed it gently. "I wouldn't leave you here if I didn't think you would be comfortable."

She knew a craven urge to cling to him for support, for he was her last link with the only life she knew. But his eyes were steady as he gazed down at her, as though he really did believe in her. In any case, she refused to show fear. It would be rude and offend her pride to boot.

She nodded and drew her hand free. "Of course."

His eyes lit with appreciation, a reward in itself. "That's my girl," he murmured and sauntered away with a mere casual wave in his sister's direction.

CHAPTER FOUR

L ILY HAD NO time to miss him.

As soon as the door closed behind him, her hostess jumped to her feet. "Come, you shall have the chamber next to mine, and we shall see what you need."

"But, my lady, you were just going out," Lily reminded her.

"So I was," Lady Masterton said, as though just recalling the fact. "It doesn't matter. I shall just be late, and no one will be surprised."

Lily had never seen such luxury as was to be hers. The best bed-chamber at the Hart, of which they were so proud, was bare, rough, and rustic by comparison. This was a much more feminine room with a huge bed surrounded by light, embroidered curtains. A soft carpet covered a good deal of the floor, and the porcelain of the washing bowl and jug seemed finer than her mother's best teacups. There were two looking glasses, a beautifully upholstered chair that matched the bed hangings, and heavy velvet curtains at the windows.

Lily tried to swallow her awe, and on Lady Masterton's instructions, opened her valise to show her meager possessions.

"The night rail will do for now, since no one is likely to see it," Lady Masterton said, tossing the garment on the bed. "I will lend you one of my dressing gowns. Have you no stays? Never mind, we shall get some. And some less *sturdy* chemises. I suppose we might share things like gloves if our hands are a similar..." She broke off with a squeak of horror as she seized Lily's hand for comparison with her own. "Oh, my dear, what has happened to your hands?"

"Nothing," Lily said awkwardly. "They are just a bit roughened and dry. From work."

"Work," her ladyship repeated as if she couldn't quite grasp the concept. "What sort of work?"

"Washing, cooking, scrubbing and sweeping, fetching and carrying, and feeding the hens and the pigs in the cold."

Lady Masterton sat down on the bed. "You had better tell me who you are. Have you...*assisted* my brother for very long?"

"Oh, no, not like this. He came several times to the inn."

"What inn?" her ladyship asked, bewildered.

"The Hart, in Sussex. My father is the innkeeper."

Lady Masterton swallowed visibly. "You speak very well for an innkeeper's daughter," she managed.

"I don't really," Lily said, lapsing into her own accent. "I just mimic our gentle guests. And I learned well at school. His lordship thought I could carry this off, but I'm not sure I can." She ended on a rather small, depressed note, which she hastily countered with a bright smile.

At once, Lady Masterton patted her hand. "I am quite sure you can," she said firmly. "Not least because Torbridge has a truly annoying habit of being right. I shan't think of you mimicking me! But we shall do better, I think, to start calling each other Cousin. I'm quite scatterbrained, myself, but I get used to things. You had better call me Cousin Millicent, or Millie, rather than *your ladyship*, which would be all wrong in the circumstances. As for your hands... Pull the bell beside you, Cousin, and we'll soak them. You will have to wear gloves in bed, too."

"Cousin Millicent" peered into her face, then touched her cheek. "Your skin is good," she said with satisfaction. "It is soft and creamy and not weathered at all."

For the first time, Lily was grateful for the lack of sun.

A breathless maid entered the room after the briefest knock.

"Bring me some warm water, a bowl of oatmeal, and a jug of cream," Lady Masterton instructed. "And send Prince to me."

Prince turned out to be her ladyship's stern-faced dresser—a very superior kind of lady's maid—who was far too dignified to show either surprise or distaste when commanded to mix the cream and oatmeal and smear it over Lily's hands.

"Such rough hands will not do in England," Lady Masterton said as though implying that in Ireland they might have passed muster. "An old pair of soft gloves, too, Prince. We'll leave the bowl here, Lily, and you can apply some fresh mixture before retiring. I wonder if I can be bothered going out now?"

"Oh, indeed, I think you should, ma'am," Lily said, distressed to think she was interfering with her hostess's pleasure. "I shall be fine here. In fact, I'll probably retire early, for I'm not used to traveling."

"Of course, you must do just as you like. And I shall spread the word that my delightful cousin from Ireland has come to stay!"

LILY, USED TO waking early and cleaning before serving breakfast, lay in bed for several minutes, listening to the noise in the streets, and the contrasting quiet inside the house. Worse, she was wearing gloves in bed, remarkably soft kid gloves, inside which her hands felt hot and moist and sticky.

She sat up, and since it was still dark, lit the lamp by her bed before peeling off the gloves. She wrinkled her nose, for they didn't smell good. She rose and went to the washing bowl and soaked her hands. They emerged from the water, looking remarkably less dried and cracked. They even felt softer.

Now, what was she supposed to do? Go and find Lady Masterton? *Cousin Millicent!* Perhaps, but she knew her hostess did want her to be seen about the house in her usual dress.

A maid crept into the room with a coal scuttle. "Oh, I beg your pardon, Miss! I didn't expect you to be up. I'm just here to light the fire. You should go back to bed till it's warmer."

To Lily, used to rising first in winter, it was barely cold at all. "Perhaps I will. Only…her ladyship mentioned an early outing."

The maid grinned. "Early means eleven o'clock to her ladyship. She won't be up much before that. It's only just after seven."

"Thank you," Lily said to the cheerful maid as she left.

With nothing much else to do, Lily smeared the last of the oatmeal and cream on her hands, returned them to the smelly gloves, and climbed back into bed. She meant to think rather than sleep, but the novelty of rest took her by surprise, and she nodded off.

It was a different maid bearing a cup of hot chocolate who woke her a couple of hours later. "Good morning, Miss. Her ladyship asks that I look after you while you're with us. I'm Emily, the chambermaid, but I help Miss Prince on occasions, and it's my dearest wish to be a lady's maid one day."

"Then I hope you will be," Lily said warmly, remembering to keep her Lady Lily accent. "Thank you."

"Ring when you're ready to dress," Emily said and departed again.

While she was still drinking the luxurious hot chocolate and wondering what was happening at the Hart, a scratching sound came from the other side of the door.

"Come in," Lily said doubtfully, expecting Emily once more.

However, it was "Cousin Millicent" in a very elaborate dressing gown who breezed into the room, bearing several garments. "Good morning, Cousin Lily! I trust you slept well?"

"Yes, I did."

"Oh, good! Look, I have brought these for you to wear this morning. The gown won't fit you, of course, for you are smaller than I, but this pelisse is very loose by design and provided it doesn't scrape the floor, should hide everything beneath. And don't you just love this

36

little hat? I decided it was too young for me and never wore it, though I never quite liked to return it."

In a barrage of information, questions, and random tangents, Cousin Millicent drew her out of bed and began throwing garments at her. Halfway through, Emily arrived to help and brushed out Lily's hair before exchanging speaking looks with Lady Masterton.

"Hair-cut," they both said at once.

In the meantime, Emily pinned it into a rather appealing but simple new style piled more to the top of her head, and the new hat was tried and approved.

Lily gazed at herself in the glass, astonished. She really did look like a lady. If one didn't see the pins and the sash, holding the gown up and in under her breasts. It was, apparently, good enough for her to be seen in the breakfast parlor, where it was possible Sir George Masterton would be discovered.

However, they had the breakfast table to themselves. Lily, used to her mother's substantial breakfasts and a lot of hard work, was glad to be able to help herself and piled her plate high with choice morsels of smoked fish, eggs, and toast. Her "cousin" nibbled at some bread. They drank coffee while the carriage was summoned, and from then on, Lily really did enter a different world.

She had never seen such subservience and eagerness to please as they were met with at Lady Masterton's dressmaker's establishment. A bewildering array of beautiful gowns in soft, delicate fabrics was shown to her. To Lily, they were all gorgeous, and it was left to her "cousin" to choose which she should try on. In a daze, she saw herself decked out in smart walking dresses, morning gowns, evening gowns, and even ball gowns.

Only when she heard Lady Masterton enumerate the gowns she wanted, including an evening dress and a morning gown delivered by six o'clock that day, did she come to her senses.

"But this is too much!" she exclaimed, then hissed in Millicent's ear. "I'm sure his lordship does not mean me to have all this. I cannot possibly—"

"Oh, he does, trust me. This is a modest wardrobe. And I would really prefer you to have the lavender evening gown today, for I thought we could have a quiet dinner at home. George will be there, and I would like you to meet him."

This was not a treat Lily looked forward to, but the prospect was still too far away to trouble her hugely. In the meantime, she was fitted with two pelisses and an opera cloak. A pair of dancing slippers, indoor slippers, and outdoor shoes were ordered from a different shop, and two new hats from a very handsome milliner.

"Oh dear, I will have ruined his lordship," Lily said anxiously as they sat in the carriage to go home, surrounded by packages.

"Oh, no," Millicent assured her. "About the only thing my father ever did for Torbridge was give him a staggering allowance."

After absorbing this information, Lily was struck by the contrasting events of Millicent's father lying in his death bed, while Millicent gadded about town buying clothes for a whirlwind of upcoming gaiety.

"I am so sorry about your father. I had selfishly forgotten. You must long to be with him."

"God, no," Millicent said with a visible shudder. "The wretched house is gloomy enough without sickness. And I don't suppose dying has sweetened the old gentleman's temper."

Lily's mouth dropped open.

Seeing it, Millicent gave a crooked little smile. "Have I shocked you? We are not close to our parents. They belonged to a generation that thought it vulgar to have more to do with their children than inspect them for fifteen minutes each evening if they happened to be in the same house. They spent most of their time in London, while we were brought up at Hayleigh. Our paths rarely crossed, and when they did, he was angry."

"What about?" Lily asked.

"Being in the country and surrounded by his children, probably. He didn't think a great deal of us,"

"Us?"

"His children. Dolph, Ella, Gilbert, and me."

"Is his name really Dolph?" Lily asked, distracted.

Millicent laughed. "Randolph. Ella called him Dolph when she was a baby, and it stuck."

"Are your other siblings in London, too?" Lily asked, accepting that they were probably not with their dying parent.

"No, not just now. Gilbert is in Spain with the army, and Ella is in the country producing offspring for her lord. Mind you, she is threatening to come up for the Season, so you may meet her. Torbridge didn't tell you any of this, did he?"

"I didn't know anything about his family at all until yesterday. He does not speak of personal things."

"Maybe not, but if you are our cousin, you should at least know how many of us there are!"

"I think he relied on you," Lily said.

Millicent stared at her. "Don't be silly. No one relies on me."

"Lord—Cousin Torbridge does. Or he wouldn't have brought me to you."

Millicent appeared to think about that for a moment. "Actually, I've no idea anymore why Torbridge does anything."

"You mean he has changed?" Lily asked. Part of her felt guilty for even asking, but the desire to know more about him overwhelmed everything else.

Millicent nodded. "Since he returned from university, or at least his travels immediately afterward."

"In what way?"

Millicent shrugged. "Oh, I don't know. When we were children, he was thoughtful, sensible, as well as fun. He looked after the rest of us. More of a father, to be truthful, than our father. Or at least, that's how I remember it before he went away that autumn. And then, when he came home, grown-up, he was more like me."

Lily blinked. "Like you?"

"On, caring for nothing but clothes and appearance and trivial things. Like propriety."

Lily frowned. "But he is not *really* like that." *And neither are you.*

"I suppose he is still fun," Millicent allowed. "And does odd things without anyone noticing. Like bringing you." For a moment, the vague eyes weren't vague at all, and then she smiled amiably and glanced out of the window. "I wonder why it's taking so long?"

Eventually, the carriage pulled up outside the Mastertons' house in Brook Street. A footman swarmed down the front steps to take the bandboxes and parcels, while Millicent sailed into the house with Lily at her heels.

Lily hoped to find that Lord Torbridge awaited them inside, but it seemed his lordship had not yet called. She and her hostess ate a light luncheon in a rather magnificent dining room. The presence of servants limited their communication to small talk, which at least helped Lily to note a few acceptable topics for future polite conversation.

Only when the servants left, did Lily ask curiously, "Do you have children, Cousin Millicent?"

"Alas, no," Millicent replied lightly, rising to her feet. "It is a matter of grief to both of us, but we have not been so blessed. Would you like to make some calls with me this afternoon?"

Lily accepted the change of conversation, though it bothered her slightly—not so much that her hostess clearly did not wish to discuss it, but the way her eyes seemed to shut down as soon as Lily mentioned children.

"Actually," Lily said, "If you would let me, I thought I might spend the afternoon looking at your accounts and so on, and see if I can straighten things out for you a little."

Millicent regarded her doubtfully. "Well, I'll show you where things are, but I fully expect you to run screaming from the room within five minutes. I won't mind, you know. I am happy to help Torbridge if I can, especially as I rather like you, Cousin Lily!"

Ridiculously pleased by this accolade, Lily followed her to the morning room, where an elegant desk stood, piled high with papers in one disorganized splaying heap. Even more worryingly, the corners of other documents stuck out of the drawers, as though they were stuffed too full to contain everything tidily.

"Oh dear," Lily said faintly. "Are those all unpaid accounts?"

"Oh, no," Millicent replied, much to Lily's relief. "There are invitations and letters I haven't answered, too."

"Perhaps," Lily said, "you had better tell me how much money you have now and when you will have access to more?"

Millicent replied in a slightly strangled voice, after which she recalled some other pressing duty and fled. Lily squared her shoulders and walked up to the desk. It was tempting just to sweep everything on to the floor, but she refrained. Instead, she tidied it into two large but relatively neat heaps on the left of the desk, leaving her space to work. It also revealed a pen in a stand.

Rummaging in the drawers, she discovered a bottle of ink, a knife to trim the pen, several sheets of expensive letter paper, and a notebook. She set to work and wrote down the figures Millicent had told her, hoping her vague hostess hadn't simply plucked them from the air. Then she began going through the daunting piles of documents, sorting them into letters, invitations, and accounts, all in order of date, and filled the wastepaper basket with old invitation cards, advertisements, and other rubbish.

She was nearing the end of the first pile when a man walked into the room. She glanced up quickly, hoping it was Lord Torbridge, but it was a stranger who met her gaze. A gentleman of medium height, impeccably dressed, his brown hair cut short, the smile on his lips faintly sardonic.

"Cousin Lily, I can only assume? I'm George Masterton."

Lily leaped to her feet, almost tumbling the chair in her hurry, and bobbed an awkward curtsey. "Sir George," she murmured in her best Lady Lily accent. "I am so grateful for your kindness in letting me stay."

Sir George raised his quizzing glass and inspected the desk. "Trust me, Miss Darrow, it will be nothing to my gratitude if you make sense of my wife's correspondence." The quizzing glass was lowered. "You are making impressive progress."

"Thank you," Lily said doubtfully. He was, she thought, an intelligent man, and not unkind. But there was something discontented, even unhappy, about him. "It shouldn't take us too long."

His lips twitched as though he recognized her attempt to include Millicent in the task for the loyal fiction it was. "I can only wish you luck. And look forward to becoming better acquainted over dinner. I understand Torbridge is also to join us."

Her heart lifted at this good news, and she smiled at its bearer. Sir George blinked, smiled faintly in return, and bowed before departing. Lily returned to the task in hand.

When she had begun on the second pile, a footman brought her a cup of tea with a plate of scones and a slice of cake. She thanked him with some delight and carried on while she ate and drank.

She was just finishing her tea and wondering about lighting the candles when Millicent rushed in with great excitement. "The new gowns have arrived! Come up at once and see!"

Obligingly, Lily set the dressmaker's respectful reminder from a year ago in its correct place in the to-do pile and followed her hostess upstairs. Emily and Prince were sent for, the bathtub filled with steaming water and scented oil, and she was sent to soak in it.

The luxury of doing more than a quick "dunk and scrub" in often cold water was unexpectedly blissful, and she was almost annoyed when Emily disturbed her to wash her hair and summon her to the main bedchamber.

Wrapped in soft towels, she emerged to discover her "court" had been joined by a hairdresser, who brushed out her hair, stared at her assessingly, and began to cut. With much of the weight removed, the natural wave of her hair was artfully used to curl around her face, while the rest was pinned high on her head. The hairdresser was dismissed, and Lily was dressed in new undergarments—a fine lawn chemise and silk stockings that seemed to caress her skin. Until she was tied into the instrument of torture they called stays.

At least Millicent granted her some reprieve here. "There is no need to lace them so tightly. She is hardly plump! Just enough to emphasize that shapely bosom. Excellent!"

The new lavender evening gown was thrown artfully over her head and laced up by Emily. Then everyone stared at her in the glass.

"Excellent," Millicent pronounced.

"Jewelry, my lady," Prince reminded her.

"Oh, the very thing! The sapphire necklace, Prince."

"Oh no, Cousin," Lily said, distressed. "You mustn't lend me all your best things! Look, I have a little necklace here…"

She pulled the small, worn box from her dressing table drawer and opened it. It was a simple pendant on a short chain of twisted gold. The pendant itself was a small gold disk with a smaller gemstone stone at its center. It had always been her pride and joy, a Christening gift from a generous lady whose name her parents did not even know.

Emily took the necklace and fastened it about her neck. Worried that it would not be considered good enough, Lily looked anxiously at Millicent.

"Perfect," Lady Masterton pronounced. Emily smiled. Even Prince nodded. "Now, I must change, too! How long do I have, Prince? Lily, don't dare go down without me! I want to see Torbridge's face when you walk into the room!"

Lily rather thought he would laugh to see the innkeeper's daughter so elegantly dressed. She certainly didn't look like Lily Villin anymore.

CHAPTER FIVE

Only fifteen minutes later, Millicent returned for her in a cloud of perfume and gauze, and swept her downstairs to the drawing room.

As soon as they sailed side-by-side through the open doors, she saw Lord Torbridge. Very smart and handsome in black evening clothes and snowy-white cravat, he stood by the mantelpiece with Sir George, laughing at some remark of his host's. They both glanced over as the ladies entered, and the smile died on Lord Torbridge's lips.

Lily's heart sank, but she had a part to play and kept her expression amiable as the gentlemen bowed and greeted them.

"Do I have to make formal introductions?" Millicent asked.

"Not at all," Sir George said. "Cousin Lily and I met this afternoon. I have to say, Millie, she has made a gallant effort to tidy your desk."

"I looked after all my father's business and correspondence," Lily said and wondered ruefully how he was coping without her. "So, it is no hardship for me."

"It seems a bit of a hardship," Sir George observed, "when my wife was busy calling on friends."

Millicent shrugged as if the criticism didn't matter to her. Lily knew that it did, though she wasn't quite sure how.

"Oh, Cousin Millie asked me to join her," Lily said. "But I wanted to make a start. I like to be useful."

"A glass of sherry," Torbridge pronounced, handing a small glass to each lady.

As Lily accepted hers, he searched her face. His eyebrow lifted infinitesimally, and she knew he was asking about difficulties. She only smiled, for if she was a fish out of water here, it was still oddly fascinating.

For Lily, the evening passed in a far from unpleasant blur. She sat beside Torbridge, which was both exciting and comforting, for she could easily see which cutlery he used for which course. The meal seemed huge, like a banquet, and much more formal than anything she had encountered before. Servants delivered dish after dish, discreetly whipped away used crockery and cutlery, and refilled the glasses. It was a lot to observe and remember, especially while maintaining her accent and keeping track of the conversation.

Lord Torbridge and his sister clearly enjoyed an easy, bantering relationship that kept everyone amused, and Sir George, although often appearing more serious, was equally witty. Occasionally, they talked of things Lily had no idea about—literature or gossip or politics—but they seemed to see when she was struggling and dropped a few words of explanation. They neither left her out nor patronized her, and she began to enjoy herself.

Especially when Millicent rose from the table saying, "Come, Lily, let us leave the gentlemen to their wine."

And Torbridge stood, drawing out her chair for her. There was a smile of approval in his eyes that almost made her preen. "You're doing wonderfully well," he murmured, and her happiness was complete.

"VERY WELL, TORBRIDGE," Masterton drawled when the door had closed behind the ladies and he had pushed the decanter of port across the table. "What the devil are you up to?"

"I?" Torbridge said innocently, pouring himself a glassful.

"You and that girl you have foisted on Millie."

"Cousin Lily," Torbridge reproved, raising his glass in a toast. "To family."

"To family," Masterton agreed. "But that girl is no more your cousin than I am."

Torbridge sat back and sipped his port, regarding his brother-in-law over the rim of his glass. "Why, who else could she be?"

"You tell me."

"Very well, if you tell me what she did or said to give the game away."

Masterton's eyebrows flew up. "Nothing. Millie told me."

Torbridge couldn't help smiling. "I hoped she would," he said vaguely.

Masterton was silent a moment. Then he said abruptly, "She would do anything for you, you know. I have no objection to her taking in this girl, but I need to know she will not lead Millie into harm."

Torbridge paused with his glass halfway to his lips and lowered it to the table. "Lord, I hope not. The truth is, she has a task to carry out for me. I don't anticipate she will have time to lead Millie astray, even supposing she knew how. I am, you will have perceived, relying on Millie to keep her on the straight and narrow."

"Then she is not a lady?"

For some reason, the question irritated Torbridge. "She is not used to society."

He met Masterton's gaze, making up his mind. He liked his brother-in-law and had always trusted him with Millie's safety, if not with always knowing the best way to deal with her. Trusting him with secrets of national security was something else entirely, but he followed his instincts. "I would like her to be invited, along with you and Millie, to Pennington Place."

Masterton's fingers tightened on his glass. He seemed to force himself to take a drink before he answered with quiet deliberation. "I do not care for Pennington."

Torbridge knew why. In recent weeks, Pennington had made Millie the object of his gallantry. Not the only one, but the flirting had been definite. Torbridge had hoped the situation would cause Masterton to make some push to keep his wife's affections. But in fact, it seemed to have the opposite effect. They seemed more divided than ever.

"Don't care for him much myself," Torbridge agreed. "He is a man of little substance. An exquisitely tailored coat, you might say, full only of wind. It's his brother who interests me."

"Jack?" Masterton looked surprised. "He's a decent sort, though I wouldn't call him a friend."

"He does seem decent," he said vaguely. "But I would like to make sure. I'm hoping there will be opportunities for Lily and me, between us, to find out."

Masterton was silent. "There is an invitation. I would prefer to refuse it." He waved one arm in irritation. "If you are going to be there, escort Millie by all means. I trust you to look after her."

He swirled the brandy in his glass. "If I were you, I would go."

Masterton's smile was bitter. "You trust her so little?"

"I think... I don't like this distance between you. Give her a reason to—"

"To choose her husband over a coat full of wind? It doesn't seem a choice I should lose!"

"It isn't," Torbridge said mildly. "But the coat gives her some attention. It is, of course, up to you. Either way, I will do my best to look out for her. Shall we rejoin the ladies?"

Masterton grunted and downed the remains of his port.

In proposing an early return to the drawing room, Torbridge was, of course, avoiding any further uncomfortable conversation about relationships, while hoping his brother-in-law would take heed of his few wise words. But he was also conscious of a pull toward Lily like an unseen but unexpectedly strong thread between them.

They found Millie sitting at the pianoforte, with Lily standing beside her, one finger hovering over the keys while she listened to whatever Millie was saying. It was a pretty vignette, and Lily deprived him of breath. Not just because she was beautiful—she had always been beautiful—but because she was *in his world.*

And that was where the danger lay. Over the last year, he had made several visits to the Hart, some for duty, others just because he couldn't stay away from her. But it had been a safe attraction, for he would not seduce a respectable girl, and any thought of marriage between people of such different classes was ridiculous. And yet, there she stood in his sister's drawing room, in a fashionable gown with her hair elegantly dressed, and suddenly everything seemed possible.

Even though it wasn't. Neither of them could change who they were.

"Do you play, Cousin Lily?" Masterton asked.

"Oh no," Lily said hastily.

"But you do sing," Torbridge said, just to see if she would. And because he had liked to hear her voice around the inn, sweet, soothing, and joyful as she went about her daily tasks.

Her eyes widened in surprise as if she hadn't realized she was overheard. "I don't think idle humming counts as an accomplishment."

"I shall be the judge of that," Millie said. "Sing, and I will play."

Of course, they knew none of the same songs, but at last, Lily broke into a soft, traditional song of unrequited love, which Torbridge knew better than to take personally, and Millie supplied an approximate accompaniment. Even here, her untrained voice was delightful, and he was glad to hear Masterton ask her for another. To his surprise, without fuss, she broke into a very different, funny song that had them all in stitches.

Torbridge's heart swelled with pride, though why he didn't know. It wasn't as if he had any hand in teaching her. But there were hidden parts to Lily, like unfurling petals, and emotion swelled within him when she came and sat on the sofa beside him.

"Well done," he said warmly. "I'm glad to see you are not easily confounded or embarrassed."

"I suppose if I was, I wouldn't be doing this at all," she mused. "Even for you." She cast him a quick glance. "Will I embarrass you in public? Will I embarrass them?"

"No, I rather think not. You have learned astoundingly fast."

"Just as well, because apparently, we are *at home* to morning callers tomorrow."

"Excellent. And I will take you driving in the park at the fashionable hour of five."

"Why?"

"The more you are out and about, the more likely you are to become acquainted with Jack Hill."

"What if he does not notice me or does not like me?"

"I think it unlikely. But the main thing for the moment is to have you invited to Pennington Place with Millie."

She nodded, a little uncertainly, causing him to ask, "Is something worrying you?"

"I'm pretending, acting. But I *feel* like…like a pig in lace," she blurted. "I'm a rough innkeeper's daughter shoved into silk, and I'm afraid everyone will see that and upset all your plans."

He knew a pang of guilt, for he'd always been aware that what he was doing was unkind to her on many levels. "I always have other plans," he assured her. "But I see no reason to fear any such thing. Your hosts have obviously taken to you."

"Yes, but they are kind, too. I went to school, but I do not have their kind of education."

"Neither do most of the other young ladies of the ton," he said sardonically. "Truly, no one likes a blue-stocking. Just giggle and tell the gentlemen they are much too clever for you. They'll believe you and think none the worse of you. And remember, a formal education is not the only kind that matters. You have more. You observe the life and events around you and learn from them."

"Do I?" she asked doubtfully.

He held her gaze. "Yes. You do."

Her breath gave a little hitch. He wanted to put his arms around her, whisk her away from everything either of them knew, and just *be* with her. Alone. He dragged his gaze free, searching for an easy topic of conversation, and became distracted by the necklace she wore, a simple pendant on a twisted gold chain.

"That is pretty." Without thought, he reached out and lifted the pendant between two fingers. "It doesn't look like Millie's."

Her breathing had quickened. He could see the pulse galloping at her throat, very close to his fingers. And his own heart hammered in response. She was not immune to him. He moved her. He didn't know if it thrilled or terrified him.

"It isn't Millie's," she whispered.

He released the necklace and sat back. "Forgive the liberty. Can I ask where it came from?"

"It was a Christening gift from a lady who stayed at the inn the night I was born."

"It's beautiful."

"Thank you."

"Do you play cards, Lily?" Millie interrupted their *tête à tête*, which had gone on quite long enough.

He stood casually and went to bring the card table nearer the fire. For some reason, his limbs felt heavy and unwilling to move away from her.

DESPITE THE SIZE of the house, Lily woke the following morning feeling trapped and longing for fresh air. Without ringing for Emily, she dressed as best she could—leaving off the stays—and let herself out of the house to go for a long, brisk walk.

Although it was hardly the sea air and open countryside she was used to, the maze of wide residential streets with patches of formal parkland was interesting enough to distract her, and by the time she returned, the exercise had restored her to more habitual good humor.

Until she was admitted to the house, and Millie rushed out of the breakfast parlor in excessive relief. "There you are! Where on earth have you been?"

"I just went for a walk," Lily assured her, touching her bonnet to make sure she had remembered to put it on. With relief, she untied it and let the footman take it from her, along with her smart new pelisse.

Millie took her arm and all but hustled her into the breakfast parlor. "Unaccompanied?" she demanded when she had closed the door and leaned on it.

"Entirely," Lily said. "It was, rather, the point."

"Oh, my dear, no, an unmarried lady should never go out unaccompanied! She should be chaperoned by a married lady and escorted, preferably by a male family member. At the very least, she must take her maid or a footman. For one thing, London's streets are not quite safe. For another..." She broke off, perhaps seeing the distress in Lily's face. "But there, I don't mean to scold you. I just know what all the old tabbies are like, and I don't want them sinking their claws into you! Thankfully, town is quiet, for the Season is not yet truly begun, and in any case, I suppose it is too early for most members of the ton to be abroad. Come and breakfast with me."

To please her kind hostess, Lily had to promise not to commit this heinous crime again, which made her feel more trapped than ever.

However, she worked some more on Millie's documents and had got as far as the papers stuffed in the drawers when she was summoned to change into her new morning gown to receive guests.

The formal morning calls were another bizarre custom of the upper echelons of society. They never lasted long, and nothing of substance seemed to be discussed with anyone. However, the people were interesting to her, as they always were, and she merely acted her way through the proceedings. She must have done well, for Millie received many compliments on her behalf and was invited to bring her cousin to Mrs. Westley's evening party that night.

"I know it is short notice, but it's just an informal gathering," Mrs. Westley explained, "since the Season has not quite begun. However, there should be enough couples to form a dance."

Millie's teacup clattered into its saucer, but no one but Lily seemed to notice.

"What is the matter," Lily asked as soon as the last of the callers had departed. "What is wrong with Lady Westley's party?"

"Nothing. Absolutely nothing, except it suddenly struck me that it would be just like Torbridge to expect you to be able to dance and not trouble to ask. *Can* you dance?"

"Oh, yes. We have many dancing parties at the inn, and friends' weddings—"

"You should cope with country dances, then," Millie interrupted. "The cotillion?"

Lily nodded.

"The waltz?" Millie asked with less hope.

Lily hung her head.

Millie rose and vigorously pulled the bell. "Send Sir George to us," she commanded the footman who opened the door.

"Sir George has gone out, my lady. He said he would return for dinner."

"Drat the man!" Millie exclaimed, scowling direly. "Wait. You must take an urgent message to Lord Torbridge."

Lily had no objection to the presence of Lord Torbridge, though she did suggest that summoning him to be her dancing master would merely annoy him.

"Who cares?" his fond sister retorted. "If he wants you in this role, he must exert himself to make it work,"

"I could just sit-out the waltzes," Lily argued.

"No, no," Millie said, scandalized. "On no account must you refuse an invitation to dance."

Torbridge duly turned up, strolling into the drawing room and asking sardonically, "Where is the fire?" However, there was a hint of anxiety in the quickness of his gaze as he took in both his sister and Lily, searching, presumably for signs of distress.

"How can you be so foolish, Dolph?" Millie demanded. "We have been invited to Lady Westley's this evening, and *you* have not taught Lily to waltz!"

Torbridge stared at her. For an instant, Lily thought he was about to make a blistering retort and stepped forward instinctively to avert it. However, he merely threw back his head and laughed.

He was still laughing when Millie sat at the piano and attempted to sober him with a loud, attention-seizing discord. "Now, Dolph! We are running out of time!"

"Oh, be calm, where is the difficulty? It's hardly complicated." He turned his still-amused gaze on Lily. "Did Millie show you the basic steps?"

Obligingly, Lily showed him.

"Very well. Now, you must do that while following wherever I go. Like this."

She gave him her hand willingly but jumped as his arm passed around her waist.

"Don't worry, I shan't come any closer," he said humorously. "And neither should you, even for the pleasure of standing on my toes."

Millie began to play. For the first few bars, he merely let her listen to the rhythm, then said, "Now," and stepped toward her.

She stumbled back a second too late, but he only grinned and carried on until she understood what was expected of her. In fact, he was so completely good-humored about the whole thing, that she soon relaxed with him into the fun of the dance and quickly learned how to follow his lead. If she was still very aware of his closeness and his touch, the embarrassment quickly left her, and she simply, if secretly, enjoyed it.

If she misstepped and caught his toe, he pulled a comically exaggerated face of pain and made her laugh. If she started to watch their feet, he made a joke of commanding her to look at his ugly face instead.

"You're meant to smile and look happy throughout," he added. "But if your partner is tedious, imagine him dancing with his head in a chamber pot, and you'll find you can keep smiling."

"Randolph!" Millie scolded.

"I know. Sound advice. I think we had better stop before it's my head in the pot."

Lily laughed.

"Stop?" Millie exclaimed, outraged. "But she needs more practice!"

"It's time for our drive in the park," he said in surprise. "Don't worry. Perhaps you should save the first waltz for me, Lily, and look on it as extra practice. But in fact, there may not even be a waltz—it's still considered a little daring, you know."

CHAPTER SIX

S ITTING BESIDE LORD Torbridge in his curricle, Lily gave a little sigh of relief as he set the horses into motion.

He spared her a glance. "That sounded heartfelt. Is my sister proving a strain on your sanity?"

"Oh, no, her ladyship is all kindness. I like her. It's just that life here is so...*hemmed in*. I used to think a lady's life must be wonderful, that she could go where she liked, when she liked, do whatever she wanted. But it isn't like that at all. There are even more stupid rules in this world than in my own!"

"Sadly, it seems to be the lot of unmarried women of whatever degree and of whatever country."

"Perhaps. But when I discovered I could not even *walk* on my own..."

"I can imagine your frustration."

She glanced at him suspiciously, but he appeared to be sincere.

"It's a little less constricting in the country," he said encouragingly. "Town is different, and in fact, it is a sensible rule considering the many dangers that lurk here. Even these respectable streets are within minutes of distinctly insalubrious neighborhoods."

She nodded. "I know, I should not complain."

"Feel free to complain to me all you wish. After all, I put you in this situation."

"I don't want to appear ungrateful," she said at once, "for indeed I am not! Look at this gown, for example, this soft pelisse! I have never worn such fine things in my life."

"And they suit you very well. I trust they are as comfortable as they are charming."

"Well, they would be, if it wasn't for the stays," she confided.

He let out a shout of laughter that attracted the attention of a lady and gentlemen they were bowling past. Torbridge tipped his whip against his hat and bowed.

"I shouldn't have mentioned stays, should I?" she said ruefully.

"I wouldn't to anyone else." A smile flickered across his lips. "Or to me, in fact. I have trouble enough keeping the line. Tell me, what do you think of my sister and brother-in-law?"

The surprising question distracted her from his previous statement. "That they are friendly, kind, and clever and would clearly do anything for you."

"Do you think them well-suited?" he asked casually. "As a couple?"

She nodded, then glanced at him. "There is some trouble between them, though. I don't know what it is, but although they get along on one level, there is a distance between them that I think hurts them both. And yet, neither can or will close that gap."

He glanced at her. "Incisive."

"It might be the debts," she said apologetically. "She has unpaid bills from three years ago, at least, and I haven't even finished going through them all."

"The debts are merely a symptom. Does she love him still?"

"Deeply, I would say." She frowned. "But you are her brother. You know both of them far better than I ever could. Why do you ask me?"

Despite the increasing traffic on the road, he turned his head and looked at her. "It's what you do, isn't it, Lily?"

"I don't know what you mean."

"Oh, I think you do. If they came to the Hart unknown to each other, would you find a way to introduce them?"

"I wouldn't need to. They would find a way to each other. I am not some matchmaker, my lord!"

"Nothing so vulgar," he agreed. He smiled faintly. "I have this strange fancy that you are the magical heart of the Hart. But look, here is Hyde Park, where everyone who is anyone must be seen during the promenade hour."

There certainly seemed to be a lot more traffic on the road leading to the park, and as they bowled along its paths, more expensively dressed people were walking and driving there than Lily had ever seen before.

Nearly all of them acknowledged Lord Torbridge and glanced curiously at Lily. To those favored few he stopped to speak to, he introduced Lily as his cousin, Miss Darrow. She met so many people, she didn't stand a chance of remembering their names or even their faces should they ever meet again.

Except one man who stood beside the path in conversation with two ladies. He was tall, fair, and handsome in a haughty kind of way. His gaze flickered over the curricle and Torbridge with a faint curl of his lip. He even gave a somehow sardonic bow before he saw Lily. His eyes widened, flatteringly, and somehow the bow became much more respectful. When he straightened, he even had his hand across his heart.

"Excellent," Torbridge murmured as they drove past. "No, don't acknowledge him, you haven't been introduced. But you are noticed."

"Why, who is he?"

"That, my dear, is James Hill, Viscount Pennington," Torbridge said. "The brother of the man we are after. And the host of the house party we wish you to be invited to."

"I don't think I like him."

"Neither do I, but I will still go."

"Are you invited? I don't think he likes you either."

"Of course, he doesn't," Torbridge said complacently. "But his mother does. And she commands the invitations."

SIR GEORGE ESCORTED his wife and Lily to Mrs. Westley's party. Although it was a fine spring evening and only a street away, they took the carriage, which gave Lily no chance to walk off her nervous anticipation. This was her most serious test yet, and she would not be able to cling all the time to Millie or Lord Torbridge for help.

However, once the palaver of the cloakroom was taken care of, she fixed a good-humored expression to her face and smiled frequently. It was no hardship to keep the Lady Lily accent in this company since anything else was unthinkable.

Sir George escorted them upstairs in the wake of other guests to a large drawing room, which appeared to be full of people. A partition had been drawn back to extend the room and allow space for a dance floor and a trio of musicians who, when Lily entered, were playing merely soft chamber music as a pleasant background to the hum of conversation.

Anxiously, Lily quartered the room for Lord Torbridge, but clearly, he had not yet arrived.

Mrs. Westley welcomed them, assured them dancing would begin in ten minutes, and introduced Lily to several young people. She answered all the smiles and greetings, including that of a young lady and her chaperone, whom she had met that afternoon. Almost immediately, she was asked to dance by a young man with very tall, starched shirt points.

Since he could barely move his head, she wondered how he would be able to dance. In fact, he seemed to have adapted and managed very well. It was Lily who felt self-conscious, for the dancing was much more restrained than she was used to, and she had to rein in her natural exuberance. But she thanked her partner as he escorted her back to Millie, claiming to have enjoyed the dance immensely.

Millie had draped herself across the arm of an occupied sofa and was flanked by two fair-haired gentlemen. "Ah, there you are, Lily," she said, and one of the gentlemen who turned at once was Viscount Pennington.

Lily's heart gave a little lurch of attention. She was not here merely to enjoy herself.

"Thank you for returning her to me, Mr. Sanders," Millie said graciously. "Lily, let me present two great friends, Lord Pennington, and his brother, Mr. Hill. Gentlemen, my cousin, Miss Lily Darrow."

In friendly fashion, Lily offered her hand to each gentleman in turn. Pennington took it first, smiling, "I am already at Miss Darrow's feet, having seen her just out of my reach in the park this afternoon."

"Did you?" Lily marveled. "I don't recall it." She gave her hand to the younger brother, who interested her far more, being the man Torbridge suspected of betraying his country.

Mr. Hill was also a handsome man, not quite as tall as his brother, but he possessed a more open and pleasant countenance.

"How do you do?" Lily murmured.

"I have rarely been so happy in my life," Mr. Hill said fervently.

Lily laughed. "You are clearly a family of outrageous flatterers. But I am glad to meet friends of my cousin's."

"Glad enough to grant me the waltz that's about to begin?" Lord Pennington asked.

"Sadly, I can't," Lily replied. "I have promised it to my cousin, Lord Torbridge."

"He isn't here," Pennington pointed out.

"Yes, he is," Millie said with a faint air of triumph and raised one hand toward the door.

Torbridge was sauntering toward them, answering various greetings with bows, remarks, and handshakes as he came.

"It always amazes me," Pennington drawled, "that Torbridge

actually waltzes at all. Not too improper for you, old man?"

Torbridge bowed to his sister and cousin and smiled rather vaguely at the men. "Sometimes fashion wins over propriety. It is quite a conflict. Coz," he added, offering Lily his arm, "Shall we?"

Lily smiled at the other gentlemen and tripped off happily on Torbridge's arm.

"Well done," he breathed. "Did one of them ask you to waltz?"

"Pennington."

"Hill is used to losing out to his brother. If you can manage it, try to choose him over Pennington. I suspect it will mean a lot and make you even more memorable."

"Providing I don't stand on his toes," Lily murmured.

"That is what our practice is for. My feet are ready to endure."

"It's not the most flattering invitation to dance that I have ever received."

"I don't suppose it is," Torbridge said, placing his arm around her. "But as long as you don't resort to the chamber pot, I shall be content."

He swung her into the dance before she could either laugh or retort, and she followed from pure instinct. His smile of approval made her ridiculously happy.

"I'm afraid I may not be very good at this," she confided.

"Waltzing? Nonsense. You have natural grace and dance very well."

"I meant attracting the attentions of gentleman," she whispered. "I've spent most of my adult life avoiding them."

"Then you'll know never to be alone with him," Torbridge said severely. "Just flatter him enough to make him think you like him."

"And that will be enough to earn me an invitation from his mother?" she asked dubiously.

"Have a little faith in yourself," he said lightly. "I do."

Enchanted, Lily smiled at him.

His breath caught. "Don't look at me like that, or Hill will think you're spoken for."

I am... She flushed, tearing her gaze free.

"It's fine," he said hastily, "I understand. Just be aware that not everyone will."

It might have taken her a moment longer to get over her embarrassment, but the sight of Millie strolling around on the arm of Lord Pennington distracted her. "You didn't tell me the brothers were friends of Millie's."

"They're not," Torbridge said coolly.

She met his gaze once more. "Sir George left almost as soon as we arrived."

"I'm afraid he is prone to do that."

"I see... I don't suppose we can go to Pennington Place via the Hart?"

"I don't think that would be very wise, do you? Besides, it isn't exactly on the way."

"It's not exactly on the way from Hayleigh to London either," she retorted.

"No, but no one was ever going to greet me as a beloved daughter."

A giggle escaped her. "I wish they would."

"Lady Lily," he warned since her accent had slipped.

"Of course," she returned in her most refined voice, and he grinned at her.

If Lily's heart beat a little too fast throughout the waltz, she was confident she hid it too well for him to notice. They ended the dance in perfect accord and strolled off in search of Millie. Lily caught sight of her in the main drawing room with a group of people who did not include Pennington.

She tugged Torbridge's arm in that direction, but he seemed not to notice. She soon saw why. Mr. Hill was in their path, exchanging pleasantries with a couple of army officers.

Torbridge nodded amiably to them and would, apparently, have passed on, except Hill said, "Well met, Torbridge. Miss Darrow."

The army officers quickly melted away to claim their dance partners, and Hill said to her, "Lady Masterton tells me this is your first visit to London. How do you find it?"

"Most enjoyable so far," she replied politely, "though I have yet to see a great deal."

"I'd be happy to show you around some of the sights," Hill offered. "If Torbridge won't eat me!"

"No, no, you carry on, old fellow," Torbridge said encouragingly. "I'm just the cousin!"

"Then you won't object if I ask Miss Darrow to dance?"

"*I* won't object, though she might."

"Will you?" Hill asked her.

"Object? Goodness, no, though I would rather sit this one out to be honest."

"Perhaps a glass of lemonade?" Hill offered.

"Perfect."

Torbridge turned to her and bowed, though one eyebrow flew up in appreciation. She wanted to laugh, although it wasn't really funny. Mr. Hill seemed a most amiable person, and she was only being friendly in order to spy on him.

She wondered how Torbridge slept at night. After all, these people were his friends. He had probably known most of them all his life. And yet, where his strange line of work was concerned, he appeared to be quite ruthless.

He had killed Pierre de Renarde and sent his widow, Isabelle, into France. He was using Lily, his friend... But that was not fair. He had already withdrawn his offer of employment before Lily had begged him to let her help.

Oh, yes, he was the most secretive man she had ever met. In fact, he was like several different men. The polite, watchful yet amiable gentleman she knew from the Hart. The witty, cultured man he was with Millie and her husband. And the proper, fashionable but slightly vague dilettate, who moved around Mrs. Westley's party, always welcome but never serious, nor taken seriously.

This last fact distressed her until she remembered what Millie had said that her big-hearted, responsible brother had come home from his travels *more like her.* Vague and worldly, Lily could only assume. The character he had adopted so no one of his world would suspect the kind of important work he did.

Whatever that was.

Catching traitors, on this occasion. The trouble was, she couldn't really imagine Mr. Hill betraying his country. She found him attentive and good company, and so accepted his invitation to the next dance. This was another waltz.

Torbridge, she noted, did not dance. He was playing cards across the hall. But Millie waltzed, with Pennington.

"So, what brought you to England?" Hill asked as they danced. "The desire for a London Season?"

"Oh, no. Penury brought me here. My cousins are very kind, and Lady Masterton insisted that I enjoy myself a little. But in fact, I am her companion."

It was the story they had agreed on to explain her sudden presence. After all, no one much cared about the family background of poor relations. But she saw at once that something had changed in Hill's eyes. Was it the lower status or the penury he disliked?

Either way, he remained pleasant company for the remainder of the dance, and only returned her to Millie with flattering reluctance.

"I hope I may call upon you both tomorrow," he said with a bow and strolled away.

"WELL?" TORBRIDGE ASKED her an hour or so later, in the Mastertons' library, where their host was pouring brandy. They had met him at the front door, and Millie had gone straight up to bed. "What do you think of our Mr. Hill?"

"I don't think he's a wicked man," Lily replied frankly.

"Not sure you can tell from an hour's conversation," Sir George said wryly, handing a glass to his brother-in-law.

"Not sure you or I can," Torbridge agreed. "Lily is a different matter."

Sir George frowned. "What do you mean?"

Torbridge shrugged. "She has an insight that amounts to a gift."

"No, I don't," Lily scoffed. "I just pay attention to people."

"Isn't that what I said?" Torbridge wondered.

"I wonder what she thinks of you," Sir George said, faintly amused.

"Or you," he retorted. "But we stray from the point. Which is, how intrigued is he?"

"I think he likes me," Lily said uncomfortably. "But he seemed uneasy that I am a mere poor relation."

"It won't concern him for long."

She took a deep breath. "My lord—I mean, Cousin—it does not seem right putting out such lures to him only to incriminate him."

"We can't incriminate him if he isn't guilty," Torbridge pointed out.

"It's the lures that concern me," she retorted.

"You haven't lured. You have merely been present. And it was the task we agreed."

"I have no intention of letting you down," she said stiffly. "But I do look forward to going back to my respectable work at the inn." She curtseyed. "I bid you goodnight."

CHAPTER SEVEN

S INCE WALKING ALONE was forbidden, Lily threw herself into work the following morning, and finally got the remainder of Millie's bills and correspondence into order. She took out the notebook and began to write down the oldest sums owed.

She was concentrating so hard, she did not hear anyone enter until a posy of flowers landed over her notebook. Glancing up, she beheld Lord Torbridge, and her heart gave its expected skip.

"Good morning," he said mildly.

"Good morning." She picked up the flowers. "These are pretty. Where did they come from?"

"A flower girl in Covent Garden. They're for you."

She set her pen in the stand, trying not to be touched by what she imagined was an apology for his insensitivity. "Why?" she asked, holding his gaze.

"It's customary to give flowers to a young lady one has danced with the previous evening. There are several more in the hall addressed to you. Including one from Jack Hill."

Of course. She laid the flowers to one side and lowered her gaze to the notebook.

"How are Millie's affairs?" he inquired. "Will Masterton have to mortgage to pay her debts?"

"No. With a little management, she can pay them off herself before the end of the year. Her allowance is generous. Even coming to the end of the quarter, she has enough left to pay the oldest of the accounts. The problem is due not so much to inability to pay as to forgetfulness."

"Well, that is a pleasant surprise. You should just hand the lot to Masterton."

"She does not wish to do it that way,"

She almost felt him shrug the matter off.

"I have tickets for the opera tonight," he remarked. "Perhaps you could mention the fact, should Hill call."

She inclined her head.

"You do that very well," he said, an unexpected smile in his voice. "You have learned how to be haughty."

"We have already agreed I have a talent for mimicry. Did you wish to discuss anything else?" She glanced up as she spoke, in time to see him blink in surprise.

A breath of laughter escaped him. "Why, Lily, are you dismissing me?"

"Yes," she said baldly. "I am busy. Thank you for the flowers." She reached for the next account on her pile and picked up her pen.

"You're welcome," he said and sauntered out of the room.

A few moments later, she heard the front door close behind him and squeezed her eyes shut. She didn't even know why she was angry with him. For failing to acknowledge her difficulties? For not caring?

He is a nobleman, a marquess the moment his father dies. I am an innkeeper's daughter. Of course, he never saw me as a real person. What else did I expect?

Nothing else. And yet, it seemed the actuality still hurt.

With her concentration broken, she stood and went down to the breakfast parlor, where she discovered Sir George eating a hearty breakfast and reading a newspaper.

They exchanged good mornings. Lily, used to serving men who communicated by mere grunts until their breakfast was eaten, made no effort to engage him in conversation but helped herself to toast, eggs, and coffee, and sat down to eat in silence.

After a while, Sir George folded his newspaper and tossed it aside. "So, what plans do you have today?"

"I believe Lord Torbridge has invited us to the opera this evening. But I've no idea what Cousin Millie's pleasure is during the day. What will you be doing?"

He shrugged. "I shall probably look in at White's at some point. Otherwise, my only appointment is a meeting with some of the other trustees of the British Museum."

"Oh, how wonderful! Do you think Millie would like to tag along with you and look at some of the exhibits?"

Sir George's jaw dropped slightly. "I would doubt it," he managed. "May I ask her?"

"Of course," he replied, amused. "But please, don't be too disappointed by her refusal. Torbridge is a better bet for that kind of thing."

Lily ate faster, but in fact, Millie joined them before she had finished. She looked surprised, though not displeased to see her husband still at breakfast.

"Oh, Cousin, I have had a splendid idea!" Lily exclaimed. "Sir George has an appointment at the British Museum, and I thought it might be wonderful to go with him and see the collections."

Millie blinked and sat down opposite Lily with nothing more than a cup of coffee. She seemed to be staring at Lily much as one might examine a rare plant or insect. Her gaze flickered to her husband, and some communication clearly passed between them, for Millie's lips twitched.

"Why not?" she agreed. "Though I am no blue-stocking, and I guarantee I shall be bored in ten minutes. *You* might last fifteen. What about you, George? Do you actually *like* any of the collections you make such a fuss about."

"Of course. Inordinately, in some cases. If we leave in half an hour or so, I shall be able to show you my favorite before the meeting."

THE OUTING PROVED an unexpected success. While Lily gawped in wide-eyed wonder at an amazing range of objects from all over the world, Sir George provided frequent witty and knowledgeable explanations. Still, it was no hardship for Lily to hang back to gaze longer at some ancient object from Egypt, leaving the couple to move on without her.

Several times, she heard Millie laugh out loud, and once she cried, "Oh, George, come and look at this!"

By the time Sir George went off to his meeting, Lily was well pleased. It seemed they had remembered they liked each other's company.

However, later that day, as Lily walked with Millie in the park at the fashionable hour, she realized she was too complacent too early.

Mr. Jack Hill had found them relatively quickly, and while he escorted them, his brother, Lord Pennington, driving a high-perch phaeton, stopped to greet them.

"Care for a turn about the park, Millie?" he invited, with rather too much familiarity, Lily thought.

Millie hesitated. "Just one turn, then. Lily, I shall expect to meet you back here in ten minutes."

Lily must have frowned as the phaeton moved on, for Mr. Hill said, "You do not mind losing your chaperone for a few minutes, do you?"

Immediately, she smiled. "Of course not. Indeed, we can see each other for most of the way. And she won't want to be late, for we are going to the opera this evening."

In fact, Millie found her before the ten minutes had expired, but the brief calm that had descended upon her this morning had quite gone. She was once more vague and oddly brittle.

"Does Lord Pennington behave improperly to you?" Lily asked bluntly.

Millie laughed. "Lord, no. We have known each other forever. It is harmless, fashionable flirtation. Neither of us means a thing by it, and the world knows it."

The world might, but Lily doubted Sir George did.

THE OPERA WAS another new experience for Lily. She liked the pretty ballet that was performed first and was totally enchanted by the main opera.

Once, Lord Torbridge leaned forward and murmured, "You are enjoying this?"

She nodded dumbly.

"Do you understand what they are singing?"

She shook her head. "No, but it doesn't seem to matter."

"It's sung in Italian."

Forgetting that she was angry with him, she cast him a quick smile of gratitude. At least there was nothing wrong with her ears.

However, she seemed to be the only member of the audience who paid any attention to the stage. The constant hum of talk and laughter had to be blocked out, as had some of the ogling young bucks with their quizzing glasses in the pit below.

And during the intervals, no one else sat anxiously waiting for the opera to resume. Everyone moved around from box to box, visiting their acquaintances. Lord Torbridge's box was generally full of young men, many of whom seemed eager to be introduced to Lily. However, one visitor must have pleased Torbridge mightily. Not only did Mr. Hill appear, but he escorted his mother, the Dowager Lady Pennington, to whom Millie presented Lily.

"So, you're one of the Darrow cousins," the fierce old lady said. "I knew your grandmother. Liked her. Though she would have done better to marry in England."

Lily had no idea how to respond to that, so said mildly, "Perhaps."

The old lady stared, then cackled. "You're quite right. Rude and unnecessary thing to say, and none of my business, besides. Enjoying the opera?"

"Oh, indeed, ma'am, it's wonderful," she enthused before she remembered that fashionable people were too overwhelmed with ennui to be enthusiastic about anything. However, Lady Pennington only smiled, and when she departed could be heard saying to Torbridge. "Very natural, pretty, and a well-behaved girl, and not just in the common way."

"Thank you, ma'am," Torbridge replied. "So, I think, too."

Jack Hill glanced back over his shoulder at Lily and grinned. He may not have liked that she was a penniless companion, but he seemed to be overcoming his disappointment. Which said more for him than for her... But then, as Torbridge had pointed out, if he was a traitor, then any means to stop him was not only justified but necessary.

As the curtain went up once more, Lily glimpsed Lady Pennington seated in her own box on the opposite side of the theatre. With her was an elderly gentleman and a downtrodden-looking female—no doubt a poor relation, Lily thought with a twinge of sympathy. There was no sign there of Jack Hill.

Although the music had begun again, she could not help looking round for him. Either he had left the theatre, or he was visiting someone else. Discovering no sign of him in her quick scan, she let her attention return to the stage.

A moment later, movement caught the corner of her eye. Her gaze flickered to a box nearer the stage in the same row as her own, and for an instant, she glimpsed Jack Hill's face emerging from the shadows, his lips moving in speech to someone else hidden from her view. Then his face vanished. There was a faint disturbance as though the unseen person rose, but his back vanished from her line of vision before she could see who he was.

A surge of excitement took her by surprise. Impulsively, she turned toward Torbridge, for this, surely, was exactly the sort of thing he wanted to know, but he no longer sat beside her. Millie's restless eyes were on the audience. Sir George, a little further back, was listening to some serious monologue from one of their interval visitors who had not departed.

Quietly, Lily stood and walked to the back of the box. Since no one noticed, she opened the door and darted into the passage. It was deserted, so she hurried along, following the curve of the wall, in the direction she had last seen Hill.

And there he was.

Hastily, she stepped back, flattening herself against the wall. Annoyingly, from where she stood, she could not even hear their voices over the music from the stage and the overlaying hum of conversation from inside the boxes. But, it was definitely Jack Hill in some kind of argument with another man who was, presumably, the one from the box, though frustratingly, he still had his back to her.

Carefully, she leaned out. They had moved slightly so that the stranger's broad, tall back now hid Jack Hill from her completely. Which meant that Hill could not see her either. Her heartbeat quickened. She could walk nearer, probably even straight past them as though heading to a box beyond them. Hopefully, she would get near enough to hear some of their conversation before they noticed her. And she would see the stranger's face.

If Hill didn't see her, well and good. She would just keep walking. If he did…she would play the silly female who had taken a breath of air in the corridor and forgotten which box she had come out of. She would even greet him with relief and ask for his help.

The plan was no sooner made than she began to walk blithely forward. The men were so involved in their low-voiced disagreement that they didn't acknowledge her approach. She passed a deserted staircase on the left and a closed box door on the right. She could make out Jack's voice now, and the occasional, slightly higher pitch of his companion's curt response.

She walked briskly on. The next door on her right was open. Was it the box they had just left? Or an unused one? The latter, surely, for no light escaped it. As she moved toward it, she finally made out Hill's words for the first time, thrown with mingled anger and contempt at his companion. "...damned money! You—"

Abruptly, a hand grasped her arm and jerked her into the darkened box.

Her mouth opened in instant protest. Her free arm flew out to fight back. But an urgent finger closed over her parted lips. "It's me," a voice breathed in her ear. *His* voice. *His* scent in her nostrils.

Emotion swamped her, but it wasn't enough to blot out the frustration that he had prevented her hearing something important to him. But then she noticed the change in the passage. Their voices had fallen silent, but their footsteps strode in her direction.

Hill had been about to see her. Perhaps he already had.

He still would, for the light from the passage penetrated into the box. In panic, she reached for the door handle pressing into her back, but there was no time to close it. God, she had given them both away, unless by some miracle, they did not glance in their direction, did not suspect they had been eavesdropping.

Lord Torbridge swung her around so that she faced the passage, though she could see nothing but him. His arms went around her, protective, strangely comforting, and his face swooped nearer.

"Play along," he breathed, the only warning she had before his mouth sank on hers, and she couldn't think at all.

She knew why he did it, of course. But he had no way of knowing she had dreamed so long and so secretly of his kiss. In her wildest dreams, even in that brief moment in the Hart, she had never imagined he would actually do it.

Cooperating with his plans had never been easier or more natural.

She flung one arm around his neck, opening wide to the blatant, overwhelming sensuality of his lips, of his body pressed so close to hers. He caught her hand at his nape, dragging it to his cheek, perhaps to hide even her glove from the men outside.

At that moment, she didn't care. Their footsteps passed on, along with some ribald commentary inspired by the sight she and Torbridge presented. But he did not end the kiss. Instead, he deepened it, caressing her tongue with his, stroking her back and her waist, gathering her so close she might have been glued to him. He filled her senses, and she never wanted it to end.

But it did. He pressed his cheek against hers.

"They're going downstairs," he whispered in her ear, and even that played havoc with her heightened senses. Her lips tingled from his stunning kiss. Butterflies still danced in her stomach, mingling with the heat of desire.

She swallowed but could not speak. Very slowly, he detached himself from her body. She hoped he couldn't feel it tremble. But he wasn't unmoved himself. She had felt his hardness against her.

"What the devil were you doing?" he demanded.

"You *told* me to kiss you," she said indignantly.

He let out a soft sound halfway between a laugh and a groan. "Not that. Following him in the first place. You must *not* put yourself in danger!"

She stared at him. "What else am I here for? Do you imagine this search is going to get less dangerous when I'm where you want me to be?"

His eyes, glittering in the darkness, stared at her.

She took advantage of his rare speechlessness to pat her hair and deal with a loose pin. Then, she stepped around him and peered up and down the corridor. She emerged and set off briskly back toward their own box. Before she had taken two steps, he was beside her, placing her hand on his arm.

But he did not speak, and she wondered miserably if he was regretting asking for her help. Regretting touching her, kissing her… With desperation, she hung on to the reason they had both been there.

"Who was that man?" she blurted. "Did you hear what they said?"

"We'll talk later in privacy," he murmured. "Let's see the last act and go back to Brook Street."

As he took his seat beside her, he murmured to Millie, "She needed some air."

For the first time, the stage and the music took second place to her own feelings. Her heart seemed to soar and plummet continually, and there was a new edge to her awareness of his physical nearness. And that was without touching.

She was actually glad when the opera ended, and they made a dash to beat the main crush to the exit. As they waited for the carriage, she kept a smile on her face and somehow joined in the conversation, though afterward, she had no idea what it had been about.

In the carriage, she and Millie sat together, with the men opposite. Stupidly, she found it hard to look at Lord Torbridge at all. If she avoided his face and looked down, there were his long, elegant legs which had pressed against her, surprisingly hard and muscled. It was safest to gaze out of the window.

"I heard an interesting *on-dit* this evening," Sir Gorge drawled as the carriage fought its way out of Covent Garden.

"What was that?" Torbridge asked.

"Why, that although Cousin Lily is Millie's companion for now, you are apparently prepared to do something quite handsome for her should she choose to be married instead."

Lily's mouth fell open.

"Are you?" Millie asked, equally startled. "Is that a good idea, Dolph?"

"No, it isn't," Lily said, incensed. "I have a perfectly good father to provide a dowry should I ever wish to marry!"

"Of course you have." Torbridge sounded amused. "I'm afraid I spread the rumor myself—only to keep Hill on the hook, so don't eat me, Lily."

"What hook?" Millie asked suspiciously. "You are up to something, Torbridge, and I won't have you upsetting Lily or the Hills!"

"I never upset people," Torbridge protested.

"Not visibly," Sir George said. "But it seems to me you've certainly caused a few upsets."

"You malign me," Torbridge insisted.

Perhaps fortunately, the carriage pulled up at the Mastertons' front door.

Sir George alighted and looked faintly surprised to be handing down his wife. "Not going on somewhere else this evening, my dear?"

"No. I want to know what Torbridge is up to."

Her brother laughed. Lily felt his breath on the back of her neck as she stepped down with Sir George's aid.

Inside, they repaired to the drawing room, where Sir George poured glasses of wine for Millie and Lily, and brandies for Torbridge and himself.

"Well?" Millie demanded, seating herself by the fire and glaring at her brother.

"Well, what?" he asked, amused. "I told you, it suited my purpose to have Lily invited to Pennington Place."

"Why? Why throw her at Jack's head? Unless for some kind of revenge, which I own would surprise me, for you were never vengeful, but what else am I to think?"

"Perhaps that you owe Lily an apology," Torbridge said. "For implying it would be some kind of punishment to be thrust into her company."

Millie flushed and caught hold of Lily's hand. "You know perfectly well I meant no such thing. Or perhaps I did, in a way, for we all know Lily is..." She lowered her voice. "... an innkeeper's daughter. No matter how perfect a lady she makes in this pretense, we all know she cannot marry Jack Hill." She glanced up at Lily. "I hope that does not upset you, my dear, but you should know where you stand."

"I have always known that, and I am not remotely upset."

"She is too good for your schemes, Dolph," Millie said fiercely.

Torbridge strolled to the sofa facing the hearth and sat down. "I shan't quarrel with you there, but we have an agreement."

Lily lowered herself onto the arm of Millie's chair. "Who was the man with Mr. Hill?" she demanded.

"A banker named Stanley."

"A banker?" she repeated. It explained the talk of money and Hill's contempt for a social inferior.

"We shouldn't be so picky these days," Millie observed, distracted. "Didn't one of the Overtons' girls marry a banker?"

"Captain Cromarty," Lily agreed. "Although he is also the Earl of Silford's grandson and heir."

Torbridge smiled into his brandy but said nothing.

"What did they discuss?" Lily prompted. "Did it tell you anything helpful?"

"Not terribly. Just that Hill owes him money—rather more than I had imagined, so he is certainly open to alternative sources of income. He is promising to pay Stanley back by the end of the month."

"Which means something really might happen while we are at Pennington Place," Lily guessed. "If he is expecting to have more money by then."

"Then you are no longer quite so opposed to him being the villain of the piece?" Torbridge asked.

"I was never opposed to the idea," she insisted. "I merely considered it unlikely. I still do, although I have to admit unlikely things do happen. And lack of money makes people desperate."

"Exactly," Torbridge said. He set down his glass and stood up. "And now, I must bid you good night. Thank you for your company this evening. Lily, will you walk with me to the door?"

She rose at once, although once out of the drawing room, she dragged her heels. "Are you going to scold me again for following them at the opera?"

He looked surprised. "No, I have said my piece on that score." He began to descend the stairs and lowered his voice. "I want to apologize for my own…rough handling. I hope I didn't hurt you."

Of course, she understood him, was even grateful for his care of her. Yet, some part of her was furious that he should be sorry for what was the most delightful experience of her life. Not trusting herself to speak, she merely shook her head.

"Good. You understand I had to hide you from Hill at all costs? It seemed the simplest solution."

She nodded.

"And the most delightful," he breathed and jumped down the steps three at a time, so that she could not possibly keep up. He snatched up his hat from the hall table and was gone before she had even reached the bottom of the stairs.

CHAPTER EIGHT

T HE FOLLOWING MORNING, Lily was surprised to discover not only
Sir George but his lady in the breakfast parlor.

"Yes, I know, I am up before eleven," Millie said, breaking the seal
on one of a pile of letters by her side. "But it seems when one retires
early, one wakes early, too. What does one do so early in the day?"

"You could tell me which invitations you wish to accept and which
to decline on your behalf," Lily suggested.

"I could," Millie agreed without notable enthusiasm. She glanced
down at her letter, while Lily helped herself to ham and eggs and
cheese. "Ah, this is what Torbridge has been hoping for! Lady
Pennington invites us to bring our charming cousin with us to her
party at Pennington Place. Which is very kind of her," Millie added,
pushing the letter across to her husband, "when I suspect I haven't yet
answered her original invitation."

"You haven't," Lily said, sitting down beside her. "But I can accept
for all of us, if you wish."

"Oh, yes, that would be excellent," Millie said. She glanced at her
husband. "That is, you *are* coming, are you not, George?"

"Apparently," Sir George said, glancing toward the opening door.

Lord Torbridge strolled in, causing Lily's heart to jolt.

It seemed the simplest solution. And the most delightful. His words had
come back to her frequently during the night, along with the memory
of his astonishing kiss. She knew the words were, in all likelihood,

mere politeness on his part, but it didn't stop them repeating in her head or in her foolish heart.

"Aha, well-timed, Dolph!" his sister greeted him. "Lady Pennington has asked us to bring Lily with us."

"Excellent," Torbridge said, sitting down opposite them. "Well done, Lily!" He helped himself to coffee. "That means we are more or less free until next week. What would you like to do, Lily?"

"Well, I should be able to bring Cousin Millie's correspondence up to date by then…"

Millie frowned. "You will need a riding habit. I never thought of that. And perhaps another walking dress." She paused. "You *do* ride, Lily?"

"Well, yes, but not with a lady's saddle."

Millie stared at her in horror. "You mean you sit *astride*?"

"It's much simpler," Lily assured her. "And if your skirts are wide enough, or even divided, it does not matter."

"Oh, it matters," Millie assured her. "You can't do it in polite society."

"Oh. Will it matter?" Lily asked in a small voice.

"No," Torbridge answered, "for we'll get you used to a lady's saddle before we go. I wouldn't join any hunting expeditions, though."

"That's what we'll do this morning, Lily," Millie said, pleased. "We'll order you a riding habit, and you may ride out with Torbridge tomorrow. What did you want in any case, Dolph?"

"I thought Lily might like to see the sights of London," Torbridge said surprisingly. He sipped his coffee.

Lily's eyes widened. "The Tower of London?" she asked eagerly. "St. Paul's Cathedral? Westminster Abbey?"

"Wherever you wish."

"Oh, my lord, that would be wonderful."

"Cousin," he corrected.

"Well, thank God," Millie said with relief. "I was afraid George or I was going to have to trail around these places. And much as I have grown to love you, Lily, I have my reputation to consider. Come with us to the dressmaker, Dolph, and then you two may go off and bore yourselves silly."

LILY WAS SURPRISED and not a little embarrassed when Lord Torbridge actually accompanied them into the dressmaker's establishment. More than that, he was addressed by name and appeared to be on familiar terms with the staff and the modiste herself. It was he who picked out the bottle-green habit and advised her to take it.

"Why that one?" she asked as Millie went to negotiate delivery.

"It brings out the green in your eyes."

Blood seeped into her cheeks, "Well, I will be glad to have one dress that you like."

His eyebrows flew up. "One? What makes you think I don't like the others?"

"Oh, nothing," she said hastily. "Merely, you seemed disappointed when you came to dinner the other night and saw me in the first evening gown."

"Disap..." He broke off. "Lily, I wasn't disappointed. I was stunned."

"In a good way?" she said anxiously.

A hiss of laughter escaped his lips. "In an excellent way. The gowns are all lovely and tasteful, and your beauty was never in doubt. I just never suspected you would enter my world with such panache. It took me by surprise. You always take me by surprise." His lips quirked. "In a good way."

She laughed and left the shop with new confidence. They waved Millie off in the town carriage while she and Torbridge walked on until they picked up a hackney to take them to the Tower of London.

FROM THEN ON, it seemed she was no longer acting. "Lady Lily" had become part of herself, and she could step out in this world as easily as in her own. Moreover, there was intense pleasure in spending so much time with Lord Torbridge.

In the mornings, he took her riding in the park, so that she got used to the awkward lady's saddle. After the initial strangeness of the position, she actually found it surprisingly comfortable and could control the horse just as easily. Since they rode early, the streets and the parks were quiet, and it was very pleasant to talk undisturbed, without fear of being overheard.

Not that they spoke much about Jack Hill and her task of discovering how information was getting from his office to France. Instead, they tended to be amusing conversations about nothing very much, interspersed, occasionally, with more serious talks about their views of the world. These gave her some hint of what had led him to begin the work he did, although he gave her no details. She understood how much he was torn between it and the ancestral duties that were about to fall upon him.

And then there were her secret moments of pleasure when he lifted her down from the saddle. He was unexpectedly strong, and his hands on her waist thrilled her. These moments when she stood so close to him, set her heart racing, yearning for what she could never have.

In the afternoons, he accompanied her around London's attractions. She was fascinated by the Tower and its menagerie. She was in awe of Westminster Abbey and St. Paul's. And she wept for the wild beasts at the Exeter Exchange.

The tears took her by surprise, and she tried to hide them from Torbridge. He helped by pretending not to notice as they returned to his carriage. Only there, in relative privacy, did he ask quietly what was wrong.

"I don't know," she whispered. "It just seems so sad to see them alone and trapped."

"You do know the tiger would eat you?"

"He wouldn't if he wasn't here," she pointed out. "All he can do is pace up and down that tiny cage for our entertainment. It's horrible for him."

Torbridge blinked. "Did he tell you that?"

"Didn't he tell *you* that?" she retorted.

He was silent a moment. "Perhaps," he allowed. "But you know, we are all trapped in some way. It might not be a physical cage, but we learn to deal with it. Perhaps he will, too. In any case, I'm sorry to have distressed you."

"You didn't distress me," she said at once. In fact, he distracted her from the imagined pain of the animals. She thought he was probably thinking about the gilded cage of responsibilities that would hem him in when his father died, and he inherited all the lands and titles and responsibilities, "How is your father?"

He cast her a quick look. "Much the same. Millie had a letter from my mother this morning."

"She does not yet summon you home?"

"For his last great deathbed scene? No." He stirred as though uncomfortable. "What pleasures await you this evening?"

"You must remember it is Millie's musical soiree. The tenor?"

"Oh, Lord, is that tonight?"

"Yes, and she is expecting you."

"Well, I shall try and look in for a little."

She regarded him. "I suppose there is no use in my asking what keeps you so busy?"

"None whatsoever."

"Then it is nothing to do with...my position?"

"Nothing. However, I will be out of town for a day or so from tomorrow. If I am not back to travel with you to Pennington Place, I shall see you there."

The idea of him not being in London with her induced a moment of panic. He seemed to have become both her protection and her pleasure, though in truth, she was in need of neither and would hardly suffer for his absence. So, she forced herself to smile, and to part from him blithely when the carriage halted at Brook Street.

She found Millie standing by the drawing room door, gazing up the length of the room. "Do you suppose it's big enough?" she asked vaguely.

"Well, we can't make it any larger."

"True. Once Alessandro has sung, we'll clear the rows of seats, and if we can induce him to sing again, he may do informally by the pianoforte. Is that a good idea?"

"An excellent idea," Lily assured her.

She had expected to find her hostess somewhat flustered, but in fact, she appeared to be going through the last-minute preparations for her party quite calmly. Perhaps because Lily had already made most of the arrangements. Between those and her jaunts with Lord Torbridge, her work on Millie's correspondence had slowed, but tomorrow she hoped to pay the accounts she could and begin on the unanswered letters.

When Lily had changed into the pale blue evening gown, she joined the Mastertons for a light and early dinner.

Millie frowned at her. "That gown again? My dear, you must have more."

"I don't see why. I've been wearing them on alternate evenings, and I have the ballgown for Pennington Place."

"We will be four nights at Pennington Place, and you have but two evening gowns. Tell her, George, she must have two more."

"Nothing to do with me," Sir George said hastily. "Take it up with Torbridge."

"I will. Though I have to say, Lily, you do look charming in that shade of blue. Do you not think so, George?"

"I do, my dear. As do you in that dark pink."

Millie's cheeks flushed with unexpected pleasure. "Do I, George? Then I am not too mature for the shade?"

"Millie, you are one-and thirty, not sixty."

Lily was delighted by the growing closeness she sensed between Millie and George. Whatever had gone wrong between them seemed to be gradually, haltingly, putting itself right again. She had the feeling some of this was to do with the absence of Lord Pennington from her life these last few days, which implied things might get difficult again during their stay at Pennington Place. She thrust that aside for worrying about later.

In fact, she had to consider it a little sooner, for among the first guests to arrive were the Pennington brothers. Millie was much too busy as hostess to pay anyone special attention, and Sir George was his usual urbane, slightly sardonic self. All the same, Lily detected a faint hardening of his demeanor, and her heart sank. She did not like his doubts about Millie, which must have been exacerbated by Pennington's familiar, almost proprietorial greeting.

"But how charming to see you, Miss Darrow," he added to Lily, "without the ubiquitous Torbridge at your side. I assure you, my brother has been seething."

"Pay no attention to him," Mr. Hill said. "I merely pined for your company—in which I now bask."

Lily laughed. "I believe you both talk nonsense. I have been plaguing my poor cousin to show me all the sights of London. Cousin Millie despairs of me, and I suspect I have exhausted even Torbridge's patience."

"But you and Millie will be attending my mother's party?" Pennington drawled. "I assume Torbridge will escort you."

"Possibly. But Sir George certainly will."

The faintest flicker of a frown was all that betrayed Pennington's irritation. He did not want Sir George there. While Millie might merely be flirting, he seemed to be aiming at something rather more serious.

Mr. Hill ushered her toward the rows of chairs. "Tell me about this tenor, Miss Darrow. Is he as wonderful as all that?"

"I have not heard him sing," Lily admitted. "But Cousin Millie tells me his voice is divine, and he deserves every success."

In fact, Alessandro was taking his place at the front of the room, and everyone was taking seats facing him. While Sir George leaned against the door, his wife wafted up to the tenor to exchange a few words.

Lily, taking her place between Jack Hill and a middle-aged lady she did not know, noticed chiefly that Lord Torbridge had not yet arrived. On either side of her, her neighbors were bowing to each other.

"Are you acquainted with Miss Darrow, ma'am?" Mr. Hill asked politely.

"No, I believe I have not yet had the pleasure." The lady had a gentle if vague smile that distracted Lily by its underlying sadness.

"Miss Darrow is Lady Masterton's cousin from Ireland. Miss Darrow, Mrs. Bradwell."

"How do you do?" Lily murmured.

No further conversation was possible because Millie was introducing Alessandro, and polite applause was necessary.

Lily lacked the experience to know if Alessandro's voice was indeed something out of the ordinary, but to her, it was certainly divine. Just as at the opera, she quickly lost herself in the beauty of the music. Rapt, she paid no attention to anyone else, and it was only as he paused between songs that she happened to glance at Mrs. Bradwell on her left. The lady's gaze seemed to be fixed on her throat, which was odd enough, but when she raised it to Lily's face, there was a haunting mixture of dread and hunger in her eyes. And her face was deadly pale.

"Ma'am?" Lily murmured. "Are you quite well?"

Mrs. Bradwell blinked. "I beg your... Yes, of course, quite well."

Alessandro began to sing again, and Lily thought no more about the odd moment until the end of his performance when she noticed that Mrs. Bradwell no longer sat beside her. Perhaps she hadn't been well, after all.

Since she was supposed to be Millie's companion, Lily excused herself to Mr. Hill, and went to see if she could be useful to her "cousin" Millie, however, was far too busy introducing influential people to her protégé, and the servants clearly had everything else in hand. A footman circulated with trays of wine, while others were removing the rows of chairs and forming them into more elegant groupings with sofas, armchairs, and small tables.

"Well, was he worth all the fuss?" Lord Torbridge's voice murmured beside her.

Turning, she greeted him with a delighted smile. "I thought so. Were you not in time to hear him?"

"I caught the tail end. There's no point in trying to speak to Millie right now. You should sit down with a glass of wine and wait to be adored."

Lily lowered her voice. "He sat beside me during the recital."

"I know. But a little competition will keep you safe and cause him to try harder."

"Are you the competition?" she asked with a quick smile, taking the chair he ushered her to.

"Lord, no," he replied with unflattering speed. "Though my approaching inheritance is bringing me much more interest from the matchmaking mamas." He was about to take the seat on the sofa next to her when he straightened again and bowed to the lady who had just stopped beside them.

"Ah, Lord Torbridge," Mrs. Bradwell said pleasantly. "Your charming cousin and I listened to the exquisite singing together."

Torbridge gave her the place nearest Lily and sat on her other side.

"That is a pretty trinket," Mrs. Bradwell observed to Lily. "May I see?"

Obligingly, Lily lifted the pendant from the base of her throat and leaned forward to give Mrs. Bradwell a clearer view. As she did so, she was reminded of Torbridge's interest in it when he had first seen it, his fingers brushing her skin, intimate and pleasurable.

"Quite unique," Mrs. Bradwell murmured, lifting her gaze to Lily's. "May I ask where you got it?"

"It was a gift," Lily replied.

"Ah." Mrs. Bradwell sat back and changed the subject. She had oddly haunting eyes, Lily thought. Or perhaps haunted. As other people joined them, Mrs. Bradwell drifted away, as did Lord Torbridge. But Lily found the woman's gaze stayed with her, and when Alessandro gave them one more song, standing by his accompanist at the pianoforte, she went in search of Torbridge once more.

Discovering him leaning against the mantelpiece, she said abruptly, "Who is Mrs. Bradwell?"

"The Earl of Fenmore's daughter, once Lady Alicia Dauntry, now the wife of Gerald Bradwell, a most respectable country gentleman from Suffolk. Why?"

"Do you know everyone's background so well?" she asked, distracted.

"Most people's. Most of the ton has similar knowledge. It's a small and exclusive world. My question stands."

"I'm not sure. She was interested in my necklace."

"It's very pretty. And it's simplicity suits you very well."

"Thank you," she said, blushing with pleasure at the compliment. "She has sad eyes. And I'm sure she was gazing at it during the performance."

"Everyone carries their own sadness with them, secretly or otherwise. Especially women."

She thought about that. "What is her sadness?"

"I don't know. Perhaps she was blighted in love. Or discovered her husband, who is not quite the rank she could have aspired to, is not the sheer delight she expected him to be."

"You are not taking me seriously, are you?"

"I always take you seriously," he protested.

"Ha! I shall ask Millie instead."

"Good luck," he murmured and nodded to someone obviously approaching behind her. "Pennington."

"Torbridge," Pennington returned. "Your attentiveness to your cousin is most commendable. You do know you are making my poor brother quite green with envy."

"I'm sure he has cousins of his own," Torbridge said wryly.

"They do not intrigue him as yours does. In fact, I have to hand it to you, Torbridge. Though I've no idea how, you have a most intriguing family. I am so looking forward to entertaining your sister at Pennington Place."

It could have meant nothing. It could have been verbal clumsiness, but Lily knew it was not. Pennington looked right at Torbridge as he said it, smiling as though baiting an imbecile who would not under-stand or a weakling who could not or would not object. A bully's trick. Lily did not know how Millie could bear this man.

Torbridge met his gaze, his expression still amiable, although he had gone very still. "I would hope such a notable host, as you claim to be, looks forward to entertaining *all* his guests. I know your mama does."

It was the faintest of insults, the subtlest accusation of ill-manners, but Lily saw the blink of surprise in Pennington's eyes. And then the dismissal, as though he couldn't quite believe Torbridge capable of such understanding or such wit.

"And I would hope such a notable...*figure* as you, Torbridge, would be aware of his own limitations."

"One never really knows one's own—or anyone else's—limitations, until they are tried," Torbridge said vaguely. "One should, at least, never be too smug to look. If I were you, I would look very carefully at my brother-in-law before you speak of my sister again. Do you know, I think she is right, Lily? I really do believe that fellow's voice is quite out of the ordinary…"

They moved away from Pennington, closer to the pianoforte.

Lily let out a breath of relief. "I thought you would knock him down," she murmured.

"I can't, can I?" he said with such suppressed violence that the words almost hissed out between his teeth. "I'm ineffectual, proper Torbridge."

Lily had never thought that of him. She had always known there was more. She just hadn't appreciated what it cost him to maintain the fiction. Perhaps neither had he.

"I said too much as it is," he said ruefully, under cover of the applause that had broken out for Alessandro.

Lily touched his hand. "No. I'm sure he'll have convinced himself already that you didn't really mean what he thought you did and that he is still the cleverest man in the room. In any room. He is not your major concern, remember?"

His eyes softened. "I'm glad you are here."

She wished beyond anything that it was true. "So am I."

CHAPTER NINE

IT WAS AT breakfast the following morning that Lily remembered to ask Millie about Mrs. Bradwell.

"Alicia Bradwell?" Millie said. "She comes up to London for a few weeks now and again, to stay with her brother, Lord Fenmore."

"What is Mr. Bradwell like?"

Millie shrugged. "I don't believe I ever met him. He prefers life in the country, by all accounts. Why, what is your interest in the family?"

"None, really. I just thought she looked sad and being curious, I wanted to know why. Does she have children?"

Millie thought. "Two sons that I know of. Not that they come to London, for they don't, but I believe Gilbert, my younger brother, was at school with one of them."

"Hmm. Did she and Mr. Bradwell have a passionate love affair and defy her father to marry?"

Millie stared at her. "Lily, what books have you been reading? Of course not!"

Sir George folded his newspaper and laid it down beside his empty plate. "In fact, I believe there was a captain of the Royal Navy she was engaged to. He died. What do you have planned for today?"

"The dressmaker's," Millie said with satisfaction.

The outing to the dressmaker's proved very successful. Not only did Millie order an evening dress and a walking dress for Lily, but a new ballgown for herself. She hadn't intended the latter, but she fell in love with a gorgeous, cream silk embroidered with red rosebuds.

Lily hoped it was not to impress Lord Pennington.

"Do you know what will look delightful with the new gown?" Millie said abruptly on their way home. "The Hay rubies. They're at Hay House—the London residence. I shall ask Torbridge to bring them round."

"He said he would be away today," Lily told her. "And might not be back in town before we leave for Pennington Place."

"Drat the man," Millie muttered. "Why does he never stay still? I suppose I could ask him simply to bring them to me there. If he remembers."

The evening's entertainment was a card party at Lady Gantry's house with a few select guests. "You are coming with us, aren't you?" Millie flung at her husband over dinner.

"I'll escort you there if you wish," Sir George said without enthusiasm, "but I won't stay. I have another engagement."

A frown flickered across Millie's face and vanished. "Whatever you prefer. If you're too busy, I'll send for my cousin Hartford. Or I daresay, Pennington would oblige me."

Lily tried not to groan. Sir George didn't even look up from his soup. "I have said I will take you."

To Lily's relief, Pennington was not even among the guests at Lady Gantry's party. His brother was there, though. His eyes lit up on seeing Lily, and she felt guilty all over again. His partiality for her company was becoming noticeable. But even if he was innocent, even if she had really been born a lady, she could not consider marrying him, for one very good reason.

In twenty years, she thought, she, too, might have hauntingly sad eyes, just like Mrs. Bradwell's.

Sir George left almost immediately, abandoning his wife to the whist table. Lily sat at her shoulder, watching. In truth, she found it a rather dull way to spend an evening, as she confided to Mr. Hill when he approached her.

"I don't find it dull," he replied. "though it's proving dashed expensive."

"Didn't you win?" she asked sympathetically.

In this strange world, gaming debts were considered debts of honor and had to be paid immediately, while tradesmen's bills could be stuffed in a drawer and ignored for months. Like Millie's. Lily saw little honor in gambling, but if Hill lost, he would have to find a way of paying. Betraying his country was hardly honorable, either, but at least it was done in secret.

"Perhaps you will bring me luck," he said lightly.

"I don't think I've brought my cousin much!"

Keeping half an eye on Hill's game, she saw him win and then lose again.

"Does Mr. Hill always lose?" she murmured to Millie when they found themselves briefly alone.

Millie shrugged. "No more than most. I suppose Pennington bales him out when necessary. But you mustn't go thinking fortunes change hand at little parties like this where the stakes are so little. It's the gentleman's clubs, and the less respectable gaming hells is where the real dangers lie."

"Does Mr. Hill frequent such places?"

Millie stared at her. "I have no idea." She lowered her voice even further. "Lily, you are not actually *considering* him as a husband, are you? Because, really, it would not do."

Lily laughed. "Of course not." *I will only marry your brother, and that is even less possible...*

For the first time, she began to doubt her wisdom in coming to London with Lord Torbridge, for being so much in his company had turned a sweet attraction into something greater, something dangerously like love. And that could never be.

"Pennington isn't here either," Millie said restlessly.

Lily glanced at her. "Does it matter?"

"No. I am used to being alone."

Even as Lily reached instinctively for her hand, Millie laughed and stood up. "Do you not think this is quite a dull party? Shall we go?"

Lily was happy enough to follow her lead, though she hoped the plan was not to go on somewhere else, where they might encounter Pennington. But Millie merely instructed the coachman to take them home.

In the friendly gloom, Lily said, "Are you unhappy, Cousin Millie?"

"Of course not. I am merely miffed at George for not being with us."

"And at Lord Pennington?"

Millie laughed. "What is the use of an admirer if he is not there to admire? Oh, look, Lily, that is Hay House, Papa's official London residence." Impulsively, she reached up and knocked to make the carriage halt.

It was a fine, tall house standing behind a wrought iron gate. It was in darkness.

"Do you know," Millie said impulsively, "I think I will just fetch those rubies now."

"Now?" Lily said, startled. "But Lord Torbridge won't be there, and it looks—"

"Oh, the servants are bound to be up still. It's only just after eleven." Millie opened the door and jumped spryly down without the steps. Lily could only follow her.

The hinges of the gate made no sound, and the paths were clearly well-cared for. But still, there was something empty, something lifeless about the house. Were there really servants here?

"When did your parents come here last?" Lily asked, nervous for no valid reason.

"Oh, years ago. My father used to come up occasionally to sneer at Torbridge, but his health has kept him in the country for the last two or three years. Mama does not like London." Millie lifted the knocker and gave a peremptory rap.

"Then Lord Torbridge lives here alone?"

"More lodges than lives," Millie said wryly. "I think he comes and goes so often that even the servants don't know when he's at home unless he rings for them."

To Lily's surprise, the front door opened to reveal a superior man-servant, presumably the butler, holding a lamp and looking displeased. However, almost at once, his eyebrows flew up in surprise, and he stood back with a bow, opening the door wide.

"Lady Millie! His lordship is not at home."

"Oh, I know, Church, isn't it annoying of him?" Millie swept in, waving vaguely at Lily. "This is our cousin from Ireland, Miss Darrow, who has never seen the house. But I've just come for the rubies. I presume they haven't been moved?"

"No, my lady, but—"

Millie handed him her cloak, which was quickly passed to an underling who had materialized behind him. Lily added her own cloak to the servant's arm while Church walked into the nearest room and lit a branch of candles and another lamp. It was a large, well-ordered room. A reception room, where less welcome visitors were no doubt deposited while his lordship decided whether or not he was at home.

"Allow me to light the way, my lady," Church said. "Would you care for some refreshment?"

"Oh, no, we'll just be in and out. Lily, wait for me here if you wish, or come up and look around."

Lily, who was sure somehow that the butler would know her for the fraud she was, elected to remain in the soulless reception room. Until Millie and the servants had retreated from her view. She waited a moment or two, restlessly drumming her fingers on the arm of the chair. But this was where Lord Torbridge lived, and she couldn't pass up the chance of looking just a little deeper, of feeling just a little closer.

She rose and picked up the lamp, walking across the hall, where she discovered a large room filled with books. It, too, had the immaculate air of little use, although a few of the shelves had erratic spaces as though books had been removed and not returned.

Besides this, she found another small sitting room, which had all its furniture in Holland covers. She began to understand what Millie meant about her brother merely lodging here. Nothing in these rooms spoke of his character, his learning, his humor...just his enigma.

She crossed the hall again, moving toward the back of the house, and here at last, she found what appeared to be a comfortable breakfast parlor. The walls here seemed more recently painted and in an unexpected shade of yellow. On a bright morning, she thought, it would look like sunshine.

She moved through the room with greater comfort. She could almost smell that he had been here. There were a few more appealing pictures on the walls, a painting of the sea, another of a countryside scene, and a portrait of a couple from the last century—a man with a gentle face and a sword at his side, and a lady with twinkling eyes.

At the far end of the room was another door, which she opened. And beheld chaos.

LORD TORBRIDGE HAD finished his business with unexpected speed and returned to London just after dark. The household was not expecting him, so he let himself in with his key and walked across the dark hallway with the confidence of familiarity.

Of course, it was always possible that one of the servants had left some obstacle in his path for him to fall over, but it had never happened yet, and it didn't happen this time. Torbridge was used to the dark. He liked it because it saved him pretending, even here with only the servants to see him.

Without difficulty, he quietly opened and closed the breakfast room door and walked straight toward his study. There he paused, for a faint but definite light showed in the crack under the door. A muttered expression of disgust preceded a dull bump of something hitting the floor. Another voice hissed angrily for silence.

Not the servants, then...

Torbridge set his hat on the table and flexed his fingers before taking a tighter grip of the cane he carried. Conscious of a suddenly fierce longing to assuage his frustrations in a fight, he walked silently to the door and threw it wide.

It was as well they had brought a light, for he could never have walked safely, let alone fought over the upturned furniture, and the books, ledgers, and papers strewn across the floor. He had time to take in that there were two of them with a shaded lantern, and that his favorite brandy decanter was in pieces by the fireplace. And then they flew at him.

Torbridge waited no longer but rushed forward to give himself momentum, crashing straight into one man while he struck the second twice with his cane. Falling back as the second man fell, he turned on the first, who had produced a pistol from his shabby great coat.

A gun changed the nature of the proceedings. If they were both armed...

Torbridge twirled the cane and slammed it into the wrist of the armed man who yelped and dropped the gun. From nowhere, the second man dived in and threw himself at the pistol on the floor. Torbridge whacked him on the back of the head, and he slumped over the weapon. Fortunately, it didn't go off.

But with fury, the first man launched himself at Torbridge, knocking him over and wrapping his fingers around his throat. Torbridge bucked and rolled, elbowing his attacker in the face, which served to loosen his grip. Then it was Torbridge on top. His stick was useless at such close quarters, so he sent it rolling across the floor. Then he struck his opponent on the chin hard enough to make his eyes roll back in his head.

With one hand, Torbridge reached up to the desk drawer where he kept lengths of rope for just this kind of purpose. His sore knuckles knocked against the open drawer, which, of course, no longer had anything inside it. Reaching around the floor, he eventually found what he wanted, and heaved his victim onto his stomach just before he began to struggle. Torbridge twisted his arms relentlessly and tied them, then his viciously kicking feet.

"You're dead!" the bound man uttered.

"Not even close," Torbridge said and stuffed his handkerchief into the man's mouth.

Rising, he found some more rope and bound the still unconscious man before lifting him somewhat gingerly off the unfired pistol. He picked that up and placed it in his desk drawer. It seemed almost ludicrous to close the drawer so tidily amongst all this mess.

He put the sofa back on its feet and dragged both men behind it and left them on their fronts. Then, with a sigh, he stepped over the carnage, cleared a space on the sofa, and sat where he couldn't see his captives.

One matter had just been concluded with efficient success, but it seemed the larger picture was shattering. He did not believe for one moment that these men were normal burglars. They had taken nothing, and they must have known that all the most valuable trinkets were upstairs. Instead, they had concentrated on one unimpressive room where he clearly worked.

From whom could they have learned that?

From whom could they have learned that he did anything of importance at all? And what exactly had they been looking for? He would ask them when they had time to wake up properly and stew for a bit. Perhaps tomorrow.

He glanced with some irritation toward the broken decanter lying in a sticky pool of brandy. Then he laid his head in his hands and tugged once at his short hair. He had begun all this, had insisted on doing it alone. He had no right to feel so isolated. He didn't even know what he wanted, except, for some reason, it seemed to have Lily's face.

And then, some faint sound made him look up. And there she was, staring at him.

That she should be here, now, was so unlikely that he blinked to clear the hallucination. But she didn't vanish. Instead, she almost jumped over the obstacles in her path, shoving others aside in her hurry to get to him. Before he could rise, she had flung herself at his feet and taken both his hands.

"Oh, my dear, what is it?" she whispered. "What has happened?"

She called him her dear, gazed up at him with such anxiety, such sweet care for him, that there seemed to be only one thing he could do. He leaned forward and kissed her.

God, he had known she would taste like this, like a flood of sunlight into darkness, like fresh flowers in winter, like everything he had ever wanted or needed. He had dreamed of her lips parting and yielding to his, just as they did now. Even before their pretend kiss at the opera, which had been so unexpectedly heady... But he had never hoped her mouth would cling quite so passionately, that she would press her breasts against him and close her eyes.

He could do nothing but deepen the kiss, savoring her breath, the texture of her lips, her tongue, her teeth, exploring and devouring. She flattened her palms on his knees, and he reached up to take her face between his hands, holding her steady for the onslaught of his mouth and the caress of his fingers across her smooth cheeks, the corners of her mouth, her long, graceful throat.

"How very sweet you are," he whispered against her lips. "Is this sympathy?"

"No. Yes. I don't know. It's everything..."

Enchanted by her inarticulate answer, he sank his mouth into hers once more. Her hand lifted to his cheek, stroking with a shy wonder that almost broke his heart.

What in God's name am I doing?

Something thudded against the legs of the sofa, and she gasped, drawing back in startlement. "What is…?"

His first instinct was to prevent her from jumping up and peering over the back of the sofa, but in truth, he was rumbled, and there was no way he could prevent her seeing—or at least asking.

She knelt beside him and peered down at his captives with shock. She closed her mouth and swallowed. "Who are they?" she asked with commendable calm.

"I have no idea," he admitted.

She frowned, and to his surprise, reached for his hand again, peering at the split knuckles she must have felt already. Her gaze lifted to his. "You did this to them?"

"They made a mess," he said mildly.

"I can see that would be annoying. Have you sent for the Watch?"

"Why, no, not yet."

She sat back on her heels. "You won't, will you?"

"Probably not," he admitted.

"You're not meant to be here," she said, as though just remembering.

He blinked. *"I'm* not meant to be here?"

A breath of laughter shook her, and he wanted to kiss her again. "I came with Millie," she said. "She wants the family rubies to take to Pennington Place."

"And she just had to collect them at midnight?"

"Well, it's not quite midnight," Lily excused her, "and I expect she'll be busy tomorrow."

"I expect she will." Pulling himself together, he rose and held out his hand to Lily.

After a moment's hesitation, she took his hand and twisted around to stand beside him. He led her inexorably to the door, and she picked up the lamp she had brought.

It gave a pleasant glow to the breakfast room when he closed the door.

"It upset you," she said quietly.

He dragged his hand through his hair, trying to shrug it off. And yet, he answered her as he would no one else. "I feel it falling apart. There should be no reason for this. No one should know to give me even a second glance."

"You have kept it secret, I think, for ten years."

Oh, yes, there was more reason than her beauty for his infatuation. The girl was altogether too quick, too perceptive. Much as he did, she put tiny pieces of information together and learned more than the sum of the parts.

"But you had to reveal something of yourself over the last year," she murmured. "To Lord Verne, and therefore Lady Verne. To Madame de Renarde. To Captain Cromarty. To Sir Marcus Dain. None of whom would betray you any more than I," she added hastily. "Or my father, who knows you are more than you appear. But word travels. A careless word, something overheard, a rumor."

He nodded. "And so, the illusion shatters, and I am useless."

"Why?"

His brow contracted.

"Does it matter if people know? It is not you, surely, but those who work for you, who need to be covert." She drew a shuddering breath. "And as for assassination by the French, surely if you are in the open, you can be openly protected?"

"And hemmed in by that protection," he felt compelled to point out.

"I do not that think it is beyond you to get around that."

He gazed at her, reading her open faith in him. Her eyes faltered, and he smiled, reaching up to touch her soft cheek one last time. "You do amaze me, Lily. How did I ever manage without you?"

"Lily!" came Millie's voice from the hall beyond. "Where on earth are you?"

Lily moved toward the door, then glanced back at him. "Aren't you coming to greet her?"

He shook his head. He had things to do. In the study.

Perhaps he imagined she was disappointed. So was he. As the door closed behind her, he knew she would not mention meeting him here to Millie. But five more minutes of her company would have been infinitely preferable to the task ahead.

CHAPTER TEN

ALTHOUGH IT RAINED for most of the journey to Pennington Place, they had set off early and arrived in late afternoon sunshine. This was what the last two weeks had been leading up to, and Lily was excited. This was where she could really help Lord Torbridge.

And if she dwelled too long and too often on his wild, passionate kisses the night before last, at least she knew better than to take them seriously. It had been a moment of weakness for him. She understood that. She knew that gentlemen kissed and even bedded without much meaning. But still, she could not help but treasure his tenderness.

She had steeled herself to ride opposite him in the carriage all day, hiding her heart. But in the end, he had driven himself in his curricle while the rain battered off his hat and great coat. They had met only during pauses to change horses and enjoy rushed refreshments.

"He'll have pneumonia by the time we get there," Sir George had observed.

"Torbridge is never ill," Millie had replied in a distracted kind of way.

And then the sun had come out when they were already on Pennington land, and they could see the magnificent house rising up from the most beautiful park Lily had ever seen.

"Oh, my goodness," Lily said, awed. "It makes Audley Park look like a cottage and garden."

Sir George laughed. "Hardly. And you aren't meant to have seen

Audley Park, are you?"

"No," Lily admitted, recovering her accent. "In any case, I've only ever seen it from a distance."

Some guests had clearly arrived earlier, for several people had spilled out onto the terrace to enjoy the sunshine. As Lily alighted from the carriage, her legs feeling stiff and awkward from the long journey, she saw Lord Torbrige laughing and shaking the rainwater off his hat as he greeted the dowager Lady Pennington and a few other guests.

Jack Hill strode across to them, grinning. "Welcome! What a pleasure to see you here. I was beginning to fear you wouldn't get here before tomorrow, but instead, you have brought the sunshine with you. Will you be shown directly to your rooms, or would you prefer to bask in the warmth first? I think Torbridge is actually steaming…"

"Let us get rid of our travel dirt, first," Millie suggested, and immediately a maid was summoned along with two footmen who carried the baggage.

As she was about to mount the steps into the house, something made Lily glance upward. From the nearest first-floor window, Lord Pennington watched them. Although his expression was impossible to read, his gaze was on Millie.

Getting to their bedchambers felt a bit like walking from end to end of an entire town, but it was worth it. If Lily had imagined her room in the Mastertons' townhouse was luxurious, this one was splendid. Its sheer size awed her, as did the intricate moldings on the ceiling, and the fine silk and velvet hangings.

"Goodness, George, we even have separate rooms," she heard Millie exclaim.

It was an odd custom of the upper class, Lily had discovered, that they maintained separate bedchambers. Sir George and Millie did at home, which Lily had always thought a shame. She thought sharing a chamber and a bed would make it easier to solve the distance between them.

In fact, when she had washed and dressed obediently in the gown Millie had told her was suitable for the afternoon, she found that Millie's chamber shared a connecting door to Sir George's, for he stood in the doorway, in suitable afternoon attire, admiring his wife's dress. She seemed quite pink with pleasure.

There is hope for them.

Sir George's gaze shifted to her. "Yet more beauty," he observed. "May I have the honor of escorting you both downstairs to the very last of the sunshine?"

"Of course, you may," Millie said. "Just as soon as my hair is pinned. What do you think, Lily?"

Lily went further into the room and duly admired Prince's handiwork.

Satisfied, Millie stood. "Then let's go down."

A knock sounded at the half-open door, and a young lady's head appeared around it. "May we join you?"

"Ella!" Millie all but squealed, flying across the room to embrace the laughing newcomer. Behind them loomed a slightly apologetic gentleman who made a vague shrugging gesture toward Sir George.

Sir George laughed and went to meet him, offering his hand.

Ella, Lily thought. This must be the younger sister of Torbridge and Millie.

"Why did you not tell me you were coming?" Millie demanded, releasing the lady to some degree and looking her over.

"I wanted to surprise you. Is Dolph here, too?"

"Yes, but I don't know where he's lodged. Oh!" She paused, realizing Ella's attention had landed on Lily. "Of course, this is Lily Darrow, our cousin from Ireland."

Ella blinked. Lily curtseyed, which the lady did not acknowledge before saying bluntly, "No, she isn't, Millie. You've been taken in."

The blood drained from Lily's face, making her dizzy. Sir George closed the bedchamber door.

Ella glared at Lily. "I don't know what she's up to, but we have no cousin named Lily."

"Well, of course, we don't," Millie agreed, somewhat taking the wind out of her sister's sails. "She isn't really our cousin, but we have to pretend she is. For Dolph."

"Oh." Ella's face cleared as if matters were now perfectly acceptable.

"Being made homeless, she came to England to see what Papa could do for her," Millie explained. "But since he's so ill, she's come to me as my companion, and been extremely helpful, I have to say. But where are my manners? Lily, this is my sister, Arabella, Lady Barham, and her husband, Lord Barham."

Lord Barham bowed, looking somewhat bemused. Lady Barham inclined her head, the clear suspicion in her face now replaced by curiosity.

"Oh, and if she decides to leave me and be married, Dolph may give her a decent dowry."

Ella's eyes widened. "Really?"

"No," Lily said. "It's just part of the lie. I couldn't marry any of his lordship's friends—or yours—if I wanted to."

"Why not?" Lord Barham asked curiously.

"Because I'm the daughter of an innkeeper."

Ella blinked. "Really? I've never seen one remotely like you before."

Unsure whether or not to take that as a compliment, Lily said only, "If you would be so good as to keep to this fiction..."

"Of course," Ella said at once.

"You, too, Barham," Sir George added as the sisters moved toward the door. "It's important to Torbridge."

Barham nodded.

Millie let out an exclamation. "But your babies! What have you done with them?"

"Eaten them," Ella said promptly.

"Seriously!" Millie commanded.

"We brought them, of course," Ella said, "with their nurse. Lady Pennington has been most accommodating. They're asleep just now—finally! But you must come and meet them before dinner, perhaps?"

Tea had been laid out on the terrace, where the sun still shone. The ladies wore shawls over their elegant gowns and sat nibbling dainty pieces of bread and butter, scones, and cakes. The gentlemen mostly stood in clumps or sauntered between the tables. Tea was served in fine china cups. Just for a moment, Lily panicked. This was not her world. She should be serving tea to those people in her parents' inn, not joining them.

But she had done this before, she reminded herself. Really, it was just like Millie's "at home", only with more people.

"Good God," a familiar voice exclaimed.

Ahead of Lily, Ella let out a cry and launched herself at her brother, quite without proper decorum, as he pointed out once he had hugged her back.

"A little more propriety here, if you please, Lady Barham," he said with a severity that might or might not have been in fun. "I have to say, you're looking extremely well for someone who has brought two more babies into the world."

"Oh, that was months ago! And you're looking pretty well yourself."

"Why, thank you." He turned to his brother-in-law, holding out his hand. "How are you, Barham?"

There was something endearingly natural in the affection of the siblings. Children who had not only survived but thrived in a home with no obvious parental love. To Lily, brought up by affectionate parents who doted on her, this was a miracle and due largely, according to Millie, to the eldest, Lord Torbridge. Not that anyone would guess, for after the first, surprised hug, he drew back to a greater distance, mostly scolding in a vague kind of way that did not appear to hurt Ella but made her sigh.

Of course, the relationship between Torbridge and his sisters was not her concern. So, when she saw the sad-eyed Mrs. Bradwell, she drifted over to greet her.

"Mrs. Bradwell. How pleasant to see you here," she murmured.

The lady glanced up, and immediate warmth suffused her eyes. "Miss Darrow. Please, join us. I gather this is your first stay at Pennington Place?"

It was the usual dull small talk, involving everyone at the table, but more than once, she caught the lady's gaze fixed on her face with an expression of almost frightened curiosity. And when the sun dipped just a little too far for comfort, and everyone began to make their way into the house, she asked Lily about her parents.

Keeping to the story, Lily replied, "Sadly, they are both deceased." For some reason, she found it particularly uncomfortable to lie to this lady. She hoped any awkwardness in her manner would be put down to grief.

"But you had a happy childhood, I hope?"

"Oh, yes," Lily said with relief at something she could answer honestly.

"I imagine they were very good to you."

It was an odd thing to say, but then she did appear to be a slightly odd lady. For some reason, Lily found this intriguing. "Very," she agreed.

"And were you really born in Ireland?"

Lily laughed. "I don't recall it, but I believe so!" By the grand staircase, she saw Torbridge gazing about him. She wondered if he was looking for her. Crushing her sudden surge of longing, she turned back to Mrs. Bradwell, realizing she had said something else. "I beg your pardon?"

"I was saying, I am still fascinated by the little pendant you wore at Lady Masterton's musical evening." Mrs. Bradwell gave a small, apologetic little smile. "I wonder if I might buy it from you?"

Involuntarily, Lily's hand flew to her throat, even though the necklace wasn't there. "Oh, no, I'm afraid I couldn't do that. It has been with me all of my life. I am too attached to it."

"Ah, of course. Perhaps I can have one made just like it."

"Good luck," Lily said. "Will you excuse me?" She hurried away toward the stairs, but by the time she got there, she could no longer see Torbridge.

"Cousin Lily!" It was Ella, beckoning to her from halfway up the first flight of stairs. Beyond her, she could see Millie and Torbridge's back.

She hurried up after them, to learn they were on their way to meet the Barham offspring. It was, of course, excellent cover to be included, but Lily couldn't help feeling guilty for intruding on yet another private family moment. Not for the first time, she recognized how trusting Torbridge's family were of her, how far they were willing to let her into their lives. Even knowing her true background. His word, his needs, clearly carried a lot of weight with them.

The Barhams had a suite of interconnecting rooms, one of which had been set up as a nursery with two large cots and a truckle bed for the nurse. Inside the first cot, an infant of perhaps two years sat up, grinning and reaching up her arms to be lifted out. In the other, lay two small babies who could only have been three or four months old.

"Well, well, tiny Barhams," Torbridge said softly.

Ella plucked the older child from her cot. "This is your uncle Torbridge, Jenny. He is quite mad but mostly lovable."

"I remember you when you were that size," Torbridge said, pointing at the other cot.

Jenny pointed, too, "Roberta. Randolph."

Torbridge glanced at Ella. "You shouldn't have."

"You *are* his godfather."

"No, really, you shouldn't have. It's a terrible name." He joined Millie in gazing down at the still sleeping babies. "But they are beautiful children for all that. Does one say, well done at such times? Probably not, but I am amazed."

Millie seemed to be amazed, too. Her eyes, full of wonder and love, filled with emotion, sparkling with some devastating sadness.

Ella laid her hand on her sister's shoulder, and Millie gasped, turning it into a laugh. "Why, you are so very clever, Ella." She beamed at Jenny. "I can't wait until you all grow up so that I may spoil you silly. I am determined to be your favorite aunt. Excuse me…"

To Lily's surprise, she drifted out of the room in her usual haze of perfumed silk and lace. Ella made a move to follow her, but Sir George stayed her. "She'll be fine. She already loves them to distraction."

Lily solemnly shook hands with Jenny and then discovered that the gentlemen were repaired to the sitting room to indulge in the strange tradition of "wetting the baby's head."

"Imbibing brandy," Ella translated dryly. "No doubt, a glass for each."

"Then I'll leave you until dinner and see if Cousin Millie needs me."

However, there was no answer at Millie's door. Lily hesitated, unwilling to barge in if she wanted to be alone. Deciding to wait, she went into her own chamber and discovered Millie sitting on her bed.

"Oh! I'm sorry." Lily closed the door and hurried forward. "I didn't realize you wanted me so quickly."

"I don't," Millie said in surprise. For an instant, she looked confused, then laughed. "Well, if I do, I don't know for what. You are a surprising comfort to me, Lily."

"I'm sorry you need comfort," Lily said, walking to the bed and sitting down. She waited a moment, then said, "You would like a baby of your own."

Millie nodded, and the tears started to her eyes again. "I had a baby once," she whispered. "A tiny, perfect son. He lived less than an hour. I barely held him in my arms."

"Oh, my dear, I'm so sorry." Lily hugged her. She had seen the pain of a lost child too often before. It was a tragedy that did not limit itself to class or lessen with the awful frequency.

Millie clutched her. "I am glad for Ella, I truly am, but when I stare at those tiny babies, I remember my own."

"Of course you do."

"I will love them as if they *are* my own."

"I know you will."

For a few moments, Lily let her weep. Then Millie drew back a little and wiped her eyes on a wispy handkerchief. "I'm sorry."

"Don't be. And you know, you are still young. You could still have babies."

"Not when my husband will not—" She broke off. "Oh, dear. I should not speak so to an unmarried lady."

"I'm not a lady," Lily reminded her. "Sir George loves you."

"He did once."

Lily frowned. "Then why should you imagine him changed?"

"Because I could not give him his son. Because he does not come near me."

So, the separate rooms truly were separate. Which was odd, because Lily *knew* they loved each other. "Did your doctors advise against having more children?"

Millie shook her head. "No. But it's true I almost died, too. And George was wonderful in those first months, even though he was grieving terribly. But the weeks turned into months, and he did not come to me. I could not persuade him, and believe me in those days, I was not too proud to try."

"And then you pretended not to care, and so did he in retaliation, and you drifted apart."

"For eight years. Lily, I long so for a baby... For *him*."

"You still have child-bearing years," Lily pointed out.

"What use are they?" she retorted, swiping at her eyes again. "Dash it, Lily. Why do I talk to you so? You have been in my household for barely two weeks!"

"It is easier sometimes to speak to a stranger."

"That's the odd thing. I don't *feel* you are a stranger at all."

"You are a kind family. You know what I am, and you have taken me in, confided in me."

"I don't think it's us," Millie said vaguely. "I think it's you." She rose to her feet. "Thank you for letting me cry on your shoulder. I shall be fine now and quite able to make a fuss of Ella's adorable children. You should wear the new evening gown. And I'll send Prince to dress your hair."

Lily watched her go while plans swirled in her head. She wished they were at the Hart.

CHAPTER ELEVEN

D INNER THAT EVENING was the most magnificent affair Lily had ever seen. She had never even imagined so many people around one table, served by an army of footmen. Despite her secret—and in part, cowardly—wish to be placed beside Lord Torbridge, she found herself sitting next to Mr. Jack Hill. Which at least focused her mind on the task in hand.

"It is good of the Foreign Office to spare you this week," she observed.

"Oh, I take leave of absence every year at this time."

"Is it a quiet time?"

"Not really. But I bring work with me if I have to. It's easy enough to communicate with London from here, too."

"Then I hope work will not spoil your leave."

"So do I," Mr. Hill said fervently. He grinned engagingly. "I shall not let it, not while you are here."

With a bewildering array of courses, cutlery, and wine glasses to negotiate, Lily had to keep her wits about her, but in the end, she felt she got through the meal without committing any major crimes against etiquette and retired to the drawing room with the ladies.

However, her relief was short-lived, for as she sat near her "cousins", old Lady Pennington deigned to notice her. "Miss Darrow, I trust you are comfortable at the Place?"

"Extremely, ma'am. The house and grounds are splendid."

"Aren't they?" she said complacently. "My husband and my son have both done a great deal to restore the fading grandeur."

Lily had no idea how much the upkeep of such a residence would cost, but she was sure it must be staggering. No wonder Lord Pennington couldn't be bothered with his brother's debts. However, before she could dwell on this, a new threat reared its head.

"I hear you sing," Lady Pennington said. "I look forward to hearing you once the gentlemen join us."

Lily opened her mouth to protest in some alarm, but Millie's elbow dug into her ribs, and she subsided with a nervous smile.

"I'll play for you," Millie breathed. "Just sing as you did in Brook Street."

"Is it normal for ladies' companions to be asked to sing?" Lily asked.

"No. But it's not normal for them to be pursued by the hostess's son either."

"Oh, dear…" Guilt surged once more, and she had to remind herself that Jack Hill was a traitor. However, she still had difficulty imagining him as such.

Any hope she might have harbored that Lady Pennington would forget her in the distraction of several other wealthier girls of higher rank was doomed. Certainly, she was not the first to show off her accomplishments, but just when she began to relax, she received the summons.

This was a very different prospect to singing for three people in Brook Street. Here she was among crowds disposed to jealousy or at least accusations of encroaching behavior from a mere poor relation. But, apparently, she could not refuse.

Well, to the devil with them all, I am Lady Lily, she told herself and raised her head to sing.

Surprisingly, her first ballad went down very well, and she was asked to sing again. Lily looked hastily to Millie for advice.

Millie nodded. "Oh, the amusing one you sang the other evening," she suggested.

Obligingly, Lily repeated that, too, and hoped to God that was the end of it. To her relief, Millie stood up while everyone else was still clapping and laughing. As she passed Torbridge, he glanced up with a quick smile, and she read approval in his eyes.

She sat down much more happy to listen to the next young lady.

As the evening wore on, it grew a little chilly for those who, like Lily, sat furthest away from the fire. Millie actually shivered.

"Shall I fetch your shawl?" Lily murmured.

"Would you?"

"Of course." Apart from making Millie more comfortable, it would look as if she was a useful companion.

"I left it on the bed. If it isn't there, get Prince to find you one."

Lily walked quickly to the door. Her heartbeat quickened when she saw Lord Torbridge standing in her path.

He smiled when he saw her and stepped aside. "I'll find you later," he murmured beneath his breath.

There was no time even to ask where or when, for he had already turned back to his friends, and Lily had no reason to linger. But it did strike her with some excitement that he might follow her or look out for her return.

The main staircase was extravagantly lit, but she took one of the waiting candles to guide her way along the winding passages to Millie's chamber. When she reached the correct passage, her heart lurched, for she thought Lord Torbridge was walking toward her.

Disappointingly, it wasn't him, but a gentleman in a well-fitting plain, black suit. He was tall and handsome, and he bowed to Lily as she passed. But he did not speak.

Intrigued, for some reason, she glanced once over her shoulder. Then she was at Millie's chamber. Entering, she found Prince was not there, but the shawl lay on the bed as Millie had told her. Snatching it up, she went next to her own room and put the shawl Millie had given her around her chilly shoulders.

Although she dawdled a little on the stairs as she returned, Torbridge did not emerge to speak to her. She could only enter the drawing room and present Millie with her shawl. By then, tea was being served, and the guests were moving around a little more. Jack Hill came to speak to her, as did a couple of other gentlemen, and Mrs. Bradwell. But Torbridge did not.

She looked around for him when it was time to retire, but once more, he was deep in conversation with friends and did not appear to notice her. There was nothing she could do but follow Millie upstairs, wish her and Sir George good night, and go to her chamber.

The lamp had been lit and the curtains drawn. Lily went to the window, wondering if she would see Torbridge below, waiting for her. There was no sign of him, and it seemed to be raining again, so she let the curtain fall back.

A knock sounded at the door, which made her heart leap. But it was only Prince offering to unlace her gown. When Prince had left, she returned to the window seat and sat there waiting for some time.

Then, with a slightly annoyed sigh, she slid out of her clothes, donned the night rail also given her by Millie, and was about to blow out the lamp when a faint scratch sounded at the door.

She froze, staring at the door, remembering for some reason, that Torbridge had been burgled. He had not seemed to believe it was connected with Hill's case in particular, but suddenly Lily was not so sure. She looked around wildly for a weapon and spied the washing jug. It was too beautiful to break but...

She was already halfway across the room to it when the door began to open. She sprinted toward the jug, keeping her frantic gaze on the door. She snatched up the jug and froze again.

Lord Torbridge stood there, gazing from her to the jug and back.

Quietly, he closed the door.

Lily set the jug back on the washstand.

"Thank God you didn't throw it. There would have been a shocking clatter, and we would both have been undone."

"I wish I *had* thrown it," she hissed. "You should have warned when and where."

He walked toward her, and her stomach twisted with wicked excitement. But he merely snatched up the dressing gown at the foot of the bed and threw it to her.

She flushed, for the nightrail was one of Millie's and made of very fine lawn that left little to the imagination.

"Sorry," she mumbled, twisting the dressing gown in suddenly clumsy hands to get it the right way around.

"Don't apologize," he said with strange fervor. Impatiently, he closed the distance between them and snatched back the dressing gown, shaking it out and holding it for her to slide her arms into it. His fingers did not quite touch her, but she felt his heat behind her as though she wore nothing. Hastily, she dragged the robe around her and swung back to face him.

He was too close, but she would not step back. She wasn't sure she could.

A quick frown tugged at his brow. "Are you quite well, Lily?"

She nodded and took a deep breath. "Are you? Did you get your study cleared up?"

His lips twitched. "Yes, I did," he said gravely.

"What of those men?"

"I thought they were what you meant."

Laughter caught her unawares. "No, you didn't. Did they tell you anything useful?"

"I'm not sure." Surprising her again, he moved away and dropped onto the floor in front of the fire, sitting with his back against the nearest chair. He looked almost like the boys who would come occasionally to the inn in winter, hoping for warmth and cake. "They are only hired bullies, but they had done work for the same man before."

"What man?" she asked eagerly, going to join him.

"They don't know his name, of course, but they called him a gentleman."

She knelt beside him with some excitement. "Not Jack Hill?"

"No, this fellow is dark, not fair. But he could certainly be connected to Hill. I'm assuming he is the means by which messages and money are exchanged."

"Then Jack does not travel to the ports because this fellow does it for him?"

Torbridge nodded. "I think so."

"Is he French?" she asked.

"They say not. Assure me they would not work for Frenchmen. But a Frenchman may sound English as easily as an Englishman may sound French."

"Either way, you need to find this man," Lily said.

"I do. And I'm hoping Hill will lead me to him. You seem to have his attention, which places you beautifully."

Somewhere at the back of her mind, she was aware he did not speak with undiluted pleasure, but her mind was still on the previous topic.

"This English gentleman," she said, frowning, "if that is what he is. Does he then know who you are and what you do? Did he send his ruffians for anything in particular? Were they meant to *harm* you?"

"I can't imagine they were instructed to treat me with kid gloves, but I don't believe they were meant to find me there at all. They chose a time when I was believed to be from home. Unfortunately, I came back early. But you are correct. I have to assume the French now know who I am, or at least what my connections are."

"It doesn't seem to upset you as much as it did."

He met her gaze. "Why, no, it doesn't. You are a lady of much wisdom."

"I'm not a lady at all."

"I don't think I believe that."

She wasn't sure what that meant, so returned to the important point. "Did you let them go?"

"Eventually. They'll be followed."

"That won't stop them talking about whatever they found in your house."

"My dear, they didn't find anything in my house for the simple reason there was nothing for them to find. I don't write anything down."

She closed her mouth. "But other people must report to you. You must surely send messages…"

"Reports are read and passed on or destroyed immediately. The same with messages."

"You really are secretive, aren't you?"

He shrugged. "I suppose I knew the day would come when this would happen."

"Then they don't know about me?"

"I thought about that. They wouldn't have been able to see you that night, and they would hardly be in a position to recognize your voice. Was that why you were trying to throw the water jug at me?"

"It crossed my mind," she said with dignity.

He took her hand. "I'm sorry. I should not be putting you in such a position. I will never let anything happen to you."

"I'm not afraid," she insisted.

He smiled and gazed down at her hand for a moment. His thumb caressed her fingers, sparking little tingles of delight. Abruptly, as if suddenly realizing what he was doing, he released her.

"Hill," he said hastily. "Do you think he trusts you?"

"I think he likes me. And he told me he likes gambling, that he has a few debts. Oh, and when he is on leave, as now, he takes urgent documents away with him to work on. He has done so this week."

Torbridge nodded. "Did he say where he works on these things? Which room?"

"No, but I can probably find out."

"Not unless the subject comes up. It would be an odd thing to ask him, but it will be easy enough to find out."

"Yes, but... How can you be sure any of these documents will have information he's compelled to pass on? He cannot send them *everything* that crosses his desk."

"I am sure."

Something in his tone made her peer into his eyes. "I should have known. You've planted a document for him to find."

"A false document," he admitted reluctantly. "Just in case we fail, and it gets through to Paris. Lily, does he give you any sense of unhappiness with his lot? Even of sympathy for the French cause? Anything that might explain these betrayals?"

Lily shook her head. "Not really. Though as we said, he does gamble and tends to lose a great deal. You must know that already. And it strikes me that Pennington, with this place to maintain, will not be happy to keep paying his debts. I suppose that is a motive but..."

"But what?"

"I still don't see him as a traitor."

Torbridge looked into the dying embers of the fire. "You like him?"

She considered. "A little, yes. More than his brother, at any rate." Thoughts of Pennington brought Millie to mind, and she frowned. "May I ask you something about Millie?"

"You would probably be better asking Millie."

"I did. She told me about losing her baby. She grieves for him still."

"I know."

"Did the doctors give any reason, any sign that she could not have more children?"

"No, I don't believe so. Though the birth may have damaged her. She was very ill afterward. Masterton feared he had lost them both. And, certainly, there have been no more pregnancies."

There was a good reason for this lack, but it was not Lily's secret to tell. She stuck to her point. "But the doctors never forbade it? Never said it could not happen?"

"Not that I ever heard. Lily, what are you about?"

"Nothing. I do not like the distance between Millie and Sir George. It makes them both unhappy. You know that."

"I know," he admitted. "But it's a rule of mine never to interfere between a man and his wife." He considered. "Unless it's a matter of life and death. In any other situation, one is liable only to make matters worse. In any case, I have thought them closer in recent…"

He broke off, staring at her. A smile flickered over his face. "I knew it was you rather than the Hart."

"I think buildings and the people who live in them soak each other up. Except your house," she added and then bit her lip, for she hadn't meant to say that.

"My parents' house," he corrected. "I own a small hunting lodge in Leicestershire." He rose to his feet. "I should go. I'll come again tomorrow night if we need to talk privately. Or we can talk during the day. There will be plenty of opportunity, I imagine."

She jumped up and followed him, even caught his arm when it seemed he would rush off. "My lord."

He turned at once. "Cousin."

She searched his face. "Have I offended you?"

"How could you have?"

"I implied your family home was cold and inhuman."

"You should come to Hayleigh."

"You have no home," she said, making the discovery at last.

"Who needs a home?" he retorted, "When one has the Hart Inn to visit?"

"You do."

"Nonsense," Torbridge said firmly as if to prove it, he swooped and pressed a quick kiss to her lips. "Good night, Lily."

"Good night," she whispered and, before he could move away, she daringly kissed him back.

With a low groan, he wrapped his arms around her and crushed her mouth beneath his. Pressed close to his body, she felt every hard, thrilling inch of him. She kissed him back, welcoming his tongue with her own. Sighing with pleasure, she threw her arms around his neck and gave herself up to the moment.

As did he, and when their lips parted for the sake of breathing, he kissed her again almost immediately. His body moved, caressing hers. His hand stroked her hair, brushing out the pins and winding the tresses around his hand.

This was bliss, what she had waited her whole life for...

He tore his mouth free, pressing his rough cheek to hers. "I have to stop kissing you," he said shakily.

"Why?" she demanded. "Because I am not of your class, your world?"

His uneven breath rushed out. "On the contrary, you seem to be a very large part of my world, and damnably at home there."

"Damnably?" she repeated, stricken.

He groaned. "Pay no attention to my ramblings. I should not be doing this. I should not be hurting us like this."

She gazed up at him, at his hot and clouded eyes, at the texture of his firm, sensual lips. "Do I look hurt? You don't."

"Don't I? But I am hurting so very much..." His mouth came down on hers once more, and she kissed him with every passion she had, as though she was *fighting* for him. Perhaps she was.

He let her go abruptly. "Good night, Lily." And in a flurry of air and the silently closing door, he was gone.

CHAPTER TWELVE

L ILY SLIPPED OUT into the garden before breakfast, called by the blessedly fresh scents and sounds of the countryside. There might not have been wailing seagulls here, and the air lacked the salty tang of the sea, but still, it reminded her of home.

Inevitably, Lord Torbridge was on her mind as she strolled alone among the formal gardens. Something was happening between them. Something was changing. The feeling warmed and excited her. Though she had no idea where it would lead, she could not prevent the hope surging within her. Hope of what was a different matter. Any closer relationship between them was still not possible.

Yes, it is. She had been brought up to recognize that marriage to a good man, be he ever so poor, was infinitely preferable to an irregular liaison with a wealthy gentleman. The latter might be handsome and charming and shower a girl with gifts. But he would ultimately abandon her.

She wished Torbridge was merely the owner of Underton, Mr. Bunton's farm.

But then, he would not have been Torbridge.

Determinedly, she pushed aside all thought of the future, all fantasy. For now, the present was wonderful, growing closer to him, knowing him better with each passing day. She would hold onto that and do her best to complete the tasks he asked of her. What would be, would be.

Children's distant laughter interrupted her reverie. Intrigued, she followed the sounds until she discovered two children of about eight or nine years old, playing a game of tag with a toddling infant who looked very like the Barham's eldest. The children were watched indulgently by a pair of nurses, one of whom was definitely the Barham nurse she had seen yesterday.

Both women curtseyed to her and wished her good morning while the Honorable Jenny Barham swerved away from her quarries to investigate the newcomer.

She grinned at Lily. "Cuz."

Lily smiled back. "Cousin Lily, that's right! And who are your friends?"

"Mr. Peter and Miss Harriet Hill," the previously unknown nurse said with pride. "Lord Pennington's children, you know."

"Goodness!" Lily gazed at the children, even more indignant with their father for his pursuit of Lily. "I didn't even know he was married."

"Widowed," the nurse whispered.

Something pulled at her mind, only to vanish out of reach as Ella and Lord Torbridge appeared around a nearby hedge and greeted her cheerfully.

Lily's stomach dived as she vividly remembered Torbridge's good night. But he wore his amiable, veiled face and merely smiled vaguely at her.

"Good morning, Cousin Lily! Breakfast is calling," he said and scooped up his niece, who squealed with delight. The other children stood, watching quietly, although they smiled when Lily waved to them. Two more children neglected by parents and brought up by servants. She wondered if Torbridge or his siblings noticed, or if they merely accepted this was how things were done.

AFTER BREAKFAST, THE morning's entertainment was a ride through the woods. Lily accompanied Millie. To her annoyance, Sir George did not, but Torbridge was there, giving far too much attention, in Lily's view, to a rather charming widow.

Lord Pennington, who led the expedition, was both amusing and knowledgeable, and Lily had hopes that he had taken Torbridge's words at the musical soiree to heart. He had been merely polite to Millie the previous evening, and there had been no flirting that Lily had seen. But then, Millie had been occupied with her own emotional problems, and Sir George had been there to support her. Now, Pennington still played the perfect gentleman, and Lily felt relaxed enough to at least appreciate the woodland scenery and the sunlight dappling between the trees.

Jack Hill rode beside Lily for much of the way, although he did not monopolize her, and other young gentlemen seemed to find her company pleasant. Cynically, she wondered how pleasant they would find her if they didn't imagine Lord Torbridge would give her a dowry. Jack Hill himself was hardly indifferent to the incentive.

"And so, do you allow yourself liberty again this afternoon?" Lily asked him as they returned to the Pennington Place stables. "Or will you be dutiful?"

"Dutiful," Jack said ruefully. "At least for a couple of hours. And once that is done, I should have tomorrow to myself before the ball. Are you looking forward to it?"

"Immensely," she assured him.

"Remember, I have asked for two waltzes!"

"But I have only granted you one."

He laughed and dismounted, letting the waiting stable lad take the reins from him while he turned to help Lily. He helped her down with a light, respectful hold, but as he moved aside, she saw his brother performing the same service for Millie.

Perhaps it would not have been noticeable to anyone less watchful for intimacy between them, but it was clear to Lily that that he held Millie too tightly, that he let her slip to the ground too slowly, and that his fingers splayed upward from her waist, sliding over her breast as she landed on the ground. Millie's indignant glare was equally clear, and she spun away from him at once, hurrying back toward the house alone.

So much for the perfect gentleman. And he saw that he had overplayed his hand, for he started after her at once, with only a quick glance over his shoulder to make sure he wasn't observed too closely. As usual, he did not even see Lily, who moved quickly, staggering into his path with an exclamation and clutching at her ankle.

"Oh, excuse me," she gasped. "I am in your way. I just turned my ankle, and the weakness made me clumsy."

His eyes sparked annoyance. She had the feeling that if other people's attention had not been attracted by her cry, he would simply have walked around her and carried on his way after Millie. As it was, he had to ask solicitously after her wellbeing and make sure she could put her weight on the ankle before he strode off.

Lily, satisfied she had given Millie enough time to reach the protection of the house and servants, met Torbridge's gaze and received the faintest nod of acknowledgment. As usual, his face betrayed little, but something about his posture was undoubtedly grim.

He caught up with her before she reached the house and held her back from the group she had been with. "What happened?"

"He treated her the way some men feel entitled to treat the taproom maids."

He swore under his breath. "You had better say nothing to Masterton."

"Will Millie not tell him? Will he call Pennington out?"

"He would, which is why Millie won't tell him. We'll have to watch out for her until I can deal with Pennington."

Short of a duel, she couldn't quite imagine how he could deal with

Pennington, though somehow, she didn't doubt that he would.

"Lily," he said abruptly. "Have men treated you that way?"

"In the taproom? Occasionally. But unlike many, my father made sure I didn't have to put up with it. He kicked out anyone who laid a finger on me. As a result, the other girls are largely left alone, too."

He strode faster, and she followed, wondering miserably if her revelation had tainted her in his eyes.

She found Millie alone in her bedchamber, waiting, she said, for Prince to come and help her change. Lily unfastened the riding habit for her.

"Has he done such things before?" Lily asked bluntly.

"Of course not. I would not be here if he had. As it is, I would have imagined it was merely accidental if I had not seen the look in his eyes." She shuddered. "Why are men so...disgusting?"

"Sir George is not disgusting."

"Not to me," Millie said with enough wistfulness to make Lily frown.

"You believe he isn't faithful?" she asked.

"How can I tell? He is gentleman enough to maintain discretion, but if he does not touch *me*..." Millie waved the rest away with impatience. "It needn't mean anything. But none of them are angels."

"Not even Lord Torbridge?" she asked and hated herself.

"Oh, he plays by the rules, and he is not married, so who cares? *I* am married. Did I ever do anything to make Pennington believe that anything beyond civilized flirting was acceptable to me?"

Lily, who did not quite understand the rules, merely shook her head. "I think the question is rather, why did he do such a thing now?"

"Because as the guest of his mother, I cannot make a fuss without creating a scandal and appearing ill-mannered to boot."

"Then we must make sure you avoid him. Lord Torbridge will help, and perhaps you should also confide in your sister."

"I thought he was my friend."

Whil, lonely and untouched by her husband, she had soaked up his admiration like a sponge. His apparent admiration.

Frowning, Lily asked, "Have he and Sir George ever quarreled?"

"Lord, no, they move in different circles, and George is not the kind of man to easily give or take offense." She paused in the act of pulling pins from her hair. "He and Torbridge knew each other at school. Pennington was a few years older, but I don't think he was kind to Dolph."

"Did Lord Torbridge tell you that?"

"No, Pennington did. He seemed to think it was funny."

And still, you called such a man friend? Lily thought indignantly.

In disbelief, Millie said, "You think in flirting with me, he was merely carrying on a childhood quarrel with my brother?"

Lily shrugged. "Not really. It would make more sense if it had been Torbridge being unkind to Pennington at school. I think he is probably just not a very pleasant person."

"I could have found a better flirt," Millie observed with a sigh. "Or none at all."

Lily leaned closer. "Tell Sir George how you feel. About everything." With that, she hurried out to change her dress, for Prince had just come in.

At luncheon, she was a little too gratified when Torbridge sat beside her. However, he spent at least as much time talking to the charming widow on his other side as he did talking to her. Piqued, she smiled at the young man on her other side. She didn't even know his name.

Only as she made to leave did Torbridge stand and murmur, "Library," under his breath.

She gave no sign of having heard him, but she knew what he meant. Jack Hill was working in the library. Although it was a sensible place to work, she couldn't help feeling it was somewhat public for sensitive information, especially if one meant to betray it to the enemy. Anyone could wander in there, as indeed Lily meant to.

After luncheon, most of the guests either retired to rest in their rooms or took walks about the elegant formal gardens. A few gentlemen played cards in one of the salons, while a group of young ladies gossiped close by, chaperoned by a severe matron working on her embroidery. Millie spent the time with her sister and her children. Of Pennington or Torbridge, there was no sign.

Lily drifted from group to group as though restless and then wandered around the huge house, looking for the library. She began to suspect that it might get to teatime, with Mr. Hill's duties completed, before she even *found* the library. Most of the doors to the great apartments were open, so it was easy to see that none of them were the room she sought. Eventually, she asked one of the footmen.

"Is there a library here?"

"Yes, Miss. This way." To her delight, he did not have to lead her far to a closed door, which he threw open for her.

"Thank you," she said and tripped inside.

It dwarfed the library in Brook Street. It even had a mezzanine gallery and an open spiral staircase leading up to it. The ridiculously high ceiling was supported on thick, Grecian pillars. From behind one of those, a frowning Jack Hill pushed back his chair and peered across the room.

He jumped to his feet. "Miss Darrow!"

"Oh, *this* is where you are working," she said. "I did not mean to disturb you, but I have finished my novel and thought I might find another here. Do carry on, sir, I shall be gone in a moment!"

Of course, it was not as simple as that, for she had no idea where in the magnificent library to begin looking for novels, and it was easy to be sincerely distracted by other works of history and science. As she moved around, she felt Hill's gaze on her, as though he was no longer even trying to work.

Eventually, she wandered close to his desk and caught his eye.

"Sorry," she murmured.

Grinning, he stood up again. "You can't find the novels, can you? I'm afraid my mother disapproves of such reading matter, so she had them all put up there." He pointed to the gallery.

"Oh dear, I think I would get dizzy up there. Perhaps a travel book would suit me better."

"Nonsense. What do you like? Scott? Mrs. Radcliffe?"

"One of each," she said promptly, not having any very clear idea about either of them.

Mr. Hill immediately sprinted across to the spiral stairs and clambered up. Behind the cover of the pillar, Lily finally let herself look at the piles of documents on the desk—almost like Millie's desk when she had been sorting through the correspondence. But these were much more official-looking documents. She began hastily with the smaller pile. One was a letter to someone at the Turkish embassy, signed John Hill. Under that was a more complicated document mentioning dates, various army regiments, and foreign-sounding places. The name Wellington sprang out at her.

Her heart lurched. Was *this* Torbridge's document?

"Have you read *Waverly*?" Hill called down.

"No, but I would love to!"

The document had a note attached, in the same hand as the letter Hill had signed. *This should not have come to me. Send directly to L. Castlereagh.*

His footsteps clattered down the stairs, and she hastily recovered the document with the Turkish letter, moved back several paces, and reached for the nearest book on the shelf, a botanical treatise.

"How will these do?" Hill asked cheerfully.

She glanced at them without really seeing them and forced a delighted smile. "Oh, wonderful! Thank you, sir. I shall take them both, and this one, if I may? I'm sorry to have disturbed you..."

She hurried out of the room, just as though she really were sorry, and closed the door behind her. Coming toward her across the empty hall was Lord Pennington.

His smile was not quite pleasant, his bow barely civil. "Miss Darrow. How is it I keep running into you?"

"Bad luck," she said promptly, "for one of us."

She spoke from instinct and anger at his earlier behavior, though she softened it almost immediately with a vague smile, worthy of Millie herself. Hopefully, he would imagine her words not rude but simply foolish. Then, clutching her books, she hurried up to her chamber to think.

AN HOUR LATER, she went down to join the others for tea in the drawing room. Encountering Jack Hill on the landing, she said lightly, "Are your labors ended?"

"Ended, bagged, and gone by morning! I may count myself a free man, provided nothing else turns up from London tomorrow! Which book did you read in the end?"

"I read the first line of *The Castle of Otranto*," she confided. "Several times. And then I woke up. It seems I disturbed you for nothing."

"Well, you have them there now for whenever you need them. And it was a pleasure to help. Shall we go in to tea?"

As she turned, she glanced over the banister to the entry hall below and glimpsed a man crossing toward the back of the house in a dignified manner. For a moment, she couldn't remember where she had seen him before, then realized it was the man who had passed her in the passage leading to her bedchamber last night when she had gone to fetch Millie's shawl. And that she had not seen him since.

"Who is that man?" she asked Jack, pointing downward.

"That? My brother's valet. Why?"

She laughed to cover her embarrassment. "Why, he looks so

grand, I thought he was a guest I had not yet met!"

Jack grinned. "That's Francis for you. I couldn't be doing with such a superior, bossy fellow myself, but he seems to suit Pennington."

They strolled into the drawing room together, and Lily was glad to see Millie seated on a sofa with Ella.

Lady Pennington presided over the teapots, and everyone helped themselves to the dainty offerings provided. Lily, watching from the corner of her eye, saw a maid speak to Ella, who stood up with a murmured apology and hurried out, presumably to her children. Almost at once, Lord Pennington dropped into the vacant place beside her.

Lily, sitting by Mrs. Bradwell, murmured instinctively, "Do me a favor, ma'am, and ask my cousin to sit beside you on some pretext." Then she stood, taking her cup and saucer with her, and went to speak to a couple of the younger ladies by the window. A moment later, she saw Millie beside Mrs. Bradwell, apparently deep in conversation, and was satisfied.

Lord Torbridge sauntered in shortly after this, but despite her impatience, she could hardly rush up and tell him everything. It was only later, as they strolled in the gardens, that she found a moment's opportunity to speak to him in private.

They were both examining the fountain in the center of an open lawn, and no one else was close by.

"If the document was something about the army and Wellington, he has it," she murmured. "It should be in a bag with the others, ready to be taken to London tomorrow."

"Still in the library?"

"Probably. He does seem almost criminally open about it all."

"He is surrounded only by gentlemen," Torbridge said wryly. He cast her a quick glance. "And ladies."

"He attached a note to the document saying it shouldn't have come to him," she blurted. "Why would he do that if he was sending it to France instead? I really don't think he is our man."

CHAPTER THIRTEEN

T ORBRIDGE HAD DONE a good deal of work, tracing the past missing documents to Jack Hill's hands. The last thing he wanted to hear was that he was wrong. And yet, he trusted Lily's judgment of character. She had said almost from the beginning that she doubted Hill was a traitor, and this newest evidence of his note did seem to back that up.

What he really wanted now was to sit down on the nearest bench with her and discuss everything, to see what emerged. The sort of conversations he usually had with himself. With Lily's insight, perhaps they could get further.

But they were on full public display, and he didn't want Hill alienated from her just yet. So, he turned away, and they began to walk back toward the terrace.

"We'll talk later," he murmured, though he wasn't sure that was a good idea either, for entirely different reasons.

Holding Lily's barely dressed person in his arms last night was a mistake he could not afford to repeat. The next time—if he allowed a next time, if she did—he doubted he would be able to leave her. Wanting her was a constant ache, blazing into a fire whenever he touched her. Whenever he looked at her. More than that, her presence was becoming so necessary to him that he felt unsettled without it.

Oh, yes, things had reached that point where he could no longer return to the Hart. When this matter ended, he could never see her again.

Unless I find a way to make this work, his brain whispered.

He shut it down at once. There was no way. He could not thrust her into a society where she would be despised and laughed at as the innkeeper's daughter, who had somehow snagged a marquess. She would be shunned and horribly isolated. Nor could he make her his mistress, depriving her of her own people's respect.

And yet, her eyes, her kisses, held such heat and passion. For some reason, she wanted him, too. Even here among much more personable and handsome gentlemen. Dear God, he was even jealous of them, of Jack Hill, whose company he had deliberately thrust her into. The whole thing was out of control.

"Lily," he said urgently before they could be overheard. "If this is wider, if we need to look beyond Jack, you have to be vigilant of everyone."

Her eyes widened, and a singularly sweet smile dawned on her lips. "You believe me."

"Of course I believe you. Why do you think I brought you?"

And then they were among people again, and all private conversation came to an end.

THE EVENING PROGRESSED much like the one before, only Lady Pennington and several of her guests agreed to retire early and sleep late so that they would be fresh for the ball the following evening. And Lily did not sing. He was pleased to see she did not allow Jack Hill to monopolize her company, but spent much of it with Millie, as was only right if she was meant to be her companion. Admittedly, a much favored and indulged companion.

He was glad, too, to see the family subtly keeping Pennington from Millie. He was never allowed to exchange more than a few words with her before she was called away or someone else joined them. Being observant, he also noticed that Mrs. Bradwell had become part of this league.

Shortly before people began to retire, he made a point of being beside Mrs. Bradwell, making idle conversation until they had a few moments of relative privacy.

"You have become quite a friend to my cousin, I think," he observed.

"Miss Darrow? She is a charming girl."

"Indeed, she is. And you appear to have found an unusual affinity in a short space of time."

She inclined her head. "If I had been blessed with a daughter—as well as my two large sons!—I hope she might have been a little like Miss Darrow."

Torbridge held her gaze. "I don't suppose you have ever been to the Hart Inn in Sussex?"

She was good. She did not blink. There was not even a twitch of one eyebrow, only the involuntary curling of one finger, which he saw from the corner of his eye. He did not look directly at her hands.

"I doubt it," she replied calmly. "I don't care for inns. I prefer to stay with friends when I travel."

"One can generally be more sure of the sheets," he agreed. "I only ask because you remind me of a lady I once met there. Incidentally, thank you for looking after my sister."

"A lady should not be *annoyed* by attentions."

"No, she should not," he agreed.

"Will you excuse me, my lord? I believe I shall retire."

He stood at once, bowing with perfect courtesy. His brain was busy with possibilities he should not even be considering. Not when he had a traitor to catch.

WHEN HE ENTERED Lily's chamber, he could not help being disappointed that she had not undressed for bed. In fact, she wore a shawl held tightly over her breasts, and with a surge of heat, he worked out why. Someone—Prince or one of the chambermaids, probably—had already unlaced her. Her gown, all her clothes would fall off with one gentle tug.

Hastily, he swung away to the window, forcing his thoughts from such dangerous channels to safer, yet more important waters. He almost succeeded before she said abruptly, "My lord, where is your chamber?"

He stared at her. "How very forward of you."

She flushed adorably. "I'm trying to work something out. Yesterday evening, when I came up to fetch Millie's shawl, I met a man in the passage. I mistook him for a guest, but in fact, he is Lord Pennington's valet."

Torbridge scowled. "Was he carrying a message to Millie's room?"

"No, for he came from farther along, and he did not stop at my chamber or hers. Are the family's quarters not all on the other side of the house?"

Torbridge nodded. "Yes. Pennington's valet would have little reason to be in this passage unless he was carrying a message. And since all the guests were at that time in the drawing room, it seems unlikely." He searched her face. "You are afraid he was searching my chamber, which is, in fact, at the end of this passage."

"Did you see signs of such a disturbance?" she asked him.

"No such carnage as they made of my study. If my chamber was searched, it was done carefully and discreetly. And it would mean our traitor is aware of my position."

She moved distractedly across the room and knelt by the fire, much as she had last night. "The valet—Francis—could be the connection between Jack and the disappearing documents."

"Yes," he agreed, covering his annoyance that she called Hill by his

Christian name, "but it's a thin connection. Here, at least, they are under the same roof. In London, Hill has his own rooms, and it's not as if the valet could simply wander into the Foreign Office to visit him."

"But he does look like a gentleman," she insisted. "At least to someone like me. Or like those villains who upended your study."

He gazed at her consideringly while he walked to the fire and sat beside her, drawing his knees up under his chin. "The valet as the conductor, the gentlemen as the players... Interesting."

She was silent, staring at him in expectation, and he followed his urge simply to talk, to share his thoughts.

"If you are right about him, perhaps Hill is innocent of everything except excessive trust, excessive openness. He and his brother meet frequently. Pennington has called on him more than once at the Foreign Office. Hill probably talks about his work. Pennington will listen, so could the valet in certain situations, with or without Pennington's knowledge. As for Jack Hill, he has all a gentleman's disregard for servants. He wouldn't notice the valet's presence."

"Then it could be the valet, or Pennington himself," she said excitedly. "I would not put it past either of them."

Torbridge shook his head. "No, it has to be both of them. Pennington undoubtedly needs the money, and he has to be involved in the loss of at least some of the documents."

She nodded. "He has children, too, including a daughter for whom he will need a dowry. He is both proud and desperate for money. Even his dislike of you could be down to the fact that you are richer, even before your inheritance."

"It could be part of it," Torbridge admitted. "For the same reason I've probably discounted him. I'm wary of attributing guilt to people I dislike. It's too easy to be misled without logic or evidence."

"Why do you dislike him?" she asked curiously.

He smiled vaguely. "Oh, children can be cruel. It doesn't make them bad adults, but the relationships made at school color what comes later. But I think he knows he is doing wrong, and he is distracting himself—or trying to—with unsuitable, even impossible liaisons. Millie is not the only woman he's pursuing."

"And the valet?"

"I shall look into him."

She jumped to her feet. "But there may be no time! The document may be stolen already and about to be sent on its way! We should be watching the doors for—"

"I have people watching the roads, ready to follow."

A smile flickered across her face. "Of course you do." She sat back down on the floor opposite him. "Then what is there left for us to do?"

"Find out if the document truly does go back to London, or if it's removed from the bag first. If it's the former, either we are rumbled, or I have been completely wrong about the whole thing."

"Is that likely?"

He shrugged. "In all modesty…no. But it is possible."

Her lips quirked delightfully, and he found it difficult to look away from them. Kissing Lily was a temptation, an addiction he found increasingly hard to resist. He knew he should go without touching her, and yet he didn't. Instead, he said, "Lily, were you born at the Hart?"

She blinked. Clearly, it wasn't what she had expected him to say, but she nodded, a little warily. Perhaps she had grown to dislike reminders of the differences between them.

"And you are the Villins' daughter by birth?"

She frowned. "Of course I am. Is there any other way?"

"Well, yes. Adoption. Did they adopt you, Lily?"

"No, of course not! Why do you ask?"

"Oh, I'm just speculating. Sometimes I think you are not very like them."

"Nonsense," Lily said indignantly. "I am frequently told I am exactly like my mother. I am proud of that."

"So you should be," he replied. "Did you go to school in the village?"

She nodded. "For longer than the other children. My mother wanted me to read and write well enough to correspond with guests who might book in advance, and to count well enough to keep accounts."

"And that is why, with so little practice, you speak with correct grammar."

"It's a bit like speaking two languages," she confided. "One for the local people, and one for more refined guests. I suppose they grew into a mixture, which is how I normally talk."

"And now you have a third language."

Her smile was a little twisted. "Lady Lily."

He couldn't help reaching out to touch her cheek. "I did not mean to confuse your place in the world or make your life difficult."

"I'm not confused. I know what I am."

He smiled. "No, you don't, Lily."

At that moment, the bedchamber door opened abruptly.

"Lily?" came his sister's voice, low but unmistakable.

They both stared at her guiltily.

She stared back, then deliberately closed the door. "Torbridge, what the *devil* are you doing here?"

"Talking to Lily, of course. We have many things to discuss."

"Not in her bedchamber after midnight, you don't."

"Oh, take a powder, Millie," he advised. "You know dashed well, there is no impropriety."

"No improp...." she trailed off and swallowed. "Is that what you would say if you found Pennington in my chamber in so intimate a scene? I don't think so."

"I am not Pennington," he said severely. "Fortunately, I think we've discussed all we need to for the night, so I am going to bed.

Good night, Lily, and thank you."

She murmured some incoherent reply as he rose to his feet. He had a feeling she was laughing, and when he glanced back, her eyes were indeed dancing with mirth. He grinned back and departed under his sister's baleful glare.

IT WAS NOT yet dawn when Torbridge rose, dressed, and made his way down to the library with a solitary candle. Even the servants were not yet abroad, although they would be soon. And then Jack Hill's bag of documents would be gone.

He kept his wits about him, all his senses on high alert, for these were the last minutes, surely, when the document could be removed. Besides which, he had imagined hidden eyes upon him since he'd arrived here, and Lily's theory about Pennington and his valet was more than possible. They could be waiting for him in the darkness.

If they were, he could neither hear nor smell them. The library door was closed but not locked. He pushed it open, leaving his right hand free to defend himself, but sauntered in as though he had every right to be there.

He closed the door, listening intently as he raised his candle high, as though examining the bookshelves. He kept up this attitude, until he passed the pillars, which were the only hiding places in the room, and confirmed that he really was alone. Instantly, he strode toward the desk on which lay a leather pouch. Inside, he found a large packet of documents, tied with string and sealed with wax at the front. Making short work of the string, he then eased open the sides of the packet, leaving the seal intact, and slid the documents out.

He went through them twice to be sure. But the Wellington document had gone.

He replaced the papers in the packet, tucked the sides back in, and rebound it with the string before returning it to the bag. He was right. Someone in this house was a traitor.

It could still be Jack, but Torbridge took Lily's opinion seriously. Now it was up to his men to see who rode out of the estate today. By his guess, there would be two messengers going in different directions. Both would be followed.

Even buried so deep in thought, he knew the moment the door began to open, slowly and silently. Halfway across the room as he already was, there was nowhere to hide. He kept walking and snatched a book from the nearest shelf, ready to hurl it at an attacker if necessary.

A solitary candle entered the room, illuminating Lily, wary, hesitant, and still the most beautiful creature he had ever seen.

Her eyes widened as she recognized him, and she hastily closed the door behind her and rushed to meet him.

"What on earth are you doing here?" she whispered furiously when she stood close enough that he could feel her breath on his chin.

"You know perfectly well, and it's gone," he murmured. "What are *you* doing here?"

She scowled. "Wasting my time, apparently. We did not discuss which of us would come back here."

"That is true. Blame my sister." His gaze drifted from her indignant eyes to her parted lips. "For future reference, your duties consist of apparently innocent inquiries and observations by daylight. Creeping about in the dark is mine. But I'm sorry we didn't get the chance to say a proper goodnight."

Her breath hitched. "I thought it was most proper with Millie present."

"It depends on your definition." He dipped his head slowly, giving her time to avoid it if she wished.

It seemed she didn't. She tilted her face toward him, and he took her mouth. With their hands full of candles and books, they could not hold each other, but their bodies touched, and he almost groaned as she melted against him.

Somehow, despite the blissful distraction and the imminent danger of discovery, he made a decision in those precious moments. He would find a way, and he would not let her go.

For now, the servants would be moving soon. He broke the kiss with reluctance and led her silently to the door. He looked into the darkened hall before he let her out, and followed her to the grand staircase, where he waited at the foot for her to run back up to her bedchamber.

He climbed slowly after her, an involuntary smile stretching his lips. He had never felt so euphoric in his life.

"DOLPH, WHAT DO you mean by that girl?" Millie demanded.

She had come barging into his room when he was only just dressed, and high-handedly dismissed his valet. Higgins had glanced at him before his departure, but when Torbridge nodded, he effaced himself with speed, leaving Torbridge at the mercy of his sister.

"Nothing ill," he assured her. "You know why she is here, why I asked you to look after her in the first place."

"It's she who looks after me," Millie said bluntly. "And not just my financial muddles. In truth, I forget mostly that she is *not* my cousin." She sat on his bed, frowning at him in the glass as he made trivial adjustments to the folds of his cravat. "But she isn't, Dolph. You know who she is, what she is, and you can't ruin her."

"I know."

"I've seen the way you look at her."

"I can look," he said mildly. Kissing might be more reprehensible, but he had no intention of sharing that with Millie.

"She looks, too."

He met her gaze in the glass, his fingers frozen on the cravat pin. "Does she?" He hoped he didn't sound as wistful as he thought he did.

"She adores you, Dolph. You have to take care. For her sake and yours."

"I know." Abruptly, he rose to his feet and swept up his coat. "Everything will be fine. The Hart, you know, is a lucky house. Shall we go to breakfast?"

He just hoped that the luck would hold beyond the inn's walls.

CHAPTER FOURTEEN

N O FORMAL EXPEDITIONS were planned that day since even more guests were expected to arrive—those not favored with a longer-term invitation. But the more energetic among the party went walking or riding in informal groups. Inevitably, Lord Torbridge was among the riders. Lily was sure he was off to hear the reports of his own men and itched to go with him.

"Stay around the house," he had murmured as they met at the breakfast sideboard. "I need you to keep an eye on things here."

She understood he meant Millie as well as Pennington and the valet, and though she was disappointed, she had to acknowledge the sense in one of them remaining behind. There was a strange awareness, a secret excitement in standing beside him in full view of several other breakfast guests with the memory of his kisses still warming her.

Something had changed. She didn't know what or when, but he meant more than casual kisses or even seduction by her. Perhaps he guessed that she loved him, that she had always loved him. Or perhaps—sweet, heady thought—he loved her, too. It was still impossible, of course, but there was such happiness in being with him, in knowing he returned her feelings, in some measure, at least. She would not think of the future.

Both the Hill brothers seemed to be enjoying a lazy day, emerging for a late breakfast and lounging around with books or idle talk. Lily drifted from room to room, always keeping the windows in view, but she saw no sign of the valet either inside or in the nearby grounds.

Torbridge came back in time for luncheon in the garden, but it was an annoyingly long time before she had the chance to exchange words with him. Only as she returned to the house with Millie, did she find him on her other side.

"Messengers from here, taking the London road at speed," he murmured. "No sign of anyone else at all. All other travelers seem to be *coming* here."

"Why would they keep the document here any longer?" she wondered. "Could they mean to pass it on to someone *here*?"

"*Another* traitor? Let us hope not! No, I think rather they're waiting until we're all distracted."

"The ball!"

He smiled and veered off to speak to friends.

Then it had to be the valet who would carry the document, she thought excitedly. For Pennington's absence would be too noticeable.

TO SAVE PRINCE having to rush from chamber to chamber, Millie summoned Lily to prepare for the ball in her room. She felt a little like a doll, letting them dress her and play with her hair. Although she insisted on wearing her one necklace, Prince clipped a pair of small, delicate amethyst drops in her ears without permission, and she was obliged to admit they looked very pretty with the pendant.

Millie, giving up feathers and turban in favor of a jeweled tiara for the evening, looked both magnificent and younger than usual, and Sir George's appreciative gaze seemed to be all the compliment she needed.

"Ah, here is Torbridge at last," Millie exclaimed. "Dolph, give Lily your arm, and let us go down."

But for an instant, Lord Torbridge didn't move. His gaze was fixed on Lily for so long that she blushed, wondering wildly if the neck of her ballgown had slipped or her hair was sticking up. Then he smiled, and before he veiled them, she glimpsed something like awe in his eyes.

"You take my breath away," he said, offering his arm. He spoke lightly, a gentleman giving a compliment to a lady in public, and yet the words and that look stayed with her, in danger of eclipsing the real importance of the evening. Pleasure and hope surged as she laid her hand on his arm and walked out of the room.

For Lily, the evening began to seem more like a fairytale than real life. This was her first ball, and it instantly cast all the other society parties and theater events she had attended into the shade. She marveled at the sheer brightness of the hundreds of candles burning in the ballroom's magnificent central chandelier and in the many sconces about the walls and staircase. Everywhere was decorated with spring flowers and greenery, and the guests glittered with jewels. On the gallery, an orchestra played quietly, a pleasant background to the hum of chatter.

Stunned by the splendor of the sight, Lily murmured, "Oh, goodness. Have you ever seen anything more beautiful?"

"Yes," Torbridge said.

Immediately, she adopted a more languid air, and he laughed.

Lady Pennington welcomed them formally to the ball, her elder son by her side. The younger hovered close by and all but pounced on Lily for the first dance, which was about to begin.

Lily would have preferred to dance with Torbridge, but since he gave her up at once, there was nothing she could do but accept gracefully and walk away on Jack's arm.

The first half of the ball passed in a whirl of gaiety. She danced constantly and enjoyed much laughter and amusing talk with her partners. In between times, she remembered to keep an eye on Pennington, who did not stray farther than the card room. If he tried to dance with Millie, he never got near her, surrounded as she was by admirers and family members.

Her one moment of uneasiness came as the supper dance approached, and she saw Jack Hill weaving through the guests toward her once more. Although from the beginning, she had used few wiles to attract him, she had to confess it was what she had set out to do. When she had believed he was a traitor to his country, the feelings of distaste and guilt were easy to banish. Now, she could not but recognize she had treated him unfairly. After all, in the real world, she would do no more than serve him ale and dinner. He would not even notice her.

Torbridge had noticed her. From the beginning, when he had carried the wounded Lord Verne into the inn.

"A waltz, Lady Lily?"

As though she had conjured him from her mind, Lord Torbridge spoke softly beside her, and since it was what she wanted most in the world at that point, she smiled and laid her hand on his sleeve. Neither of them asked permission of Millie, her formal chaperone.

With her hand in his and his arm at her waist, she followed his steps without thought, gliding and turning across the floor to the beguiling rhythm of the music. Every nerve seemed to spark into excited awareness, and yet it wasn't remotely uncomfortable. It felt very close to bliss.

"I almost feel this is not real," she confided. "Like a dream. Or as if I've stepped out of some children's tale, the kitchen maid dancing with the prince."

"Sadly, I can't fetch you a prince from this company, but then, you were never actually a kitchen maid."

"Close enough."

"It's all silly, isn't it? The luck of birth and the rules laid down to maintain people like me."

"I know no one else like you. Besides, your worth doesn't come from your birth."

"Nor does yours." He was silent a moment, then said in a rush, "Would you marry Jack Hill if you were born a lady?"

She didn't have to think about it. "Lord, no."

"And yet, you like him."

"I like Ned Bunton, too. When he doesn't paw me. Besides…"

"Besides what?"

"He would not look at me in real life." Her heart lurched with the sudden fear that she was about to ruin the moment, the friendship, everything she valued between them. And yet, she didn't stop the words tumbling from her lips. "I think you looked. I think you saw me as more than the wench at the Hart."

"Wench *of* my heart," he said lightly. "And what did you see when you looked at me?"

"Secrets and mystery. Kindness. Responsibility."

His lips twisted slightly. "It will make a dull epitaph."

Dear God, she had hurt him… "I could not read you," she blurted. "Because my own feelings got in the way. I never could think, never imagine the perfect lady for you."

His gaze never wavered, though the rare turbulence in his eyes thrilled her. "Why not?" he asked huskily.

"Because I wanted it to be me," she whispered.

His fingers tightened. So did his arm, although he forced it to loosen almost at once. They didn't miss a step. His searching eyes did not release her. "And now that you know me better?"

"I want it more. But don't be afraid. I know it can never be, and I will never follow you around—"

"But would you walk by my side, Lily Villin?"

She stared at him. "What are you asking me?"

He muttered something under his breath and quite suddenly whisked her through the open French doors from the ballroom onto the terrace. The cold fresh air shocked her, and she clutched at his shoulder as he all but dragged her away from the windows to the side of the terrace.

"I'm asking," he said unsteadily, "if you love me."

And suddenly, there was only honesty. A smile flickered across her lips as she tenderly touched his cheek. "I have always loved you. I always will."

Her mouth was crushed under his in a wild, passionate kiss that bent her backward with its force. She threw both arms around his neck and clung, kissing him back with all her love.

"And if I can find a way for us to be together?" he whispered against her lips.

"Don't. I know it can't be. But I wanted to tell you just once."

"Trust me." He straightened them both. "But I am playing fast and loose with your reputation here. The proper Lord Torbridge would never do such a thing. I think you were overcome with the heat and must be taken back to Millie, now that you are recovered."

"Yes, but this is still our dance, and then it is supper."

He offered her his arm. "What a splendid ball this has turned out to be."

"Do you suppose Francis is even now bolting for the coast with your man behind him?"

"I hope so, for our host is quite definitely here." He bowed her solicitously through the door to the ballroom, and the first thing Lily saw made her smile involuntarily.

"Look," she said, nodding to the left of the dance floor, where Millie waltzed in the arms of her husband—a social *faux pas* they clearly didn't care about. "I believe I have brought the luck of the Hart with me."

IT WAS NOT in Torbridge's nature to lose himself in fantasy, but the very real nature of his own feelings and Lily's did threaten to overwhelm him. He had to fight this novel bubble of warmth and joy to remember his duty and make sure of Pennington's continued presence. And Jack Hill's. But he was sure that the message would reach him soon that the valet, Francis, was traveling at high speed to one port or another.

In the meantime, he took pleasure in eating supper with Lily, Millie, and Masterton, in making plans for leaving Pennington Place.

"No, you have monopolized Lily for long enough, Torbridge," Millie said stoutly as he prepared to accompany them back to the ballroom. "Go away!"

He laughed and bowed with good grace, holding back while they joined the throng ahead, for Mrs. Bradwell had caught his eye. Something about her hesitant smile was inviting, almost pleading, and she was, in fact, just the person he wished to speak to. Maneuvering himself across to her, he bowed and offered her his arm.

"If we wait here for a moment," he said kindly, "we may avoid the crush."

"I would not keep you from your next dance, my lord."

"I would not keep you from yours," he replied at once.

"I am too old to dance."

"Of course, you are not. I will ask you myself unless you really don't wish it."

"I would rather talk to you," she admitted. "But it is so warm in here. And in the ballroom."

"Then, if you don't mind the cold, we can go this way." Pulling back the curtain at the side of the room, he revealed a door. "Perhaps it should have been left open."

She cast him a look of amusement. "You like to know your surroundings."

"I do," he admitted, unbolting and opening the door. "It comes in useful. We can walk from here around to the ballroom if it isn't too cold for you."

She stepped outside and gave a sigh of relief. "Perfect."

He closed the door behind them. "Is there something, in particular, you wish to discuss?"

"So many things," she said ruefully. "You asked me some unexpected questions when we last talked. You took me by surprise. You still do, but I find now I want to answer them if it helps her. For some reason, I trust you. I may be wrong to do so. And if I am, and you betray my confidence, I will simply deny everything."

"I would never betray a confidence."

Mrs. Bradwell halted at the terrace steps, and by the light of the lanterns there, peered into his face. "How did...*my necklace* get from the Hart to Ireland?"

"It didn't," he admitted. "It seems we are sharing confidences. The necklace has always been at the Hart."

Her lips parted. "But she is..."

"A lady? She is many things. Here, chiefly, she is obliging me for reasons that have nothing to do with you or your past."

"*Obliging* you?" she repeated with distaste. "What do you mean by her?"

"People keep asking me that," he complained. "Nothing ill will have to suffice for now, though you could help me, if you chose, to make it something good."

Mrs. Bradwell leaned against the low terrace wall and closed her eyes. "I cannot claim her," she whispered. "I could not so dishonor my husband or my sons. And even if I did, what good would it do her?"

Torbridge leaned beside her. "I'm not sure any of this has been good for her. I took her with me on impulse, mostly selfish, I admit. I would not ask you to ruin your life or your family's. I merely want to know the truth, to understand what to do next."

From the ballroom, the music had begun once more, a merry country dance. Mrs. Bradwell lowered her head and began to speak very quietly so that he had to strain to hear.

"When I was young, before I married Mr. Bradwell, I was engaged to marry Captain Alfred Horsham, one of Lord Carborough's younger sons. It was considered a good match by our families. And it was very much a love match. He was ordered to set sail, but we were to be married as soon as he returned. I'm sure you can imagine the excess of emotion on parting, and what it led to... He was killed only three days out of Portsmouth, a stray shot from a ship already fleeing.

"All I had of him was the pendant Lily wears, which was his parting gift to me. And the child I carried. Of course, my family covered up the scandal. I was bundled into the country, where no one knew me, amidst claims that I was ill and pining for Captain Horsham. And in Sussex, we met a young innkeeper and his wife, who were desperate for a child." Her eyes squeezed shut. "I gave them mine," she whispered. "Along with the necklace Alfred had given me, and a coral teething stick I had bought in Finsborough when no one was looking. One hour I held her in my arms, and then we left the inn, and I never saw her again.

"My family encouraged John Bradwell. He would not have been considered good enough for me before, but now, *any* husband was favored." A smile flickered. "It turned out to be a good decision. He is a good man who understands my past. But he could not tolerate public proof."

Torbridge touched her hand. "I understand. But what of Horsham's family? Did they know?"

She nodded. "I felt it my duty to tell them. His lordship didn't want to know. Even Alfred's older brother, the current Lord Carborough, couldn't bear his hero brother's name tarnished with an illegitimate daughter. They gave me money, which I gave to the Villins."

Torbridge thought that somewhat cold. But then, his own father would probably behave in precisely the same way. "Thank you for telling me this."

She raised her head, her eyes glistening with unshed tears. "Then, she really is my daughter?"

"I think you know she is."

Mrs. Bradwell straightened. "Then do not abuse her trust or mine, my lord."

"I won't," he said, but without waiting for him, she was already hurrying up the steps to the terrace.

Torbridge followed more slowly. He had no reason to doubt Mrs. Bradwell's story. It explained many things, including the odd affinity between her and Lily. But his next steps would have to be carefully judged.

Illegitimate children were a fact of life in the upper echelons of society as elsewhere. Most went unacknowledged or were passed off as the husband's rather than the lover's. Lily's case was a little different, but…

He found himself at the door of the ballroom, gazing in, and some movement at the back caught his attention. A swish of green silk vanishing abruptly around the corner toward the supper room. He would have thought nothing of it, except that green was the same shade as Lily's gown. And there had been a man with her, although the tiny glimpse was not enough to see who that was.

Entering, he searched the dancers, and those seated along the walls, looking for Lily as he moved inexorably across the floor in the same direction as the vanishing silk. She was not among the dancers or with Millie or Ella or Mrs. Bradwell.

His stomach tightened with unease, for although Jack Hill was dancing, there was no sign of Pennington.

He had been paying too much attention to the future and not enough to the present. The matter of the traitor was not yet settled, and until it was, he should not have allowed himself to be distracted.

Reaching the short passage to the supper room, he saw the lights had been dimmed there. He strode toward it. He did remember to glance left through the anteroom door on the way.

Lily stood alone by the window, shaking her head urgently as he swerved with relief toward her. It was a moment's warning, but not enough to avoid the blow.

CHAPTER FIFTEEN

WHEN LILY, STILL in her foolish haze of Torbridge-induced happiness, noticed Lord Pennington was almost upon them, her first concern was for Millie.

Millie, however, was deep in laughing conversation with friends. Not that Lily gave Pennington the satisfaction of actually looking, but she could hear the voices behind her as she moved subtly into his path, meaning to distract him for as long as Millie needed. She couldn't quite remember if Sir George was with her still or had wandered away.

"Ah, Miss Darrow, the pride of Ireland. And now, England. I do hope your evening is agreeable?"

"Very," she replied appreciatively, although the comment about Ireland, where she had never been, made her uneasy. "The ball is delightful."

"Then you will do me the honor of dancing with me?"

It was unexpected, for ever since the incident with Millie in front of the stables, she knew he disliked her. And in truth, she did not want to touch even his hands in the country dance. However, there seemed to be no one to step in and claim a prior commitment. She could not, with civility, refuse.

"Or perhaps, so soon after supper, you would prefer a more gentle stroll around the ballroom?"

"I believe I would," she said gratefully. "It was a splendid supper. Too splendid!"

He took her hand, placing it on his arm. So much for avoiding his touch.

"Too splendid?" he repeated. "You are not used to civilized ballroom suppers, perhaps? Or can you just not get out of the habit of consuming everything in sight for fear of when your next meal will be possible?"

The insulting words were spoken in his most amiable voice, so although her stomach tightened unpleasantly, she answered in the same manner. "I assure you, Lady Masterton keeps an excellent table."

"Better than the Darrows?"

She stared up at him, deliberately haughty. "I am not so vulgar as to compare them."

An ugly expression sparked in his eyes. His lip curled. "But I think vulgar is exactly what you are. You are no more a Darrow than I am, and I very much doubt you are related to Torbridge at all. You are, instead, some low creature he has foisted upon us under false pretenses."

So, the gloves were off. There was a certain relief in that. She just hoped the valet was already on his way to the coast.

"That is hardly civil conversation," she pointed out.

"I believe we have a few uncivil things to discuss." He was guiding her back the way she had so recently come, toward the dining room.

She tried to draw her hand free. "I believe I would prefer our discussion to be in public."

His hand clamped over hers on his arm. "Oh, no, you wouldn't," he sneered. "Only think what might be overheard and how damaging that might be for you."

"How can you damage a low, vulgar creature foisted on society under false pretenses?" she retorted, throwing his own words back at him. But since she could not escape without an undignified tussle, she decided to follow his lead, to discover what he knew, what he suspected, and how far he was involved in the stealing and passing on of information from his brother's office.

He did not guide her to the dining room but to the smaller ante-room beside it. The room was lit with two lamps and contained a low table and two chairs. Although she refused to be frightened, she was glad he made no effort to close the door.

Until she saw the man behind it.

Francis, the valet, who should have been galloping away from Pennington Place with Torbridge's men in covert pursuit.

Unease sharpened into alarm. In the best traditions of the class she was impersonating, she ignored the presence of a mere servant and returned her gaze to Pennington.

"Sit," he invited, releasing her to indicate the nearest chair by the window.

"I would rather stand," she replied.

"No matter," Pennington said indifferently. "So, do tell us, Miss Darrow, who the devil are you?"

"You already told me who I am. I was brought up never to contra-dict a gentleman."

His lips stretched humorlessly. "No matter. I don't really care. It's Torbridge I mean to punish."

"For catching out two filthy traitors?" she spat.

"For planting a spy on my family. For being the too-wealthy imbe-cile, he has always been. You may say goodbye, but you will have to do so very quickly."

Too late, she saw the wicked knife in the valet's hands, and shock swiped the breath from her body. They meant real harm to Torbridge. Murder.

She should have known it. Torbridge knew the truth, the only man of any standing who did—certainly as far as Pennington knew. More than that, she was the bait that would draw him into the trap.

She lunged forward, but Pennington seized her by the arm and jerked her backward into the chair she had refused to sit in.

"Let us wait for him in comfort," he said smoothly. "I don't know how long it will take the dolt to notice you and I are both gone."

She regarded him curiously, for clearly he seriously underestimated Torbridge, which gave her hope. "You don't think a great deal of him, do you?"

Pennington laughed. "From the first punch at school, I knew he was weak, soft, and lacked understanding of anything but the rules. He cannot even see what's under his—"

"Sh-sh," the valet interrupted from behind the door, and with dread, Lily heard quick footsteps coming along the passage from the ballroom. She did not know that it was Torbridge, but her heart was in her mouth. If it wasn't him, perhaps she could use the newcomer's presence to escape, to find and warn Torbridge.

Lord Torbridge appeared outside the doorway and glanced in.

She shook her head violently, but she should have known nothing would keep him from her. Pennington's hand clamped about her nape. She did not even have time to shout out before Francis hit him a devastating blow on the back of the neck, and he fell forward onto the floor.

At the same time, Francis kicked the door shut, muffling Lily's helpless cry of rage and fear for the man she loved.

Torbridge, however, took them all by surprise. Before Francis had recovered his balance from kicking the door, Torbridge kicked viciously backward, tripping the valet, and then rolled out of his way so that Francis landed hard on the floor.

Lily, who had had enough of playing bait—or worse, hostage—wrenched herself free of Pennington, who actually laughed as he strode forward, aiming a kick at Torbridge's head. But Torbridge moved too quickly. He leaped to his feet, crashed his fist into Penington's jaw, and as he reeled, swung around to face Francis, who now held his wicked blade in his right hand.

Torbridge lunged, slamming him back against the wall and grasping his right wrist. The valet struck him a couple of quick body blows with his left hand, but it was in desperation, for the inexorable squeezing of his wrist was opening his fingers.

Pennington, meanwhile, was recovering his senses. With a grunt of fury, he launched himself at Torbridge's back. Lily stuck her foot in front of him, and he staggered forward helplessly into Torbridge's outthrust elbow.

The knife clattered to the wooden floor. Lily scuttled to pick it up, while Torbridge jerked Francis forward and back so hard that the valet's head struck the wall with a sickening crack. Before the servant even slid to the floor, Torbridge spun around, blocked Pennington's flying punch with his arm before punching him in the midriff. And as Pennington doubled involuntarily, Torbridge's devastating fist shot back up into his chin and knocked him back against the wall.

Dazed and open-mouthed, Pennington stared up at him from the floor.

Torbridge swung on Lily, grasping her by both shoulders, devouring her with his eyes. "Did they hurt you?"

"They didn't care about me," Lily gasped. "It was you... I think they meant to kill you."

Torbridge laughed. "Pennington has only ever beaten someone smaller. Which is why, no doubt, he brought his valet."

"I beat *you* often enough," Pennington said viciously.

"But not today," Torbridge said.

Against the opposite wall, the valet groaned and stirred. Neither man seemed to be paying him any attention.

"Learned to box a little, did you?" Pennington sneered.

"Amongst other things," Torbridge said evenly. "I thought it might help in my new line of work."

"Protecting your sister and your whore?"

Torbridge held his gaze for so long that Pennington began to look confused. Across the room, the valet sat groggily upright, clutching his head, gazing at the scene opposite. Lily tried to catch his eye to warn him Francis was conscious, but something told her to stay silent.

"Do you really think I won't hit you again?" Torbridge said softly. "Just because you are down? I'm not the man you thought me, Pennington."

"He never was," Lily said.

Pennington's gaze flickered past her to Francis, but Torbridge still seemed oblivious of the valet's recovery. He, too, had taken a few blows.

And then the valet hurtled to his feet, bolted across the room, and threw himself through the window in a cloud of shattering glass and splintered wood.

The crash and the tinkle of glass faded into silence save for the valet's receding footsteps. As those left behind stared at each other, a sharp breeze whipped into the room. Outside, a horse snorted, and then hooves galloped away into the distance.

Pennington laughed. "But you see, you still lose, Torbridge. Francis has a valuable document in his pocket, which is also the only proof you have against me. You shouldn't have let him get away."

"Oh, we will let him get away," Torbridge said gently. "All the way to France."

It took several moments for that to sink in before Pennington's frown of consternation vanished into a flash of horrified understanding. "You planted it. The plans are false."

"Utterly," Torbridge said.

The door burst open, and Millie and Sir George all but flew inside. They halted, stunned, presumably by the carnage of the fallen table, the shattered window, and a bruised Pennington on the floor looking sick.

"Close the door," Torbridge said mildly.

Sir George obeyed. "What the devil has been going on here?"

"Oh, Pennington's valet just resigned in a spectacular manner.

What did you want?"

"A footman was looking for you and couldn't find you," Millie said. "He had an urgent letter." Her gaze met her brother's, and Lily understood.

So, it seemed did Pennington, who laughed maliciously. "That's right, Torbridge. Run off and play at being marquess. Millie and I will carry on where we left off."

Even without the dead or dying parent, the remark was in abominable taste, clearly designed only to sow discord. And indeed, Millie whitened, as though she could see all her recent closeness with her husband evaporating once more.

"I am at a loss," Sir George drawled. "Not even some scum from the gutter would refer to my wife in such a way. I can only assume you refer to some other Millie, which is hardly appropriate or gentlemanly in the circumstances. Or you are an imbecile."

Pennington laughed. He probably meant it to be sardonic, but it sounded merely angry.

"Since you have clearly hit him already, Torbridge—several times by the look of him—I'll leave him there."

"His hospitality certainly palls," Torbridge agreed, strolling past them to open the door. "Shall we go and find this message?"

"I wouldn't, George, I wouldn't," Millie whispered passionately to her husband as they filed out in front of Lily.

"I know. You have more taste."

She seized his arm almost desperately. "I do, but that is not the reason. I would never, *could* never, consider a lover. Because I have only ever loved you."

Sir George came to an abrupt halt. In spite of everything, Lily had to hide her smile as she brushed past them to catch up with Torbridge. He was silent, unusually grim. She didn't speak either, merely walked beside him until, at the ballroom stairs, they encountered the footman with the silver tray.

The footman bowed to him. Torbridge took the letter with a mechanical word of thanks and turned his back on the ballroom as he broke the seal.

Lily looked anxiously up into his face, watching his eyes scan the paper. Then his hand dropped to his side.

"Is he dead?" she whispered.

"Not yet. But he won't last more than a day or two according to the doctors. He wants to see me."

Millie and Sir George appeared, and without a word, Torbridge passed his sister the letter. She looked almost frightened. There seemed to be little love between the children and their father, but still, the death of a parent was a solid rock taken away.

"It's an excuse to leave," Lily said shakily.

"Then let us take it," Torbridge said briskly. "Begin packing. I will speak to Lady Pennington."

IT WAS AN understandably subdued party that left Pennington Place around the same time the ball was ending. Sir George and Millie sat side by side, tightly holding each other's hands. Torbridge stared out of the window.

"Was it done?" Millie asked him at last. "Whatever your business was here."

"Oh, yes, it's done. I was wrong about the culprit, but Lily kept me right."

"Lily," Millie repeated, frowning at her. "What are we to do with you now?"

Lily smiled painfully. "Let me off at the nearest town, preferably with a little money for the stagecoach. It's time I went home."

"Not yet," Torbridge said abruptly.

Millie blinked at him.

Lily, clutching her leaping heart, waited. But he seemed far away from her, from everyone. It was neither the time nor the place to be discussing inappropriate love.

"Exactly," Millie said brightly. "More than ever at Hayleigh, I shall need my companion."

CHAPTER SIXTEEN

HAYLEIGH HOUSE WAS probably even larger than Pennington Place, but parts of it were clearly much older, including the original medieval great hall which served now as the entrance hall. Although it was too dark when they arrived to make out details, Lily thought it was surrounded by parkland and forest, but nothing so frivolous as formal gardens or mazes.

It was only nine o'clock in the evening, so there was no shortage of servants spilling out of the house to see to bags and horses, ushering everyone up the imposing front steps into the house.

No distraught mother ran to receive or offer comfort. Instead, a lugubrious butler informed Torbridge that her ladyship was in the small drawing room.

"And my father?" Torbridge asked.

"Still with us, my lord, God be praised. But I believe her ladyship would like to see you first."

Lily, after being swept up an impressive staircase and along a broad passage to a set of double doors, wondered if she should wait outside for the emotional greeting. But Torbridge merely took her elbow and ushered her in before him.

The room was dimly lit by the standards Lily had become used to, but it was enough to see a thin, severe lady seated in the chair nearest the fire. She looked up at their entry, her eyes sharp, her lips thin. As they drew closer, Lily sensed unease but little grief in her.

"Well, Torbridge," the lady said coolly, extending her hand.

Any hopes Lily harbored that this was not Lady Hay were immediately dashed when Torbridge replied with equal coldness. "Mama." He took her hand, pressed a perfunctory kiss on her cheek, and stood back.

"Sir George," Lady Hay acknowledged, offering her free hand to her son-in-law before her daughter. "Millicent." Inevitably, her gaze landed on Lily. "Who is this?"

"My companion, Miss Darrow."

Lady Hay immediately dropped her hand back into her lap. "What do you want with a companion? You aren't yet thirty years old."

"I'm one-and-thirty," Millie replied. "And I have found her most helpful."

Lady Hay, clearly, was not remotely interested. "Where is Ella?"

"Following with Barham," Torbridge said impatiently. "Your letter said my father wanted to see me."

"Indeed. He has a list of instructions as long as your arm, and he does not trust you to read it. Or understand."

"He gave me them the last time," Torbridge said.

"Then he will reinforce them on this occasion. You had better go up and get it over with. All of you. I imagine, Millicent, you'll need Miss Darrow to carry your smelling salts."

It was, Lily suspected, an opportunity for malice, mingled with an aversion to entertaining a stranger of little rank. Lily, while grateful not to be left alone with a woman who chilled the blood in her veins, doubted she wanted to be anywhere near the marquess.

It was only the stiffness of Torbridge's figure in front of her that prevented her from hanging back in the dressing room. In some way, she didn't understand he needed her support. He needed her there.

An elderly valet answered the door to Millie's timid scratching. "Oh, my lady," he almost wept. "My lord, come in. His lordship has been asking for you constantly."

"Stop sniveling, man," came a weak yet profoundly irritable voice from the depths of the huge bed that loomed before them. "Can't see what you're complaining about. It's not you who's dying. If that's my son, bring him here."

They walked further into the room, although Lily then hung back, as did Sir George, letting Torbridge and Millie face their father on his death bed.

"Ha," uttered the fond father between rather horribly wheezing breaths. "Did you read the papers I gave you?"

"No," Torbridge replied. "I shall probably tear them up."

The only man's fingers curled around the bedclothes in fury. "Is that supposed to be funny? I cannot bear you to ruin everything I have built here."

"Of course, he won't," Millie said indignantly, and immediately attracted her father's ire.

"What do you know of men's business?" he snarled.

"Nothing," Millie replied. "But I know my own brother. As should you."

"Ha. My daughter grows claws. You should beat her, Masterton."

"He won't beat her," Torbridge said at once. "He is not a monster."

"Bah." The marquess's hand lifted feebly in dismissal, then fell back on the covers. "You were always too soft, too cowardly to be the son I wanted. But you're still my heir, and you will do my bidding. For God's sake, don't be more of a fool than you can help."

"Why do you insult him?" The words fell from Lily's lips before she could stop them. She didn't know why, except that he didn't deserve the insults, and that the very air in the room felt poisonous.

Everyone stared at her, even the sick old man in the huge bed, who peered at her with more curiosity than anger. "Who the devil's this?"

Lily stepped forward. "My name is Lily, and I think it is a shame you are not prouder of your son, who works tirelessly for his country and has done more to prevent French victory than most other people you know put together. Moreover, he is nobody's fool, but a man of great courage, wit, integrity, and wisdom, and if you cannot see that, then I pity you."

Torbridge turned his head, gazing at her with something approaching wonder. Millie moved instinctively to draw her back out of the line of fire, then dropped her hand because Sir George said simply, "She is right."

"And who is *she*?" he demanded. "Well, little girl?"

The old eyes were fierce in his sick face. The eyes of a man who was always obeyed and rarely crossed, directly at least.

She leaned forward. "Lily. I'm no one, just an innkeeper's daughter."

To her surprise, he laughed, which turned into a fit of coughing, and the valet appeared to shoo them all out.

"Come and see me tomorrow, Lily, the innkeeper's daughter!" he called breathlessly as they left the bedchamber. "I'll still be alive then, whatever the stupid quacks say!"

LILY WOKE THE following morning after a long and refreshing sleep. She lay for a few minutes, soaking up the atmosphere of the house, and shivered. Sitting up, she pulled open the bed curtains. Sunlight squeezed through the cracks in the shutters, enticing her to slip out of bed and throw them open.

Her chamber looked out over a magnificent lawn and the edge of a wood. Blackbirds were singing on the roof above, then stopped and flew over the lawn toward a glistening lake. Drawn to it, she hastily washed and dressed as best she could without help, and hurried downstairs to find the quickest way outside, preferably without encountering the marchioness.

A cheerful maid scrubbing the passage floor pointed her to a side door and laughed as Lily tried to avoid where she had already washed. With a feeling of relief, Lily followed the path away from the house, then skirted the woods, and headed toward the inviting lake.

As she drew nearer, she noticed a male figure sitting at the water's edge, throwing stones into the lake and watching them bounce across the surface. A child's trick the local boys had practiced at the beach below the Hart. Ned, she remembered, had been the champion.

But this was not Ned. This was Lord Torbridge in a shabby coat and muddy boots.

"Good morning, Lily," he said without turning.

She came and sat beside him. "How did you know it was me?"

He picked up a stone from the little pile at his side. "No one else brings peace and comfort with them."

"It's not a peaceful or a comfortable house," she noted.

"Far from it." He threw the stone, and they watched it bounce four times across the water before it sank. Finally, he turned his head and looked directly at her. "The house is better with you in it."

She swallowed. "You seem to look on me as some kind of magical creature or a talisman."

"Perhaps you are."

"No. I'm just a woman. Out of her class and out of her depth. And I was rude to your father."

"Good for you. No one's been rude to him for years, except me, and most of my incivilities go over his head."

"You hide from each other."

He shrugged. "I suppose it makes life bearable for both of us." He picked up another stone but didn't throw it. Instead, they sat in silence until, slowly, she laid her head against his arm. She felt rather than saw him smile. After a few moments, his arm came around her, drawing her closer, and they sat in silence, gazing out over the lake.

RESTLESS AND ON edge, Torbridge wished his father would die. It wasn't a totally selfish wish. The old man was clearly in terrible pain and discomfort, and his son wanted his suffering to end. He knew how helplessness irked his father. But he also hated the purgatory of waiting, of this weird space he seemed to inhabit. Although his relationship with his father would be difficult and hostile up to the end, he understood he would still grieve in his own way. And he wanted to move on.

Lily.

Lily felt like his anchor, his rock, as well as the center of all his hopes.

"That girl of Millicent's," his mother said abruptly after a tense luncheon, just as he was about to follow the others out of the dining room. "She calls your sister 'cousin'. *Is* she one of the Darrow cousins?"

"Something like that," Torbridge said vaguely. "I believe her to be well connected."

"But poor."

Torbridge acknowledged it with a nod of his head and waited impatiently for his dismissal.

"Sit down, Torbridge," his mother said impatiently, indicating the chair opposite her own.

He owed her that much. Walking back to the table, he sat, and waited, meeting her frowning gaze.

"Have you thought about this place?" she asked abruptly. "This will all be yours in a matter of days. Hours even. How do you want to arrange things? I suppose you will leave it up to me."

"No, I won't do that," he said gently. "But I suppose you are asking what your position will be. I mean to marry shortly, so you should consider what you would like to do and where you want to live. There

---

is the Dower House, or if you prefer somewhere farther away—even London or Bath—I am happy to accommodate you."

For a moment, she looked stunned and then outraged. But it was her gaze that fell first.

"I hate this house," she observed. "It always felt like a mausoleum."

"You certainly made it so. I have different plans for it."

"You, Torbridge?" she sneered. "You never had plans in your life."

He smiled faintly. "Mother. You only say that because you never before inquired what they were."

"You mean you will finally dare to do something once your father is dead?" she snapped.

"No, Mother. I don't mean that at all. I believe that is Dr. Gordon coming up the drive. Shall I take him to his lordship?"

His mother shrugged, and he rose to his feet. Halfway across the room, he paused and turned back to her.

"It will be a release for you, too, you know. Freedom to go where you wish and do what you wish. Who knows? Perhaps you will finally be happy."

She looked merely affronted at the accusation that a noblewoman of her stature should aspire to anything as vulgar as happiness. But when he glanced back before closing the door, her expression was thoughtful.

A smile flickered across his lips as he went to greet the doctor.

"To be honest, I did not expect him to survive the night," Dr. Gordon confided when Torbridge asked about his father's condition. "Perhaps he has been hanging on to see you and your siblings."

Torbridge made a noncommittal noise.

To his surprise, they discovered Lily in the sick room, sitting by the marquess's bed. The old man was awake, and they seemed to be deep in conversation. Lily glanced up and smiled, melting his heart as she always did.

His father seemed to be staring at him as if he didn't know who he was. Oh, yes, the old man was dying. Fast.

Lily made way for the doctor, letting Torbridge escort her from the room.

"Is he saying much?" Torbridge asked her. "Is he making any sense?"

"Mostly, he listens," she replied unexpectedly. "But his responses are perfectly lucid."

"The doctor is surprised he's still alive." He grimaced. "He imagined the old man was waiting for me."

"In a way, perhaps he was."

Torbridge regarded her with curiosity. "What did he say to you?"

"Oh, he asked about my life, and Millie, and you."

"What did you tell him?"

"The truth. Will you stay and talk to him?"

Torbridge shrugged. "If he wants me. Which is unlikely in the extreme."

Unlikely or not, the doctor emerged into the dressing room, looking very solemn and said, "He wants you both. I'll just step downstairs and have a word with her ladyship. Oh, I've given him a heavy dose of laudanum, so he may fall asleep."

Lily smiled at Torbridge triumphantly, and there was nothing for him to do but follow her back into the bedchamber.

His father was propped up on the pillows, his breathing labored. "Read to me, Lily, if you can. The Odyssey. It's on the bookshelf in the other room."

Obligingly, Lily tripped back through to the dressing room.

"Is she really an innkeeper's daughter?" his father wheezed.

"Not by birth."

"And she's not Millie's find, either, is she? She's yours."

"I brought her to Millie," he admitted.

"Why? What do you want with her?"

"To marry her," Torbridge said.

The old man stared at him. Lily came back in, carrying the large, leather-bound tome that contained both the original and the translation of the Odyssey. She sat down beside the bed and began to read in English.

After a few moments, Torbridge lowered himself onto the side of the bed. His father's eyes began to close, no doubt as the laudanum began to take effect. But he seemed still to be listening to Lily's voice. As she read on, his hand moved feebly across the top of the coverlet until it touched Torbridge's, slid over it, and rested.

Torbridge stared at his father. The man he'd never truly known and who'd never known him. And now they never would. He swallowed. Slowly, he turned his hand and clasped his father's.

The old man's lips twitched. Torbridge had never seen him so peaceful. Lily read on.

Torbridge slipped his fingers over the pulse in his father's wrist. Just for a moment, he closed his eyes, then opened them and released the lifeless hand. "Lily."

Lily stopped reading and met his gaze. She knew at once. Tears started to her eyes. "I am so sorry," she whispered.

"You brought him peace at last. Even with me."

"I tried." She put down the book and rose to put her arms around him, drawing his head to her breast. He held her for a long moment.

Then, as the new Marquess of Hay, he stood and went to tell his mother and sister that his father was dead.

WHEN SHE ARRIVED with her husband and family around teatime, Ella wept to hear that her father was dead, though fortunately, she was easily distracted by the needs of her children. Lady Hay regarded the children with odd fascination and occasional irritation, but it was noticeable she did not ask Ella to take them away.

With everything already set in motion for the burial and the reading of the will, the family retired early—all except the new marquess, whom Lily found walking laps around the outside of the house, deep in thought. He carried a lantern with him, for the whole house was in darkness.

He smiled when she joined him but did not stop, merely took her hand, and threaded it through his arm so that they could walk together.

"What are you thinking about?" she asked.

"Lots of things. But chiefly that I don't know my own name anymore. I have been Torbridge as long as I remember. Now I'm Hay."

"They're only your titles. You still have the same name. But I take your point. You have always been Lord Torbridge to me."

"How silly," he said, stopping by the broad arch that led into the courtyard. He placed a hand on her shoulder, and the lantern light flared over his handsome face, emphasizing the high, sharp cheekbones. His gaze dropped to her mouth. "I have kissed those lips, and they have never even called me by my Christian name."

As if he couldn't help it, he bent and kissed them again.

"Randolph," she whispered, and his lips smiled and sank deeper.

Almost abruptly, he straightened and started walking again. "I have plans for this place, for the house and the estate. All the estates. Do you think the house will ever be *comfortable?*"

She knew he didn't refer to the physical furnishings, but to the atmosphere of the place.

"When you make it yours," she said. "Like the London house. You might stay there, but you do not live in it."

"They need a wife, children. Love."

She nodded, smiling, although she couldn't prevent the pain twisting through her stomach to her heart. It was his duty to marry, but she could never be his wife. Even though she rather suspected he loved her. Perhaps he would grow to love another. She tried to hope so, for she couldn't bear the thought of another generation brought up by cold parents without love for each other. At least he would love his children and show it.

"Your father died proud of you," she blurted.

He glanced at her uncertainly, as though he didn't quite understand why he wanted it to be true. "What did you tell him?"

"About you. The things he didn't know, didn't see, had long stopped looking for. The things you hid from him in your perverse pride."

He was silent for a little. "Did it give him peace?"

"I believe so. I think he did love you, all of you, in his own way."

"Perhaps." He walked faster, but his hand closed over hers, squeezing, drawing her with him.

She had never felt so close to him as now in the midst of his conflicted grief and sense of freedom. Stepping into his father's shoes was a new challenge, a smaller cause, perhaps, than the one he had taken on for his country, and she knew he was already planning ways to do justice to both.

Entering the house, he closed and bolted the door, then lit two candles from the lantern, which he then blew out and left by the door. She took one of the candles from him, and they walked through the dark house hand-in-hand.

Just for these moments, she let doubts about the future go. There was something very natural, very right, in treading these passages, climbing these stairs at his side. This house could be a warm, loving home, full of fun and laughter.

She didn't recognize the corridor in the darkness, for they had approached from a different direction, but she had seen the table littered with candle stubs before and knew that opposite it was her bedchamber door.

Her heartbeat quickened.

He set his candle down on the table and turned back to her. "It has been a strange day. I am so churned up inside, I don't know what I would have done if you were not here."

"You would have coped, as you always do."

His hand lifted, touched her hair. "And yet, you have become as necessary to me as breathing." His quiet voice grew husky. "And if I kiss you now, I don't believe I'll be able to walk away."

Her heart seemed to dive into her stomach, spreading heat and desire. She understood him, and she ached for him. She had always ached for him.

Mutely, she lifted her face to his and parted her lips. For two heartbeats, he didn't move, although she could feel his labored breath on her skin. And then he groaned softly and buried his mouth in hers.

She reached up, tangling her fingers in his hair, drawing him closer, wishing she could simply drop the candle she still grasped and hold him with both arms. His hands on her hips held her so close against him that she could feel his hardness. Heat surged through her, and she stumbled back against the bedchamber door. His hand moved, opening the door, and they almost fell inside the room. Without breaking the amazing kiss, he kicked the door closed, took the candle from her at last, and set it on the table by the door.

A long moment later, he disentangled their lips and tongues, but only to throw off her cloak and kiss her throat instead. He traced a line of fire across her shoulders. And downward to her breasts, where the fabric of her gown got in the way. Even through the layers of clothing, his mouth thrilled her. Then with another groan, he straightened and pressed his rough cheek to hers, holding her to him while his breath came in pants.

"I can't do this to you," he whispered. "If something happens to me, like Mrs. Bradwell's captain, killed three days after their parting... My selfish comfort is a small thing."

"It doesn't feel small to me."

Surprised laughter hissed between his teeth, stirring her hair. "We shall have such fun, you and I..."

"If you are not killed in three days? Do you expect to be?"

"No, of course not. It's just an example of the uncertainties of life. And I will not take advantage of your pity."

"*Pity?*" she repeated, drawing back to stare at him.

"Deny that it's there," he challenged, and, of course, she couldn't. His difficult father was dead, and even without the confused emotions of that, his life was changing forever. Of course, she pitied him. And wanted him.

"I love you," she whispered.

His mouth hovered over hers. "And I love you. More than my life," He kissed her as if it were the sealing of an oath and slowly, reluctantly, released her. "Soon," he breathed, another promise, and then he left, unusually clumsy as he fumbled with the latch and closed the door behind him.

CHAPTER SEVENTEEN

THE OLD MARQUESS was buried in the family vault in the village churchyard, and his will read to his family and friends by his solicitor from London. There were, apparently, no surprises, despite the length of the instructions for his heir and a sizeable sum left to Gilbert, the younger son currently fighting in Spain. His wife received an equally large stipend, guaranteeing her independence to live where she chose. She declared her intentions to remove to Bath for the next month while the Dower House was prepared for her.

"I may not stay there for long," she told her son. "But I take it I am at liberty to do so for as long as I wish."

"I have already said so," he replied. "I shall be away for at least a week or two myself, with matters to attend to in London. And elsewhere."

"We're going back to London tomorrow," Sir George said. "Come with us, if you like. I suppose you will be with us in any case, Cousin Lily."

Since the marchioness was moving around the drawing room some distance from the others, perhaps working out which objects were her personal property and which the estate's, Lily replied low. "You have been so kind to me, far beyond what his lordship asked of you. But my task is finished. It's time for me to go home."

She almost saw the readjustment to reality cross their faces as they remembered she was not really their cousin or even Millie's paid companion. She was just an innkeeper's daughter with a talent for mimicry.

The new marquess—Randolph—said, "I will take you on my way to London."

"It isn't on the way," she pointed out.

"Yes, it is," he said gently.

"We will take her," Millie pronounced. "Imagine what it would do to the poor girl's reputation for you to drop her off after all this time."

He opened his mouth, then hastily closed it again, a frown of rare irritability on his brow. Lily was sure he had been going to say it didn't matter. And in truth, she was finding it very hard to care. She was in the midst of an internal struggle with Randolph at its center.

They left Hayleigh the following morning in a large cavalcade of coaches. Lily, gazing out of the window, was sorry not to have seen more of the countryside and the people. She glanced back at the house once, wistfully, for it came to her at odd moments how to soften its appearance, make it welcoming and warm. But whatever she became to the marquess, such matters would never be for her.

They stayed the night at a coaching inn, which Lily found herself examining with professional criticism, and in the morning, the Barhams went on to London, while everyone else took the back road to Finsborough. Lord Hay drove his curricle, which had been brought to him at Hayleigh from Pennington Place, and she, Millie, and Sir George took turns joining him there for a breath of fresh air.

"Will you stay?" she asked once.

"Tonight, I will. I need to speak to your parents. But I need to be on my way tomorrow."

"There will be much for you to do," she agreed, trying desperately not to be disappointed.

Was this where it was to end after all? Perhaps the Hart would work its magic. It would need to, for she could find no way out of this but parting. It seemed he had come to the same conclusion. He could not marry her, and he would not dishonor her.

She was with Millie in the carriage when the Hart finally came into view, solid and unpretentious. And abruptly, everything else flew out of her mind. She could not wait for the steps to be lowered but threw herself out of the carriage and into her parents' arms, laughing and crying at once.

She was home.

MILLIE, EVERY INCH the gracious lady, thanked the Villins profoundly, and in full hearing of several customers and Jem the ostler, for lending her their daughter. She exclaimed with delight over all the ways Lily had helped her whip her life into order and look after her and her father on his deathbed.

And not one word was a lie. Randolph—he could not yet think of himself as Hay, but he was no longer Torbridge—stood back, with no need to intervene.

They were given bedchambers and the private parlor, where they dined and then drank the excellent brandy Lily brought them. It felt odd to be served by Lily now, odder still to watch her walk out of the room, back in her old work-a-day dress.

Millie and Sir George watched her, too, suddenly uncomfortable with this reality of her life. Fortunately, they retired early to their chamber, and after a few minutes, Randolph strolled across to the taproom, where Villin was throwing out a few customers with too much ale inside them.

"When you have a moment, Villin, step into the parlor, if you would," Randolph said amiably. "Mrs. Villin, too, when she's available."

Within five minutes, they had joined him, and he quickly got the business part of their arrangement out of the way. He had already paid to employ a maid for a month to replace Lily, but he now pushed a purse across the table to them for Lily's salary.

"She was invaluable," he said warmly. "To both my sister and to me. You may believe, if you keep it to yourselves, that the country is safer and Bonaparte nearer defeat because of your daughter. I added a bonus because of her additional help when my father died."

"You do not need to pay her for that," Mrs. Villin said stoutly. "Of course, she would help at such a time."

Randolph smiled. "Of course. You have brought her up to be a kind and compassionate young woman, as well as an efficient, intelligent, and educated one."

The Villins exchanged proud and gratified glances.

Randolph sat back in his chair. "Does she know you adopted her?"

Both heads jerked to face him, stunned.

Villin was the first to recover. "I don't know what you mean," he said loftily.

"Yes, you do. You adopted her from an unmarried lady—we will not name names, but I have this from her—who gave birth here at the Hart and left her child with you, along with a pendant and a coral teething stick."

Mrs. Villin so far forgot herself as to lean across the table and grasp his sleeve. "You have not told Lily this? We would not spoil her life with discontent and wishing for more than we can give her."

"When I first suspected, I asked her if you were her birth parents. She answered indignantly that you were. I was sure she believed it, but I did not." He regarded the agitated hand on his sleeve but did not draw free. "As to what you could give her, you have already given her more than most of everything that truly matters."

"Then you will not try and take her from us?" Villin blurted.

"Don't be silly," Randolph replied. "I could not take her from you if I tried. You are her parents, and she loves you."

Mrs. Villin released his sleeve, and they both relaxed.

"However," Randolph said ruefully, "I think you should tell her the truth. Her mother is now married with a family of her own and will not hurt them with this revelation. But there is also her father's family."

"I understood they would not acknowledge the child," Villin said. "Sir, for the love of God, please don't go stirring all this up. Lily is content with this life. What good will it do her to be the bastard daughter of some nobleman whose family doesn't want to know?"

"Well, they are my next call," Randolph confessed.

Villin stared at him, his eyes no longer so friendly or even remotely submissive. "Where is your interest in all this, my lord?" he demanded. "What exactly do you mean by my daughter?"

Randolph raised his eyebrows. "I mean to marry her."

EVEN WITH THE help of Molly, the maid who had been employed to do her work at the inn during her absence, Lily's time vanished in a daze of cleaning, washing, and serving breakfast. Her softened, pampered hands began to nip.

It panicked her to think *he* would soon be gone. There were so many things she had still to say to him, private things.

From the kitchen window, she saw Jem harnessing the spirited horses to his lordship's curricle. She bolted from the kitchen, drying her hands on her apron, and ran through the house and out the front door.

The Mastertons' servants were stowing their trunks on the second coach, where Prince and Sir George's valet traveled, along with the under coachman. There was no sign of the Mastertons themselves or of Randolph.

With a sigh of relief that she had not yet missed them, she watched Jem leading the skittish horse and curricle around to the front yard.

Randolph's voice inside the house distracted her, and she turned to see him striding toward her in his driving coat, talking over his shoulder to Millie and Sir George.

And then all havoc broke loose.

There was a bump, as though the curricle's wheels had gone over a stone, and then the horses screamed. She swung around to see them rearing up, with poor Jem still hanging on to the reins while trying to get out of the way of their lethal hooves. Randolph sprang past her, running toward the horses, who were now trying to bolt, only something was dragging at them. The wheel seemed to have buckled. Randolph launched himself at their head, catching the reins from Jem and pushing him to safety.

Stroking their outraged noses and murmuring to the horses, he persuaded them to stand still and calm to mere eye-rolling.

"Are you hurt?" he threw over his shoulder at Jem.

Lily, already beside the ostler with no real memory of moving there, scanned him anxiously.

"I'm fine," Jem told them both. "Something just startled them. Something broke." He brushed past Lily and crouched down by the wheel now bent at a mad angle, peering around it. "The axle broke," he called up. Then he frowned, peering more closely.

"Don't," Randolph said. "Not until it's free of the horses. They're still unsettled."

Jem stood. "I can tell you now," he said grimly. "The axle didn't just break. That's a clean cut more than halfway through it. Someone must have done that deliberately. It was always going to break."

Lily stared from him to Randolph. "Dear God, what if it had broken while you were driving at full tilt along the London road?"

Deliberately, it seemed, Randolph smoothed his brow. "Your father is quite right," he observed. "The Hart really is a lucky house."

By then, Jem seemed to have realized the awkwardness of his position, considering what he had just revealed. "It weren't me, my lord! And I'd never allow anyone into the coach house but your own servants."

Randolph dropped a hand on his shoulder. "Don't worry, I've no intention of accusing you. I know exactly who did it. Or at least caused it to be done."

"Pennington," Lily breathed, staring at him. "He must have done it before he sent it on from the Place."

"Or had his man do it before he left Hayleigh. How stupid of me not to think of such retaliation. Criminally stupid. You or Millie could have been with me when the axle snapped." A shudder passed through him, and he turned away. "Jem, can you have this fixed today?"

"I'll send to Finsborough right away, my lord," Jem said eagerly, clearly relieved not to be under suspicion for such a terrible act.

By then, Sir George and Millie had joined them and caught up with events.

"What an utter blackguard," Sir George said darkly.

"And to think I once found him amusing!" Millie exclaimed. "Vile creature. But Dolph, why isn't he arrested already?"

"Perhaps your brother has had other things on his mind," Sir George said wryly.

"We all did," Randolph said. "But that isn't the reason." He hesitated, then said quietly, "It was decided, though not by me, that it would not be good for the country at this point either to arrest a peer of the realm for treason or to dismiss his brother for gross negligence."

Lily frowned. "So, nothing happens? Is everything as before? As though we did nothing?"

"Not exactly," Randolph said. "We have fed the French false information, which will make Wellington's job a little easier. And we have stopped the flow of information. Francis—or Francois, should we say?—will not be back. Jack will have been warned by now that no documents are to leave his office for any reason, that he is to receive no visitors, and he is not to discuss his work with anyone. Pennington will be...observed, and his household vetted, secretly or otherwise. But to be frank, I cannot see it happening again. I doubt he went out looking for someone to betray his country to. He's an opportunist, and Francis was his opportunity to make some much-needed money."

"And this?" Lily demanded, waving one hand at the curricle now being detached from the horses. She didn't know whether to be angry, relieved, or frightened for him.

Randolph shrugged. "Malice," he said. "Pure malice. He could never stomach losing. Certainly not to me."

"What the devil does he have against you?" Sir George asked in outrage. "Everyone else likes you."

A smile flickered across Randolph's lips. "There you have it. Plus, my father was a marquess, his, a mere viscount. My allowance was larger. He couldn't even beat me up without arousing the ire of those he considered his friends, so he had to leave me alone."

Millie spoke in a small voice. "Is that why he made up to me?"

"I don't know," Randolph replied. "It's probably why he overstepped the line."

Millie sighed.

"Do you mind?" Sir George asked her, brushing at an imaginary speck of dust on his sleeve.

"I mind being an idiot," Millie admitted, taking her husband's arm. "Shall we go home, George?"

In spite of what had just happened, Lily smiled to herself to see them climb into their carriage together. She rather thought they were happy with each other and that Millie's hope of a baby was no longer unreasonable.

Her parents came out in time to help wave the Mastertons off, before they turned on Randolph, demanding to know about the curricle.

"Deliberately?" Villin exclaimed when Lily gave him an abbreviated version. "Dear God, who would do such a thing?"

"An old enemy of mine, I suspect," Randolph said.

Few people had ever accused her father of stupidity. He stared at his noble guest. "This would not be the same enemy you took my daughter in pursuit of?"

While Lily tensed, searching rapidly for something to say, Randolph met his gaze. "Actually, yes, it would. It seems I need to further clip his wings. I never thought of him resorting to this. Excuse me."

As he strode off after the horses, her father gazed after him with bleakness in his eyes. "You know, I never had him pegged as a *dangerous* toff."

"You wouldn't want to get on the wrong side of him, certainly," Lily said warningly, uneasy at her father's expression.

"Or be anywhere near him when he gets on the wrong side of anyone else," her father muttered. "I should never have let you go with him."

As MORNING TURNED into afternoon, and the curricle was being repaired, Lily felt less concerned with her parents' sudden hostility to Lord Hay than with his eager departure. She couldn't help being hurt that he was in such a hurry to leave her.

Restlessly, she abandoned the washing-up and walked around to the stables to see what progress was being made.

"Just about done," Jem reported. He was brushing her father's old cob, ready for his visit to the Finsborough market. "He can be off within the hour."

Her heart sank. "But it will be safe now?"

"Of course!" Jem grinned and went back to work.

A shadow fell over the door. Randolph, once more dressed for driving.

"Ready to go, sir?" Jem asked. "Shall I harness the horses?"

"If you please, Jem."

Jem dropped the brush and cheerfully left the cob to lead out Lord Hay's fine thoroughbreds. Lily watched him go before she slowly turned her gaze to Randolph.

"Come here," he said softly.

Her heart drumming, she went to him, and his arms wrapped around her, holding her tenderly. "A short farewell, Lily, no longer than a fortnight, and then I will come for you."

"Wait," she whispered, grasping his face between her hands when he bent to kiss her. "There are things I have to say. You say you love me, and you know I love you. I know you can't marry me, and I don't expect it. I will go anywhere with you. But Randolph, only for a little. Only until you are married, for I won't share you, won't compete for you with a wife. That would be fair on none of us, least of all on the children you will have."

He gazed down at her, a faint frown tugging at his brow. "You mean... you would give yourself to me for a couple of years, or months, and then face the ruin, alone and unmarried?"

"It is either that or say goodbye forever now. Randolph, I want this happiness with you—more than anything!—but you have to know..."

"Do you think you could?" he interrupted. "Do you think I could let you go?"

"My dear, you wouldn't have a choice," she said shakily.

He searched her eyes. "Do you trust me, Lily?"

"Of course," she replied at once.

A smile flashed across his lips and was gone. "Then don't worry yet about such choices. Wait for me." He kissed her, long and thoroughly, and all her doubts fell away like autumn leaves, leaving only the warmth of his love.

Because of that, she could smile as she stood between her parents and waved to him as he drove his curricle out of the yard. He smiled and tapped his whip against his hat in a farewell salute.

Chapter Eighteen

Having called at Lord Carborough's London house and discovered that his lordship was at his club, Randolph repaired to White's. The club was quiet since it was only mid-morning. Only a few gentlemen sat around reading newspapers and drinking coffee.

Carborough's stout and balding figure was easily discovered behind *The Morning Post* nearest to the fireplace.

"Good morning, sir," Randolph greeted him.

Carborough frowned, clearly irritated to be addressed at all, and grunted without looking up from his paper. Randolph continued to stand there patiently until Carborough's newspaper gave an angry little shake, and his lordship glowered upward.

The newspaper lowered. "Torbridge, old chap. That is, my Lord Hay, I was so very sorry to hear about your father. Deepest condolences."

"Thank you, sir. It wasn't unexpected."

"I suppose you are up in London sorting out the business end of things. Sad work but has to be done."

"Indeed, I have a few errands in London. One of them, I hope you can help me with."

"Of course," Carborough said in surprise. "Anything I can do, dear fellow. Sit down."

Randolph dragged a chair nearer, having no wish to have his conversation overheard. "It's a bit of a delicate matter, concerning your brother, Captain Horsham."

"Alfred? Was he a friend of yours?"

"I don't believe I ever met him, but of course, I know he was a hero, being killed in the line of duty and depriving the country of a captain who could have surpassed Nelson himself."

Carborough nodded sagely, a genuine sadness seeping into his eyes. "He was my favorite brother, you know. Hit me very hard at the time."

"I can imagine. I believe it hit his betrothed very badly, too."

"Alicia?" he said quickly. He blinked several times. "Yes, poor girl. She was devoted to him. I believe she was ill for some time. Married some dull old stick in the country eventually. She comes to London occasionally."

"We were thrown together at Pennington Place a week or so ago," Randolph said. "And she was, eventually, confiding enough to tell me something of her story. Of course, there was a reason for that, but despite her newer family, she grieves still for your brother's child."

Carborough's face reddened as he sat up straighter, making blustery puffing noises. "Here, now, Hay, you can't go around saying things like that! Not fair on my brother or poor Alicia."

"Or poor Lily?" Randolph suggested mildly. "Yes, that is her name. She has been brought up by a kind innkeeper and his wife, but by some quite unconnected chance, she recently met Mrs. Bradwell."

"I won't have my brother's name sullied like this!"

"Sullied?" Randolph stared at him with deliberate astonishment. "My dear, sir, he has a daughter of incomparable beauty, intelligence, and sensitivity, who, despite her upbringing, can pass—indeed did pass—as a member of the ton in both London and Pennington Place. A wealthy nobleman wishes to marry her. Would Captain Horsham not, rather, be proud? Would not his name, and yours, be the better for such a connection?"

Carborough stared at him.

"It has been more than twenty years since he died," Randolph said quietly. "Is it not time to rethink a decision made in the midst of grief?"

"What decision? What do you want of me?"

"Acknowledge her as your niece. There will be talk, yes, but it will be behind hands, nothing that will touch your family's, or even Mrs. Bradwell's. The girl has already been introduced to society as my cousin, so it will not be difficult to add the connection to you."

Carborough blinked rapidly. "But Tor... I mean, Hay, *why* am I to do this? I don't understand why you introduced an innkeeper's daughter as your cousin—"

"Because she isn't really an innkeeper's daughter, is she? She is your niece, would have been your favorite brother's beloved daughter. Don't you think this is something he would want?"

Carborough dragged his gaze free and stared into the flames of the fire. It was still a little cold for April. Randolph did not interrupt the silence.

Abruptly, Carborough looked up. "Who is this nobleman who wants to marry her?"

Randolph smiled. "Me."

Carborough uttered a short laugh, tugged once at his lower lip, then lumbered to his feet. "Come back to the house with me, Hay. It's chaos there. My youngest is coming out this Season, and I'm always falling over dressmakers, hairdressers, suitors, flowers, tantrums... Can't call the damned place my own. But we'll shut ourselves into my library and enjoy a quiet sherry. I want to show you something."

Randolph went with him willingly—it wasn't a long walk—and Carborough House turned out to be more or less as he had described it. A mountain of posies waited in the hall, wailing could be heard upstairs, and maids appeared to be running around with great purpose. Carborough had let them in with a key, and when any of the dashing servants tried to acknowledge his presence, he simply put his finger to his lips.

Entertained, Randolph followed him quite happily as he crept upstairs and along the passage and eased open a door at the end. Closing it behind them with obvious relief, he grinned at Randolph, looking suddenly much younger. "Made it. Sit down, Hay, sit down. Try this sherry, and tell me what you think."

When Randolph was settled in a comfortable armchair with his glass of sherry, he gazed around the shelves of books that seemed, surprisingly, to be frequently disturbed. Against all appearances, Carborough, or someone in the house, was an eager reader.

Carborough went to the desk by the window and took a box from one of the drawers. He took a folded paper from the box and brought it to Randolph before he sat heavily in the chair opposite and picked up his glass.

"Read that," he instructed. "I've never shown it to anyone before. I was ashamed of Alfred, and then of me."

Randolph opened the letter which had clearly been folded and unfolded so often before that it was likely to tear. It was from Alfred to his brother Justin—now Lord Carborough—written, it seemed, after his injury. A letter from a dying man who clearly knew his fate.

I won't survive this one, and I won't have time for all the farewells I would choose. You must do them all for me. You have always been the best of brothers, and so I beg one last favor of you. Look after Alicia, whom I love with all my heart. And if there is a child of that love, bring it up as your own...

"I didn't." Carborough took a sizeable gulp of sherry. "I gave her money, offered doctors, remote estates for her to stay and have her child, but I never did as he asked. I didn't want to distract from the heroism of his death. And so, you're right. I let his child, all we had left of him, be brought up in poverty by strangers."

Carefully, Randolph folded the letter again.

"It wasn't very long before I began to wonder if I'd done the right thing," Carborough said. "I even wrote to Alicia, who told me she was marrying Bradwell. That seemed good enough reason to sweep my doubts under the carpet along with the letter. Mostly, I stopped thinking about it, though every so often, I would read the letter again and wonder." He took another sip and set down his glass on the table beside him. "You'll think me a villain. Heartless at best, criminal at worst."

"No," Randolph said. "Grief affects us in strange ways."

Carborough met his gaze. "What do you want me to do?"

RANDOLPH'S PLANS WERE proceeding nicely when he returned to Hay House to discover his sister Ella waiting for him.

She was in his study, eyeing her surroundings with disfavor. "Dolph, this is dull. You have a huge house here! Why do you live in a cupboard?"

"It's one of the many things I'm about to improve in my life. What do you want, Ella?"

"Why should I want anything?"

"Because you never visit me here. I'm in a bit of a hurry, so spit it out."

She sighed. "Wretch. It isn't that I want anything. It's just that I'm...slightly uneasy. About something I may have said."

That caught his attention. He frowned at her. "What did you say?"

She drew in her breath. "Lady Pennington called the day before yesterday with her condolences for Papa."

"Go on," Randolph said steadily.

"Well, she asked after you and Millie. I said you were all on your way back to town but had stopped for the night at Finsborough. I may have mentioned the Hart. It just sort of slipped out, I suppose because it was mentioned so often that last day. But she is hardly going to go haring off there and discover Lily, is she? In fact, I saw her earlier this afternoon, so clearly, there is no harm done."

"Was Pennington with her?"

"No, of course not. I would have been much more on my guard if he had been."

"But you're still worried, aren't you? Otherwise, you wouldn't be here."

"Barham thought he saw the back of Pennington's head," she blurted. "In St. James."

"And his mother might have told him I'd gone to the Hart..."

"Why would she?" Ella asked brightly. "Who would care?"

"I don't know," Randolph said, unease seeping through his bones. "But I think perhaps I had better hurry back there." He frowned. "Immediately after I speak to Jack Hill. It will be fine, Ella, just go home and don't worry."

He was already halfway out of the door as he called the last words over his shoulder.

JACK HILL WAS on his list of people to see while he was in London, but Ella's admission added new urgency to the conversation. Fortunately, he found Jack in his rooms and didn't have to trail around London looking for him.

As he was admitted, Jack wandered through the doorway to the room beyond. In his shirtsleeves and fastening his waistcoat buttons, he stopped dead at the sight of Randolph. "Tor... that is, my lord," he said nervously. "I was not expecting you."

"Sadly, I don't yet have a card to send in to you. Mine all say Torbridge still. How do you do?"

"Oh, well enough. Just off to dinner with friends." He swallowed. "Look, I'm so sorry for what happened. It never entered my head that my brother... But you should know I've been jawed to death by everyone from Castlereagh downward, so I doubt there's anything you can say that isn't already dinned into me. To be—"

"Where is your brother?" Randolph interrupted.

Jack gave a rueful shrug. "Not sure. We were worried about him after…well, you know. So, we brought him with us to London, and he was with Mama. Only he vanished this morning."

"Vanished?"

"He wasn't in his bed. The man valeting for him knew nothing, and we haven't seen him since."

"Damn," Randolph said with unusual grimness.

"It's been hard on him," Jack offered, then threw up his hands. "No, don't eat me. I've been worried about him for some time, though it never entered my head he'd do anything so… It wasn't like him, Torb—Hay, you must see that?"

"I never saw him as a traitor," Randolph admitted.

"The estate is struggling," Jack said bluntly. "He has his managers and bankers jabbering in one ear and my mother in the other about keeping up appearances. He's always needed approval to function well, and suddenly it just wasn't there. I didn't know how to help."

"You could have stopped gambling to begin with," Randolph said mildly.

Jack flushed. "I always thought just one big win would at least let us tread water for a bit, give us time to get on our feet, financially speaking. But it just made it worse. And now, with this selling of documents. I know it's hushed up, but my mother obviously knows, as do you and I and all my many superiors at the Foreign Office. He feels the disgrace on top of everything else."

"So he damned well should," Randolph said frankly. "Did you know he damaged my curricle? Deliberately to cause an accident? I could have died. More to the point, so could my sister or Miss Darrow, both of whom spent time in the vehicle with me."

Jack whitened, dragging his hand through his hair. "Dear God, this is bad. This is awful. God knows what he will do now! Seriously, Hay, he needs a doctor and peace. I'm the only one who has a hope of reaching him when he's like this. We—"

"Get your coat," Randolph interrupted. "We're going to find him."

LILY WAS NOT altogether surprised when her parents sat her down on the morning after Randolph's departure and explained how desperate they had been for a child, that God had not favored them until He had brought a lady to the inn who was already going into labor. The lady's betrothed had been killed at sea, and she was unmarried. Rather than disgrace her family, she had given her baby up to the awed and grateful Villins.

"Mrs. Bradwell," Lily said slowly. "That is why he asked me if you had adopted me. You did."

"But we love you as much—more!—" her mother said anxiously, "than if you had been made from our two bodies."

Lily brought her distant gaze back to her parents and took their hands. "I know," she said warmly. "You *are* my mother and father. It makes no difference that I am the illegitimate child of a lady. He still can't marry me."

"I wish that didn't make you so unhappy," her mother said huskily.

"Oh, I am not unhappy," she insisted, "for I still love him, and I have you."

"Lily," her father said with difficulty, "don't rely on him coming back."

"He said he would."

"He won't. To give him his due, he won't ruin you. But for your own sake, don't think of him, girl."

There was no chance of that. Missing him was already a deep, hollow ache inside her, and he had said he might be gone as long as two weeks.

On the fourth morning without him, she found herself at the inn gate, staring wistfully up the road as though she could *will* him to appear.

And just as she began to turn back to the inn, something moved in the distance. She held her breath until the blob resolved into a solitary horseman. This was how he often came to the Hart, a sudden, impulsive decision. As though he had come early because he couldn't stay away.

She picked up her skirts, actually took a couple of steps down the road, meaning to run to him, when something in his posture stopped her. She couldn't put her finger on what it was, but even at this distance, he did not ride like Randolph. Almost certainly, she had been mistaken.

Hastily, she turned back into the yard. There were beds to change in two of the guest rooms.

She and her mother had just finished in the first room when her father called upstairs for them.

"Gentleman wants to eat," he said, jerking a thumb over his shoulder toward the coffee room. He looked at Lily. "Ned's in there, too."

Lily's heart sank, largely with guilt. Although she had done nothing to encourage Ned, she had a greater understanding now of the feelings he must have been struggling with. If he truly loved her as she loved Randolph.

"If you're not ready to see him, I'll take in the meals," her mother offered.

Lily squared her shoulders. "No, I might as well get it over with. We've always been friends, after all."

The delicious scents of her mother's spicy beef stew were already permeating the inn when Lily walked briskly into the coffee room with plates and cutlery for the two guests.

Ned, by the window, jumped to his feet at once, his face worried as though he were afraid she wouldn't speak to him.

"Morning, Ned," she said cheerfully and glanced over to the table nearest the hearth to greet the other guest.

Lord Pennington sat back and smiled.

CHAPTER NINETEEN

L ILY NEEDED ALL her quick wits. Whether he had landed here by accident or design, she knew what to do. What she had always planned to do if anyone from Randolph's world happened to drop in to the Hart.

Squashing any last trace of the "Lady Lily" accent, she forced a welcoming smile to her lips. "Morning, sir," she greeted him, and though every hair stood up on the back of her neck, she walked over to him and set his place. He already had a bottle of the decent claret and was idly playing with the stem of his glass, watching her every move.

She moved quickly across the room to Ned, performing the same service. "Mother's beef stew," she told him.

"Lily, sit and talk a moment," he pleaded.

"I can't right now. I've got a lot to do. But we'll speak later." She turned away, trying not to look at her other guest.

"Lily," Lord Pennington repeated, his voice mocking. "Where have I heard that name before?"

"It's not uncommon, sir," she managed.

"Such a similarity of appearance, too. Perhaps you have a sister. Also called Lily."

Lily shrugged noncommittally and went on her way. There was no doubt about it. She was rumbled.

The question was, of course, why was he here? Had he received some hint of her origins and come to prove it as some bizarre revenge on Randolph and Millie? Perhaps he imagined she had tricked them into believing she was their cousin? Or had he come simply to hurt her? Because she had helped to uncover his infamy? Did he know Randolph was not lying injured or dead after the curricle accident? Was he going after each of them in turn? In which case, she would have to warn Millie and Sir George.

And then, as her mother shoved a heavy tray into her hands, she suddenly understood.

At the Pennington Place ball, he had used her as bait to bring Randolph to him. He lacked the imagination to change tactics, and after all, it had worked up to a point. The speed of Randolph's reactions had merely taken him and Francis by surprise. This time, Pennington would be ready.

"We need to send to London," she blurted.

"After you serve lunch," her mother said firmly, "and clear up, you may do as you choose. Go."

"Mother, that man, that gentleman—"

"Go! I've had my fill of your *gentlemen!*"

Her mother's rare spurt of ill-nature had its effect. She took the tray to the coffee room and served Lord Pennington his bowl of beef stew with newly-baked bread and butter. She did so briskly, and again he watched her, like a spider with a fly.

She did the same for Ned and then fled the coffee room in search of fresh air and wisdom.

"Lily?" her father said from the taproom where he was gossiping with a couple of local farmers on their way home from the Finsborough market. She waved to acknowledge him but kept going.

A few moments later, he ambled outside and sat beside her on the bench. "What is it?"

She drew in her breath. "The gentleman in the coffee room. I know him. I met him when I was working for Ra—Lord Hay."

Her father's eyes narrowed. "He recognizes you? Just play dumb."

"I have. He doesn't believe me. You might say he is an enemy of Lord Hay. Of the country, in fact."

Her father blinked and scowled. "What the devil is he doing here?"

"I don't know. That's what worries me."

Searching her face, his hand clenched. "Has he ever laid a finger on you?"

"No, no," she said hastily. "Well, not beyond dancing."

"Will I throw him out anyway?"

Lily smiled and brushed her cheek against her father's shoulder. "You would, too, wouldn't you? No, Dad, we'll just watch him and wait for him to leave. I'm afraid he's looking for Lord Hay, to finish off what he started with the curricle."

His eyes widened. "*He* damaged the curricle?"

"We think so."

"Then, *I* think we should send to the magistrate and have him arrested!"

"It's not as simple as that. He's a peer of the realm. Even Mr. Lacey can't just arrest him. Besides, I doubt Lord Hay will be here before another week." She stood decisively, "All the same, I think we should check for any strangers here, not just at the inn but lurking around the country. Randolph beat him so thoroughly before that he won't risk a trap without allies."

Her father nodded. "I'll send the lad and ask Ned to look around, too." He rolled up his sleeves, through which the muscles of his arms bulged comfortingly. "And *I* will be keeping a close watch on our fine guest."

They walked inside together in time to see her mother emerge from the coffee room. "He complimented me on my stew," she said proudly. "And he has bespoken the parlor *and* a bedchamber."

Which definitely meant the man was up to mischief. Gentlemen like Pennington did not choose to stay at country inns for no reason.

And he had plenty of time to get to Finsborough before dark, or even Brighton if he hurried.

After scribbling hasty warning notes to both Randolph and Millie, she gave them to the stable lad, asking him to post them in Finsborough while he was out looking for any strangers there who might be connected to Lord Pennington.

After that, she helped with clearing up the midday meal and making preparations for the evening. Lord Pennington installed himself in the parlor with the remains of his lunch-time wine.

During the afternoon, one good thing did occur that gave her hope.

Pennington had opened the parlor door, just as she was passing—which almost made her wonder if he had been watching through the keyhole for her—and asked for tea.

"Of course, sir," she replied, for he had not yet told anyone his name, and she had not quite given up hope of convincing him she was unrelated to Miss Darrow.

At that moment, the front door opened, and Lady Verne from Finmarsh House walked in, closely followed by her husband. Lily was always pleased to see them, for she counted them as proof of the Hart's luck. But today it struck her that their friendly treatment of her as simply Lily the innkeeper's daughter whom they'd known for years, might well help her cause.

She dropped the newcomers a curtsey and a smile. "Welcome, my lady, my lord! How can we serve you today?"

"Ah, Lily, how good to see you," Lady Verne said in her naturally friendly way. "Tea, please, if you would. How are your parents?"

"Very well, my lady. The parlor is engaged, but if you'd step into the coffee room..."

Inevitably, Lady Verne's gaze took in Pennington, still standing by the parlor door. He bowed with unusual jerkiness, as if this arrival threw him somehow, perhaps forcing him into a world of his peers where setting lethal traps for a gentleman was not *done*.

Lady Verne paused, then went toward him, extending her hand. "Lord Pennington! What a pleasant surprise. We were so sorry not to come to your mother's party this year, but we were visiting my brother. Are you acquainted with my husband, Lord Verne?"

Pennington, recovering his grace, bowed over Lady Verne's hand and then greeted her husband with interest. "I have not had the pleasure."

"Verne doesn't go to town much," Lady Verne said cheerfully. "Except when I drag him. What brings you to our corner of the world?"

"Oh, looking for a friend I heard was here. A friend of us all, I believe. Lord Hay."

"Torbridge?" Lady Verne asked quickly.

"Before his recent elevation."

"Is he here?" Verne asked Lily.

"No, my lord. He left the inn several days ago. He would have gone with Sir George and Lady Masterton, but there was an accident with his curricle." She let her gaze flicker to Pennington, who was watching her with that same spider-like smile on his lips.

"Oh, dear, was he hurt?" Lady Verne asked anxiously.

"Not in the least," Lily replied. "Fortunately, it came apart when there was no one inside it, though the horses reared and narrowly missed kicking our poor ostler in the head."

"Then it could have been a lot worse," Verne observed.

"Considerably. Apparently, he had driven Lady Masterton for part of the journey from Hayleigh."

"And what of Miss Darrow?" Pennington asked.

Lily stared at him. "I beg your pardon?"

"Miss Darrow, their cousin. Did she also go in the curricle with Lord Hay?" His eyes were both mocking and vicious.

"I could not say, sir," she said woodenly.

"Then, she was not here at the inn?"

"I don't believe I saw a Miss Darrow, sir," she said firmly.

"How curious. She must have disappeared into thin air." His gaze moved with apparent reluctance. "Don't let me keep you, Lady Verne."

"You are welcome to join us for tea," she said amiably.

"How kind, but I have some urgent letters to write, so I won't intrude. Charming to run into you here." With another bow, Pennington stepped back inside the parlor and closed the door, while Lily finally showed the Vernes into the empty coffee room.

"What's going on?" Verne asked quietly. "Where the devil is Tor...Lord Hay?"

"In London, we believe." Lily cast a quick glance at the door. "*He* means him ill. I'm sure he was responsible for damaging the curricle."

Verne's eyes widened. He was not often surprised by the evil of his fellow men.

"Oh, surely not," Lady Verne exclaimed. "I know they don't much care for each other, but Pennington *is* a gentleman,"

Lily, who should have known better than to speak ill of the man to one of his own class, merely curtseyed and hurried to the kitchen to fetch tea for everyone. Oddly, she felt more rattled by Lady Verne's unwitting reinforcement of her social inferiority to Randolph than by Pennington's mocking questions about Miss Darrow.

After a brief argument with her mother—who wished to serve Pennington only in order to give him a piece of her mind—Lily took in his tea and left her mother to deal with the Vernes.

Lord Pennington sat by the fire, staring into the flames. A bottle of brandy and a half-empty glass sat by his elbow. Uneasily, she wondered how much of it he had drunk that afternoon, but at least it had quietened him. After his deliberate baiting of her in the hall, he seemed to have lost interest in her. He responded with a mere grunt when she informed him tea was on the table.

Only as she left, with a quick, worried glance at him over her shoulder, did he turn toward her. His eyes glittered, and there was an ugly curl to his lips.

Returning to the kitchen, she found Pete, the stable lad, returned from Finsborough. "Didn't see no obvious villains," he reported cheerfully. "Apart from the ones that live there already. The strangers at the inn all had good reason to be there, and no one's been asking questions about the Hart."

"Surprising," Lily mused. "Here, have something to eat before you go back to the stables."

Only a little later, word came via one of the Bunton's farm servants that no one of dubious character, in fact, no strangers at all, had been seen lurking in the vicinity of the inn.

Why would Pennington come here alone to face Randolph? Lily wondered. *What on earth is he up to?*

She had just taken a fresh pot of tea to the Vernes when she heard someone else enter the coffee room. The hairs on the back of her neck stood up. She knew it was Pennington.

"Come to join us, Pennington?" Verne said, indicating the free chair at their table.

"No, actually, I was looking for the girl. Lily…what *is* your name?"

"Villin, sir," she said woodenly. "Lily Villin."

He laughed. "What a charmingly apt name. Well, Lily Villin, what does it cost to hire your…services?"

He could have meant anything, but she did not like his contemptuous tone, nor the faint hesitation before the word *services*.

"My services are not for hire, sir. I am the innkeeper's daughter, and I am needed here."

"I'll pay as much as Hay did. If you perform the same services."

She felt the blood rise into her face. "I don't know what you're talking about, sir."

"Oh come, I know he hired you, foisted you on polite society to spy on us, and prevent the delectable Millie from rushing into my arms."

Verne said sharply. "Sir, this is not civil conversation."

"No, it isn't," Pennington agreed. "But it is a public room. You are at liberty to leave, although I can't imagine Hay is a friend of yours. I know he pursued your wife for long enough. How much, Lily Villin, to draw him back here? And share my bed as you did his?"

The sheer force of his malice drove her back a step, and he advanced with a mocking laugh.

But to her surprise, Lord Verne jumped to his feet and strode in front of Pennington. "That is enough. More than enough. Lily, go to your father."

Lord Verne could be a thoroughly intimidating man when he chose to be. And he chose it now.

But Pennington seemed merely surprised. "Do I have to deal with your father for you?"

Lord Verne stared at him. "What is the matter with you? Leave the girl alone, she has already answered you."

"So many protectors," Pennington marveled.

"You're right there," her father said ominously from the door.

Lily had seen her parent cope with fights, drunks, and ill-behavior of many kinds. Usually, he didn't even need any help, but on this occasion, he had the formidable Lord Verne on his side.

"Time for you to leave," her father said, advancing into the room, his hands clenching in obvious threat.

"It's your choice," Pennington drawled. "I'll leave with your daughter, or I'll wait here, but I'm going rapidly off your hovel, innkeeper."

"Then don't let us keep you," Lady Verne said coldly from Lily's side. "Lily goes nowhere with you, and you are a boor to suggest it."

"Before you, perhaps I am," Pennington said, thoughtfully. "I apologize for that. But you would not defend the minx if you knew

203

what she was."

"And what is that?" asked a soft, totally unexpected voice.

Randolph. Lily's heart soared and plummeted. He strolled into the room at his most casual and unthreatening. He was dressed for driving, in a many-caped coat and shiny black boots. Only a few fresh mud splashes revealed he had traveled far. From his demeanor, he might have dropped in to Brook Street from Hyde Park. Unless one knew him as Lily did.

His eyes might be bland and amiable, but every inch of him was poised, every careful movement exuded danger.

"You should not be here," she said huskily.

"Not the welcome I was hoping for, but I suppose you have had a difficult day." As he spoke, Randolph cast her a quick, assessing glance in which she saw all his anxiety. He was no longer the same, intriguing mystery to her. She knew his thoughts, his fears, his every expression as though they were her own.

"You asked me a question," Pennington observed.

For the first time, it struck Lily that the frightening glitter in his eyes was not simply brandy but some insanity none of them could reach.

"I did," Randolph agreed. "And you should be very, *very* careful how you answer."

"I will be," Pennington assured him with a smile. "You asked me what she is, this Lily of many names. She is, of course, your spy and your whore."

Verne let out an exclamation of disgust, seizing his wife's arm and plucking her further away. At the same time, her furious father and Randolph charged forward. Her father's fists were already raised, but Randolph caught him by the shoulder.

"It's not you he's trying to rile, it's me," he said.

Pennington smiled. "Challenge me," he taunted. "Call me out."

Lily's blood ran cold. "No," she said hoarsely.

This was the one thing she had not thought of. He had set no trap for Randolph, who had already proved he could beat him in a fight and avoid murderous tricks. He had come for a straightforward duel, where one of them would die. *Don't answer him. Don't dare...*

"No," Randolph said deliberately.

Pennington laughed. "Same coward you always were. You witnessed it, Verne! Very well, my lord Hay, *I* challenge *you*."

"On what possible grounds?" Verne demanded before Randolph could even speak.

"Insulting my mother's hospitality by bringing his whore to Pennington Place. I demand satisfaction."

"Don't," Lily said in a strangled voice.

Randolph didn't even look at her. "Very well," he said. "Outside."

CHAPTER TWENTY

As PENNINGTON LEFT the room, exuding a weird kind of relief, Lily turned on Randolph.

"What are you doing?" she demanded, stricken.

"Don't worry," he said vaguely.

It was rare that he said anything stupid to her, and she could only stare at him in disbelief.

"Wait here," he said, already striding toward the door. "Verne, I think you'll have to serve as second to us both."

"Randolph," Lily blurted as a confusion of feelings and understanding struggled urgently for recognition. "I think...I think he *wants* you to kill him!"

It caught his attention, but only for an instant. "Don't worry," he repeated gently, and went out, Verne and Villin at his heels.

Lily and Lady Verne looked at each other. As one, they walked across the coffee room and followed the men outside.

By then, Pennington had fetched a box containing dueling pistols, which Verne opened and took out, testing the weight of each.

"Be careful," Pennington warned. "They're loaded and have a hair-trigger."

"My first duty," Verne said, "is to attempt a reconciliation. To my thinking, the matter is easily arranged. Hay, if you took an uninvited guest to Pennington Place, you must apologize. And you, Pennington, may easily apologize for your crude and unkind words about the young lady of the Hart."

"Can't do that," Pennington said before Randolph could even open his mouth.

"Why not? You know it was only to rile him. And she does not deserve such treatment from people who regard themselves as her betters. I'm serving as your second, but I own I'll think the worse of you for this fight."

"It doesn't matter. Give me the pistol."

"This is idiocy," Verne warned. "We don't even have a doctor present."

"Not yet," Randolph murmured vaguely. He took the other pistol gingerly from Verne. "But, before we do this, Pennington, satisfy my curiosity. Why are we really doing this?"

"It's all there is left." There was a wealth of pain in those few words, piercing even Lily's fears so that she stared at him, frowning. Pennington laughed. "Either way, I win. If I shoot you, you're dead. If you shoot me, you'll stand trial for murder, or flee the country."

"Flawed logic. If you kill me, *you'll* stand trial for murder."

"It won't matter. I'll finally have beaten you."

Randolph paused, eyeing him curiously. "Is that really what all this about? Beating *me?*"

Pennington blinked, as though confused for a moment. Then the breath hissed between his teeth in a mirthless laugh. "It does seem to have come down to that. There you stand, Lord Perfect Manners, Lord Wealthy, who never makes a mistake. The future marquess, top of all his classes and of sports teams. Sought after by hostesses and matchmaking mamas alike. Everything always came so easily to you, didn't it? Because of who your father was, who you would one day be, everything just landed in your lap, from wealth to success. Even the one thing I could do, beat you, literally, no longer works!"

Randolph frowned, regarding him with genuine interest. "Is that really what you think? That it was easy? Did you not know I worked for those marks at school? That I used what I was good at—making friends—to combat physical fights I couldn't win? And if you are thinking about our little contretemps at Pennington Place, that wasn't easy either. When I decided what I wanted to do with my life, to look after my country, I decided there would be times when I would need more...aggressive skills. I hired people to teach me. And trust me, I spent a lot of time bruised from head to toe before I began to hold my own."

Pennington's gaze was riveted to his enemy. He seemed to be only half-understanding.

"We can't help the family we're born into," Randolph said. "But we are not born with skills or knowledge. I learned mine, often with great difficulty, and I'm still learning. What are you doing?"

Railing at a world that let him be bested by someone he'd tried most of his life to despise, Lily thought. Without making any effort at all. Even his betrayal of his country had been opportunistic, easy. Given the strength of his spite, perhaps the world should be grateful he never truly tried.

"What am I doing?" Pennington repeated slowly, then smiled savagely. "Dueling. Ten paces, Verne, you count them."

"Ten?" Verne said, startled. "Twenty, for God's sake. Let's not make it too obvious a killing matter."

But Randolph, after a quick glance toward the inn gate, merely shrugged. "Ten, it is."

"No!" Lily exclaimed, propelled into action by the sheer stupidity of all the males concerned, including her father, who merely scowled, and Lord Verne, who seemed to be facilitating the murderous duel, if only to prevent outright murder, perhaps.

She threw herself forward, meaning to charge between the duelists, but her father suddenly caught her round the waist.

"Oh, no, you don't," he said grimly. "Stay well clear."

After one giant but useless heave to be free, Lily stilled, for she finally heard what Randolph clearly had—the carriage bowling along the road outside, the horses' hooves slowing as they neared the inn.

"Someone's coming," she said triumphantly. "You can't duel here. It's meant to be in secret, isn't it? Because it's against the law!"

"What is law compared to honor, eh, Pennington?" Randolph asked. He was pacing away from Pennington on Verne's steady count.

A curricle swung through the gate, and with astonishment, Lily recognized Jack Hill driving, with a completely unknown man at his side. The horses halted abruptly.

"Dear God!" Jack exclaimed, his voice echoing around the yard. "No, James!"

Presumably, this meant Pennington, for she heard his voice answering, though she couldn't make out what he said before he turned to face Randolph.

"Don't worry," Randolph said, not to her this time, but to Jack, she was sure. "It will be fine."

Jack stared at him, then jumped hastily down. "Stop, James. Apologize. Don't fire."

"Verne won't drop the handkerchief, will he?" Pennington said, referring to the signal to fire, Lily could only assume. "It's up to you and me, Hay."

"James, don't!" Jack yelled, striding toward him. "You can't win! He'll delope!"

Delope? Lily searched desperately for the meaning of the word. *To fire in the air, an acknowledgment of wrong.*

Pennington's face twitched. "Then he'll die! Why should he delope? He knows he's not in the wrong!"

"Because you *are*, James. You're ill, and he knows it. He won't fire on you. And you can't fire on him. Because you are in the wrong, and you know it."

Silence hung in the air. The two men stared across the inn yard at each other, pistols raised and aimed at arms' length.

Pennington did not lower his arm.

"James, please!" Jack uttered.

Deliberately, Randolph raised his arm, pointing his pistol high in the air, and fired.

The noise was deafening, the smell of gunpowder immediate and terrifying. The horses whinnied in distress, forcing the curricle passenger to grab the reins and calm them. Jem came running from the stables, and two men fell out of the taproom, goggling.

"Delope," Jack said. "It's the only way to win."

But in a sudden rage, Pennington hurled the pistol from him. It exploded as it hit the ground, and the horses snorted, trying to back the curricle into the outside wall.

Jack strode forward, throwing his arms about his brother. The passenger stepped down from the curricle, leaving the open-mouthed Jem to deal with the horses, and took Pennington's other arm, speaking low and soothingly. He gave him a flask, and Pennington drank.

"He's a physician," Randolph said quietly beside Lily. "Pennington's been ill like this before. They'll take him away traveling for a year or two until he's better. Pity, in some ways, but there it is."

"A pity?" She stared at him. "Why?"

"I still don't like the bastard," Randolph said and walked back into the inn.

THE HART WAS chaos for several hours, with people coming and going, and long conversations going on between Randolph and Jack, then Randolph and Verne, and finally Randolph and her parents. Lily kept away from it all, angry with everyone for allowing the duel to get as far as it did. The thought of Randolph actually dying terrified her.

In the end, with Pennington's party gone, Lord and Lady Verne decided to have dinner at the inn and to hear from Randolph all that had been going on. Verne had once been—perhaps still was—involved in the relay of messages between British spies in France and the government, a network she knew her father had aided. And which had been run, she had long suspected, by Randolph himself. So, these two knew and trusted each other.

And Lady Verne, whom once Randolph had wanted to marry. Lily was not used to jealousy, but the rare anger within her seemed to twist her emotions toward Randolph's old love, too.

She and her mother served them dinner. She sensed Randolph watching her, uncomfortable. *At last,* she thought sadly, *he is realizing the impossibility of our relationship.* Her heart ached.

As she brought in the dessert, he said suddenly, "Sit and join us, Lily."

She set her mother's delicious fruit tart on the table beside the cream and slowly lifted her gaze to Randolph's. "That wouldn't be appropriate, my lord, would it?"

"Lily—"

"Enjoy the tart. It's particularly good today," she said and fled.

The ache grew worse.

However, she joined her parents and smiled as they waved off their noble patrons, the Vernes.

"Until tomorrow!" Lord Verne said cheerfully as he closed the carriage door.

"Clear up in the parlor, Lily," her mother said, yawning. "I'm off to bed."

Lily nodded and preceded Randolph into the room, clearing the remaining crockery from the table onto a tray, but leaving his brandy glass. "Can I get you anything else?" she asked.

"Lily." He came up behind her, folding his arms around her and drawing her back against him. "Stop. It's time we talked."

"No, we've talked too much already!" she burst out. "That's why we are in this mess, why we dreamed and imagined things to be possible that simply aren't. Randolph—" The rest was lost as he turned up her face and leaned round to kiss her lips.

Just for a moment, she allowed the sweetness of his mouth on hers, the comfort of his warm embrace. She even leaned back against him and kissed him back. But tears started to her eyes, and a sob rose in her throat.

"Lily, Lily, what is it?" he whispered, turning her in his arms.

"You must see," she gasped. "I will always be serving you and your friends. I will never be your equal! Oh, I know, if it is just you and friends like Lord Verne, perhaps, as your mistress, I might join you, but I cannot sit at the same table with Lady Verne or Lady Masterton. We cannot even go away, for you are needed here and—"

"Oh, hush, my love, my sweet," He pressed his cheek to hers, and in spite of everything, she loved its warm roughness against her skin. "Let me tell you what I've been doing. Trust me, I will not allow the world any reason to disrespect you."

And somehow, she was sitting in the fireside chair, and he knelt at her feet, holding her hands, which he kissed.

She swallowed, blinking away the tears. "My parents told me about my birth, that they adopted me from Mrs. Bradwell when her betrothed died."

He nodded. "I hoped they would. I got the whole from Mrs. Bradwell at Pennington Place, but for the sake of her husband and sons, she will not let me speak."

"It makes no real difference," she said gently. "Being some gentlewoman's natural daughter does not make *me* a gentlewoman."

"No, but if your father's family acknowledged you, it would."

A frown tugged at her brow. "My father is dead."

"Yes, but his brother, the Earl of Carborough, is very much alive. He behaved badly to you, through grief and confusion, but he will make amends. He has already acknowledged you as his niece, with a suitable dowry, and if you will do me the honor, you can be Lady Hay tomorrow."

Her mouth fell open. "No. It cannot be that simple."

"It will not be regarded as a great match by people like my mother, but no one will cut you. You will be invited everywhere and may sit at any table you choose. Including Lady Verne's."

"But they know me as Lily Villin! Half of your friends already know me as Lily Darrow, and now I am what? Lily Carborough?"

"Lily Horsham, but we shall marry quickly to avoid any awkwardness around so many name changes. The Darrow connection may be easily explained—there is always some connection between aristocratic families. It will only serve to prove you were brought up a lady and that Carborough's acknowledgment was a little later than it should have been. As for the local families of quality, like the Vernes and the Mayburys, I believe we may count on their discretion."

"Then...then I would your wife? The Marchioness of Hay? And I would be the lady of that huge house?"

"Which we will make our home, full of love and children, friends, and laughter."

Her breath caught. "Oh, Randolph." Her voice cracked, and she clung to his hands as he kissed them again. "It sounds so right, so wonderful. I can't believe it can be real. Oh, but my parents—my parents *here*...I cannot leave them!"

"Well, you'll have to," he said reasonably, "unless you want them to live with us, which I doubt they'll agree to. But there is no reason why we cannot both come and stay here whenever we wish. You know I would not try to keep you from them. That fruit tart alone is reason enough to haunt your mother."

Laughter caught in her throat, and she leaned forward to kiss his lips. "Is it possible?" she whispered.

"More than possible," he said and wrapped his arms around her.

Sometime later, as she sat in his lap in the fireside chair, her head on his shoulder, she said suddenly, "How did Jack know you would shoot in the air?"

"When I told him I was coming straight here while he fetched the doctor, he warned me how Pennington might react to my presence. He wanted me to wait for him, but I could not leave you to face Pennington alone. Even an hour or so seemed of vital importance. I promised that I would not hurt Pennington unless he threatened you or your family."

She shifted her head, staring at him indignantly. "But what of Pennington hurting *you*?"

Randolph shrugged. "I would have talked him out of it eventually. Seeming to go along with it merely took away any reason for temper. Believe me, I had lots more to say, and between that and your natural effect on people, I was sure he would never shoot me. And then I heard Jack arrive, fortunately ahead of schedule, and trusted in his efforts."

"Is he mad? Pennington, I mean."

"Not really sure what mad is," Randolph confessed. "He certainly has spells of...irrational behavior and illogical thought. I think stress brings it on, and he has been under a great deal of stress recently, repairing the house to his mother's exacting standards, dealing with his own debts, and his brother's. And then his solution, the selling of secrets to the French, must have put enormous strain on him, for he understood perfectly well the consequences of what he was doing."

"So, traveling will take his stress away?"

"Hopefully. And Jack will stop gambling for good."

"Will Jack go with him? Doesn't he have to work?"

"In the circumstances, a sabbatical will be arranged for him."

"It's a lot of trouble to go to," she observed, "over one traitor that you don't even like."

"I want him out of my hair so I can marry you."

That seemed perfectly reasonable to Lily, so she smiled and laid her head on his chest. Which was such a delightful place to be that she didn't even notice when she fell asleep.

CHAPTER TWENTY-ONE

"L ILY!"

Her mother's outraged voice dragged her from sleep. She raised her cheek from a warm crushed shirt and the hard yet ultimately appealing pillow of Randolph's chest. The pale light of early morning flooded the room as her mother pulled back the curtains and the shutters.

Randolph's arms closed more closely around her as he stood and deposited her in the chair with a light kiss on her head.

"I am surprised at you, my lord," her mother said bitterly. "I thought you would have more care for my daughter's reputation than to compromise her in this way."

"We fell asleep, Mother," Lily said hastily.

"After which you just happened to fall into the same chair?" her mother said with heavy sarcasm.

"You know exactly why we were in the same chair," Randolph observed. "And you also know that your daughter is as pure this morning as she was yesterday. It was unwise, perhaps, but makes no odds since we will be married today."

Lily blinked. "We will?"

Her mother's mouth dropped open, but the sound of an approaching carriage in the yard distracted her. Her father called. "Customers!"

Lily's mother glared. "Get washed and dressed at once. I'll need you."

"Perhaps," Randolph said, reaching for his coat, "it would be a good time to send for the girl you employed before? And perhaps a couple of other helpers, to free your own and your husband's time."

"For what?" Lily's mother demanded.

"Lily's wedding, of course."

Lily laughed. "You can't be married so quickly."

Randolph took a document from his coat. "You can with a special license."

Lily's eyes widened. "Today?" she asked shakily.

"Now."

"Who is in the carriage?" Lily's mother asked, sounding so frightened that Lily went and put her arms around her.

"I believe, Lily's mother and uncle," Randolph replied.

Her mother's grip tightened. "Then...then what you said before, you've made it happen?"

He nodded, and her mother's eyes squeezed shut.

"Mother," Lily said urgently, but her mother pulled away. "We have guests."

Lily shook out her crumpled dress, picked pins up off the floor, and hastily rolled up and pinned her hair.

"Lily," Randolph said, taking her hand. "Will you marry me?"

"Oh, you know I will," she whispered, pausing only to smile at him before pulling him toward the door. "But I have to be with her when she meets them."

"Of course."

He held back as Lily went to join her mother, who curtseyed stiffly to the lady who had just come in. Mrs. Bradwell. Behind her came a stout, well-dressed gentleman, looking dubiously about him, as though wondering if he had made a terrible mistake.

Mrs. Bradwell paused. "Mrs. Villin," she said, and her voice not quite steady. "I never thought I would see you again." She came forward, holding out both hands, which Lily's mother was too stunned to ignore. She took them in something of a daze. "You were so good to me, and you have made her such a wonderful..." She broke off, dashing her hand across her eyes.

"We didn't make her anything," Lily's mother said gruffly. "She just is."

"She had help. I can see that." Mrs. Bradwell turned to Lily, offering her hand again. Her gaze was pleading. "Can you forgive me?"

"Easily, ma'am." Lily took her hand. "There was nothing else you could do. And I have always been content in my life."

"I think you will always be content. It is a gift you did not get from me." Her fingers and her gaze both clung to Lily. Then, as if forcing herself, she released her and turned to the stout gentleman behind. "I would like to introduce you to Lord Carborough, your uncle."

Lily curtseyed. Carborough's gaze slid away, then came back to her with determination. "I should have done more. Didn't behave well, not even to my beloved brother's child. I intend to make it up if I can. But you should know your father was a great man, a hero."

Lily read it all in his eyes, the shame, the hope, the uncertainty, the love for his dead brother. And she smiled before a shadow made her glance around to the taproom door, where the man she had always called father stood, stricken.

She went to him, taking his large hand in hers. "Then, I have two heroes to thank for my life."

"I'm no hero, girl," her father whispered.

"But you are. You don't just stand up against wrong—thieves, traitors, bullies, swindlers—you do something about it. I've learned there are many kinds of heroes." She pulled her father's rough hand to her cheek and met Randolph's gaze. Her own hero, the hero of a whole country that would probably never know.

He said, "Perhaps you should change for the wedding."

"Perhaps you should, too."

He ran one hand over his jaw and chin and laughed. "Most definitely."

Lily glanced at her mother. "Mother? Help me?"

And her mother smiled with relief to be asked. Only at the foot of the stairs did she pause and turn determinedly back to face the others. "Mrs. Bradwell, will you join us?"

Unshed tears still stood out in Mrs. Bradwell's eyes. She smiled but shook her head. "No. I am just glad to be able to see her married, and to such a good man."

RANDOLPH, DRESSING AND shaving while dealing with unexpected nerves, had cause to regret the absence of his valet. Surprisingly, it was easier when Verne came up to jolly him along. All the most important events of his life had been faced alone, by choice, so it came as something of a surprise to discover he had a friend. And, soon, a wife.

Wife. He paused, his hand hovering over his cravat. "She won't take fright and cry off, will she?"

"Lily?" Verne said in disbelief. "Don't be ridiculous. It's time to go. The cut on your chin has stopped bleeding, you look beautiful, and Walsh is here."

Walsh was the local vicar, who had been summoned to perform the ceremony.

"Beautiful?" Randolph complained. "I wish to be taken seriously on my wedding day."

Verne eyed him sideways as they walked to the door. "It has been a long time since I regarded you in any other way. You play a good part, but Lily always saw the truth."

"I can't hide anymore," Randolph observed. "What I do has been too exposed by the Pennington affair."

"Will you stop?"

He shook his head. "No. I will just have to change the way I work.

Be more apparently open. It will be better for Lily, too, to be married to someone who is not a figure of fun."

"You were never that."

Randolph scowled. "Damn it, I worked hard to be thought so!"

Verne laughed and pushed him out the door.

The parlor was full of people, though neither Lily nor Mrs. Villin were present. Villin was there in his Sunday suit, standing self-consciously by the door. Carborough was making conversation with him about the state of the roads. On the sofa, Cecily Verne and Mrs. Bradwell had their heads close together in low conversation.

Of course, the wedding was no surprise to the Vernes. Randolph had told them last night about Lily's true background and what he meant to do. After their first shock, they had seemed to realize the rightness of the marriage.

"There was always something special about Lily," Lady Verne had mused. "And apart from her birth, she would always have been the perfect wife for you. Since you have dealt with that one problem, there is no question in my mind that you are doing the right thing. She will make you very happy, my lord. And I am glad."

He had smiled at her with genuine affection.

"However," Verne had added sternly, "you had better make her happy, too. I am very fond of Lily."

"I know of no one who isn't," he had replied. "Men of all degrees. And yet she never looked at any of them."

"Except you," Lady Verne had said. "She always looked at you."

"I don't know why."

Lady Verne had laughed. "I do."

He blinked the memory away, walking across the room to shake hands with the vicar and deliver up the special license.

And then the door opened once more, and Lily walked in.

She wore the simple, pale blue walking dress, with Mrs. Bradwell's necklace, and her hair was dressed simply but softly, piled at the top of her head. Her skin seemed to glow, her eyes sparkled, and she smiled with such pure happiness that Randolph thought his heart would explode. She had never been more lovely. In that moment, although he had always striven for the good of the whole country, she was his entire world.

She took Villin's arm, and he brought her to stand beside Randolph. She smiled up at him trustingly, catching at his breath.

The ceremony was brief, the words familiar from his sisters' and other weddings he had attended. But he had never before properly understood the hugeness of the vows or appreciated the joy of making them. And then, Lily was his wife.

It took a few dazed handshakes, a torrent of congratulations, and then the rising happiness seemed to burst inside him, and he wanted to dance and sing and run all at once, with her hand in his.

He couldn't do any of those things just then, but he stored them up.

Perhaps his own happiness combined with Lily's to infect everyone else in the room, for the lingering awkwardness seemed to vanish, and by the time they trooped through to the coffee room for a hastily assembled wedding breakfast, everyone was laughing and chattering together, mirroring his own high spirits.

And when she left, Mrs. Bradwell hugged both Lily and Mrs. Villin. Lord Carborough, who was traveling back to London with her, actually shook hands with the innkeeper as well as with Randolph, after which he kissed Lily's cheek and bowed to Mrs. Villin.

The Vernes left shortly afterward in a flurry of embraces, leaving Lily and Randolph temporarily alone in the inn yard.

He closed his fingers about hers and swung her arm. As she smiled up at him, he said, "Walk with me?" And then at last, clear of the inn's gates, he ran with her across the meadow toward the woods.

Halfway there, he swung her into his arms and sang words of love in a popular waltz tune and danced with her.

LILY HAD ALWAYS suspected this rollicking, fun side of his nature. She had caught odd glimpses of it in the past, but never before seen it in action. Now, he swept her along in his mad dance, and she laughed at his hastily made-up words of love, twisted around to fit the rhyme and the rhythm.

Lapsing into silence at last, they stilled for sheer lack of breath, still smiling at each other. As his smile faded and changed, desire flamed in his eyes, causing the butterflies in her stomach to take flight. He bent his head, and her lips parted to receive his kiss. His mouth touched hers and then he drew back, moving again toward the woods, his arm around her waist.

"I suppose this is not the way Lady Hay should behave," she said lightly.

"I hope it is the way Lady Hay will always behave."

"Though perhaps not in public?"

He grinned, as though imagining. "Perhaps not," he agreed. "I have a reputation for propriety to keep up."

"Randolph?" she said as they entered the woods.

"Yes, my sweet?"

"What if I really had been the innkeeper's daughter, with no aristocratic blood in my veins at all? Would you still have married me?"

"Of course." He didn't even think about it.

"You would have been sneered at for such a marriage. So would I."

"Under no circumstances. I would simply have lied."

She stared at him. "Lied? In what way?"

He shrugged. "Like the Darrow connection, only more. And I would have made it work. I will not allow you to be unhappy, and if I cannot change the world to achieve that, then I can change the story we tell the world. And supply 'proof' if necessary."

Perhaps she should have been appalled at this lack of morality, but she saw only the determination and the love.

She halted, gazing up at him. "You would have done that for me?"

He brushed a strand of hair from her face. "I would do anything for you." He bent his head, and this time, he kissed her properly as she had wanted to be kissed since he had walked into the coffee room to face Pennington yesterday.

Birds sang joyfully overhead, and a soft breeze caressed her cheek. Within, there was only love, the thrill of his touch, and her own sweet, heady desire. And it didn't stop. One kiss grew into the next, shrouding them in an increasingly sensual veil that hid the rest of the world.

She moaned as he lifted her, still kissing her, and carried her to the hollow by the large oak, where he laid her down on the soft, spongy ground. He took off his coat, folding it under her head for comfort, and then lay close to her, loosening her gown while her heart drummed with excitement. He caressed her more intimately than ever before, making her gasp and arch with pleasure as he kissed her naked breasts and shoulders, stroking her leg and thigh beneath her gown.

She clung to him with growing wonder, stroking the hot, smooth skin of his back as she burrowed beneath his shirt. It all happened so naturally, and yet so quickly, that she didn't fully grasp his intention until the full weight of his body stretched out on hers. Almost at once, he eased up on his elbows, but the shock of urgent, thrilling need caused her to press up against him.

He gazed down at her, his breath labored, his eyes clouded and wild. "Now?" he whispered.

She tightened her arms around him. "Now," she pleaded.

And there, in the privacy of the woods, with sunlight dappling through the trees, he made her his. She wanted to close her eyes in awe and bliss, and yet she could not bring herself to look away from his face as he concentrated on her every pleasure, shaking with the effort of holding back his own lust to care for hers. And the ecstasy, when it swept her up in a tangle of cries and kisses and gasped out words of love, belonged to them both.

AFTERWARD, WHEN THEY had refastened clothing and brushed each other off, they picked the grass out of each other's hair, and he helped her replace her pins. Then they began to walk slowly back to the inn.

"I hope you didn't mind my impatience," he said, watching her.

She smiled. "Did I appear to mind?"

"No," he admitted.

"Actually, I'm glad. I could not imagine retiring with you at the inn under the eyes of my parents. And my bedchamber is tiny."

He considered, "I would like to see your bedchamber, but we might be more comfortable in mine for tonight. Then we can decide where you would like to go for your wedding trip."

This was something she had not even thought of. "Oh goodness," she breathed. "What does one do on a wedding trip?"

"Go somewhere new, get to know one another better, stroll around seeing the sights, eat, drink, and be merry. And make endless love."

Blood rushed into her face, more desire than embarrassment. "Endless?" she murmured unsteadily.

He smiled and kissed her. "Endless."

EPILOGUE

FOUR MONTHS LATER, mid-way through August, the Marquess and Marchioness of Hay held their first party at Hayleigh House.

It was not a huge event like the one at Pennington Place. For one thing, much of the house was still under renovation and redecoration. For another, Lily wasn't quite ready to receive vast numbers of the ton with whom she was not well acquainted. Instead, she invited friends: Lord and Lady Verne, Sydney and Henrietta Cromarty, Sir Marcus and Lady Dain, Millie and Sir George, Lord and Lady Barham, Mrs. Bradwell, and Lord and Lady Carborough. Lily had also invited the Duke and Duchess of Alvan but had received only a very kind note in return, for the duchess had just given birth to a son.

The Dowager Marchioness, Randolph's mother, had received an invitation at her new abode in Bath but had declined on the grounds of being in mourning.

"Mourning, my foot," Randolph had said amused.

And in fact, the dowager came anyway, looking around her with astonishment. She was, of course, the last to arrive.

"What have you done with the place?" she demanded in the great hall.

"An excellent job, I believe," Randolph said mildly. "Maintaining a little old-world grandeur while being rid of the mausoleum look. We like it."

The dowager sniffed.

"What's she going to think of the drawing room?" Lily murmured.

"Who cares?" Randolph replied.

In fact, Lily didn't mind greatly whether or not her mother-in-law approved. She had worked hard with Randolph's full support to lighten and brighten the great house, gradually making each apartment warmer and more welcoming in appearance. She had enjoyed herself hugely in the process, in between learning about her duties as a great lady, not just of the house but of the surrounding estate and all the people who depended upon them. Her upbringing had made her an excellent housekeeper, and her nature made her both an empathetic and practical help to those who were now her inferiors. It seemed very strange when she troubled to think about it, but she loved her new life.

And the cold emptiness of the house had already receded, drowned in the liveliness, and the sheer gladness of its new owners at being together. The servants, even Chives, the lugubrious butler, now moved around the house cheerfully, talking to each other and greeting their lord and lady without fear.

This party, however, made Lily distinctly nervous, for nearly everyone knew her true origins. And she was half-convinced the dowager had come merely to see her set-down.

Tea was being served in the bright, redecorated drawing room, where the dowager was greeted with courtesy and presented with tea and cake.

"This cake is delightful," Captain Cromarty observed. "I'm about to ask Lily for another slice."

"No need," Lily said at once, offering it to him. "It's my mother's recipe."

The dowager choked on her tea and had to be patted on the back by a solicitous Lady Dain.

From the window, sitting in the sunshine, Lady Verne said, "I love that little garden just below us. Can we walk there?"

"Whenever you wish," Lily said at once. "It opens from Randolph's study downstairs so that he can enjoy a little beauty while he works."

"Works?" the duchess repeated. "*Randolph?*"

Everyone laughed, as though it were an excellent joke instead of a sneer, and the dowager looked thoroughly bewildered.

After tea, the older members of the party retired to their chambers, as did Millie and Sir George, for Millie, glowing with health and happiness, was at last expecting a child, and her husband was most solicitous.

The younger people went down to admire Lily's new garden. Lady Verne, who was quite heavy with child, eased herself onto a bench with some relief and lifted her face into the breeze.

"I'm so glad you came," Lily murmured. "Surprised you could face the journey but delighted you did."

Lady Verne laughed. "I'm restless if you want the truth! I know my little mite will not enter the world for a few weeks yet—no, don't ask me how I know, I just do—and coming to see you is the perfect antidote to simply *waiting.*"

The aged butler appeared with a tray bearing a decanter and several glasses. While Lily and the other ladies walked around, Randolph poured sherry for anyone who wanted it. Lily began to feel contented.

"When do you expect your baby?" she asked Henrietta Cromarty, for whom she held a special place in her heart. Henrietta had once saved her life.

"Not until November."

"I believe I shall have a baby, too, in the spring," Lady Dain said, blushing faintly. Once the governess to Henrietta's family who lived near the Hart, she seemed newly vibrant and contented.

Henrietta hugged her with delight, and Lily blurted, "As shall I, God willing."

"Oh, my dear, I am so pleased for you, too!" Henrietta cried. "It seems we are all contributing mightily to the population!" She smiled. "Truly, Lily, I'm delighted to see you so happy. You deserve it."

"I'm not sure about that," Lily said deprecatingly. She moved toward the lemonade, which had been placed on the table next to the brandy decanter.

"*I* am," Lady Verne said. "I hold you and the Hart personally responsible for all our marriages—and my brother's!"

Lily blushed but smiled. She was proud of anything she had done in that respect. "Well, the Hart is a lucky house, but it was Randolph who was responsible for our marriage. I never thought it was actually possible." She began pouring lemonade from the jug for the ladies.

"None of us were possible by society's standards," Captain Cromarty said wryly. "I was a smuggler and a banker. Verne had the reputation of Beelzebub."

"I was merely a penniless governess," Lady Dain added.

"And don't forget Isabelle de Renard and her dashing Frenchman," Sir Marcus added. "I know you were responsible for that, too, Lily, despite the supposed impossibility."

"I remember when no one thought my sister Charlotte would marry at all," Henrietta mused, referring to the Duchess of Alvan. "She was meant to be the unmarriageable one of my sisters and cosigned to look after my parents in their old age! Until she went to the Hart and met Alvan. Believe me, Lily, you are not alone!"

Randolph raised his glass to all, though his eyes came to rest warmly on Lily, who slipped under his free arm. "To the unmarriageable. May they always find happiness despite their lot."

"The unmarriageable!" echoed several fervent voices. And everyone drank.

About Mary Lancaster

Mary Lancaster lives in Scotland with her husband, three mostly grown-up kids and a small, crazy dog.

Her first literary love was historical fiction, a genre which she relishes mixing up with romance and adventure in her own writing. Her most recent books are light, fun Regency romances written for Dragonblade Publishing: *The Imperial Season* series set at the Congress of Vienna; and the popular *Blackhaven Brides* series, which is set in a fashionable English spa town frequented by the great and the bad of Regency society.

Connect with Mary on-line – she loves to hear from readers:

Email Mary: Mary@MaryLancaster.com

Website: www.MaryLancaster.com

Newsletter sign-up: http://eepurl.com/b4Xoif

Facebook: facebook.com/mary.lancaster.1656

Facebook Author Page: facebook.com/MaryLancasterNovelist

Twitter: @MaryLancNovels

Amazon Author Page:
amazon.com/Mary-Lancaster/e/B00DJ5IACI

Bookbub: bookbub.com/profile/mary-lancaster